3/11

D0524449

The Easter Rising 1916

Molly's Diary

PATRICIA MURPHY

HANDS ON
HISTORY

Published 2014
by Poolbeg Press Ltd
123 Grange Hill, Baldoyle
Dublin 13, Ireland
E-mail: poolbeg@poolbeg.com

© PATRICIA MURPHY 2014

Typesetting, layout, design, ebook © Poolbeg Press Ltd.

2

A catalogue record for this book is available from the British Library.

ISBN 978-1-78199-974-5

Typeset by Poolbeg

Cover illustrated by Derry Dillon

Printed and bound by CPI Group (UK) Ltd, Croydon, CR0 4YY

www.poolbeg.com

About the Author

Patricia Murphy is an award-winning Producer/Director of documentaries for BBC and Channel 4 and a children's author.

Many of her groundbreaking programmes are about children and include *Children of Helen House* for the BBC about a children's hospice, *Raised by the State* on growing up in care and *Caravan Kids* about the children of New Age Travellers. She devised and directed the launch programmes of *Born to Be Different*, Channel 4's pioneering series following the lives of six children born with disabilities in the 21st century. She also made *The Worst Jobs in History* with Tony Robinson, *Behind the Crime* (a controversial series about criminals) and several films on the environment.

She is the author of *The Chingles* Celtic fantasy trilogy published by Poolbeg.

She grew up in Dublin and graduated from Trinity College, Dublin, with a degree in English and History. She now lives in Oxford with her husband and young daughter.

Dedication

In memory of my father Charles Murphy (1937-2013) who died while I was writing this book, and all those who lost their lives in the 1916 Rising

*E*aster 1916. The Great War rages in Europe with two hundred thousand Irishmen fighting in the British Army. But a small group of Irish nationalists refuse to fight for Britain and strike a blow for Irish freedom. Caught up in the action in Dublin is twelve-year-old Molly O'Donovan. This is her diary.

Molly's Diary

📖 📖 📖

9 o'clock, Saturday morning, 22nd April 1916 – MY BIRTHDAY!
My bedroom, 9 Sackville Street, Dublin, Ireland,
Second City of the British Empire.

My name is Molly O'Donovan and I am twelve years old today. Hurray! My father is Chief Technical Officer at the General Post Office (GPO for short) and makes sure everyone gets their telegraphs and telephone calls. My mother is called Bessie. She is a Quaker from Enniskillen in the North of Ireland. We live opposite the GPO in Sackville Street, Dublin, the widest street in Europe, in a tall thin house above a tailor's shop.

My brother Jack is two years older than me – and teases me something rotten!

I had hoped to fill my new diary with elegant words and clever thoughts but all I've had are constant interruptions. I only had to pick up my new fountain pen earlier at breakfast for Jack to make fun of me.

"Why on earth would a boring girl need a diary!" he jeered. "Dear Diary, today I broke a comb in my awful red hair, I played nurses with my silly dolls. Blah, blah, blah!"

Jack tried to swipe the diary from me but I held it out of reach.

"Die, Imperial Enemy! God save Ireland!" he cried and the eejit tried to bayonet my diary with his fork.

"Shush! I'm writing down EVERYTHING that happens. So you'd better stop jumping off roofs and marching with rebels!" I made a face at him but he made a worse one back and stabbed again at my lovely diary. "Hands off! It's the best present ever!"

It's true. It's vellum and hand-bound in leather with my name carved on the front. It has a little lock and all. Mother's friend, Addy, who works in Eason Stationers, made it.

Then our char Nancy Maguire chimed in. "Janey Mac! Would yeh ever stop actin' the maggot, young Jack," she scolded. She is quite old and crinkly and her face is sooty from cleaning the grate.

Jack mimed shooting at me with a rifle, the dangerous galoot.

"At least your sister's not hangin' outside old Fenian bomber's tobacco shops like you and our Anto," said Nancy.

Anto is Nancy's fifteen-year-old son, a messenger boy with buck teeth and sticky-out ears. Jack thinks the sun shines out of his scrawny backside.

"Nancy, who are the Fenians?" I asked.

"A shower of no-account troublemakers from way back who want to bomb us all into bein' an Irish Republic," she said, shaking her brush. "I'll give them the tail-end of this if they come too close."

Jack was going to rugby-tackle me so I jumped up on my chair to hold the diary out of arm's reach.

In all the rough and tumble we hadn't noticed that my father had walked into the room and heard what we'd been saying.

"What's this about Fenians?" he asked sharply.

"If I catch our Anto with dem bowsies marchin' around like tin soldiers," said Nancy, "I'll box his ears and theirs too."

My father suppressed a smile. He thinks Nancy is very funny.

3

"Lookin' for an Ireland Republic while my poor aul' husband Mossy and Jemsie me firstborn are fightin' the Germans," continued Nancy.

Both are soldiers with the Dublin Fusiliers in Flanders. So Nancy is one of the 'Separation Women' who wait to get money every week from the Post Office because their husbands are off fighting the Germans.

The Kaiser in Germany started the war. It's a long story. A madman in Serbia shot a duke and now everyone is fighting everybody. It all gets very confusing because some of the Irish, and not just the old Fenians that Nancy wants to wallop with her brush, won't fight for England against Germany and want an independent Ireland. Friends of Jack, I'll have you know.

"'We serve neither King nor Kaiser but Ireland!'" said Jack defiantly. He'd told me he saw this slogan on a big banner outside Liberty Hall down on Burgh Quay. It's the headquarters of the Trade Unionists who want the employers to give their workers more money and rights. They are yet another group who have their own army. There are so many armies marching about it's surprising they don't all bump into each other.

"I'm amazed you could even read that banner on Liberty Hall," I said to Jack. This was unkind and I immediately felt bad. Jack has problems with reading.

"If I ever see that Kaiser, I'll make him sit on his big pointy helmet – that'll put some manners on him," said Nancy.

"Nancy should be the Prime Minister," I giggled.

"And that fella Tom Clarke in the tobacco shop around the corner," she went on. "What that aul' Fenian bomb-maker says is more dangerous than the matches he sells. As for yer one, Countess Marzipan!"

"Countess Markievicz. Her husband is a Polish Count, though she herself is Anglo-Irish," corrected my father who is a stickler for accuracy.

"Whatever she's called, she's a bit of a consequence with her smokin' and trousers and big hats," said Nancy. "Turnin' all those young boys to devilment!"

"Isn't Anto in the Countess's Scouts –" I began, but Jack pinched me hard and looked daggers at me, so I bit my tongue. Luckily Nancy didn't hear me and was going on about how the Countess should stick to making soup for the poor.

"At the Post Office we maintain a neutral stance," said my father sternly to Jack. "I suggest you do the same, young man."

Jack kicked the chair leg. "I'll do as I please," he mumbled.

"Not when you're in my house," said Father. "Go to your room."

Jack skulked upstairs. My father hurried out. I was left standing on the chair, holding my Dear Diary, like a scarecrow. And my father hadn't even noticed!

I heard my father in the hall, taking his hat and umbrella from the hallstand, and then his exclamation of "Good God!"

He rushed back into the room and I thought I was in for it.

"Molly, I nearly forgot to wish you Happy Birthday!"

I jumped down and embraced him, for I love my daddy dearly and wish I could spend more time with him – but he is always so busy keeping the General Post Office going and says it is the most important building in Ireland. Not a telegram would be received nor a telephone call put through without my daddy looking after all the wires.

We heard a clatter at the front door. It was my mother arriving back with the delivery boy from the Dublin Bread Company, known as the DBC. As it's Holy Saturday it's closed for the rest of the day. The stout little boy was juggling several packages, including my birthday cake! His name is Tommy Keenan and he looks like he eats most of the cakes. He was wearing a little tricolour badge, the green, white and orange flag of the Republicans, so I think he is a Fenian too!

"Where's our wee Jack?" Mother asked anxiously in her soft Northern Irish accent. (Jack is heading towards six foot and is not at all wee!)

My father pointed up towards the ceiling, with an expression that indicated he had been sent to his room in disgrace. He kissed my mother on the cheek.

"The telegraph wires are always humming, holiday or no holiday," he said, heading for the door. This make me think of busy bees humming in a hive.

"Don't forget we're taking Molly to Bewley's Café when we come back from Howth Head," said my mother.

My father brightened up. "Make sure Jack goes to the sea. The fresh air will blow those silly notions out of his head."

"I'll write it all down in my diary!" I said excitedly.

"We better all watch our pee's and poo's so," proclaimed Nancy.

We all laughed. Nancy, of course, meant P's and Q's. Though I confess that doesn't make much sense either.

My mother gave her a bundle of old baby clothes and I helped her carry them to the door. I can't think why she needs baby clothes. Nancy is an old woman with lots of wobbly teeth and more like a grandmother – though I know she doesn't have grandchildren.

As she left Nancy whispered to me, "My Anto and Jack are good boys really. If Mossy were here, he'd tan Anto's hide to knock some sense into him."

"My mother won't let Father hit Jack," I said. It's because she's a Quaker and they are against war and violence, but Father would not like to do it anyhow.

"Yer da is as daecent as any man who ever wore a hat, and yer ma is a saint," said Nancy.

That is true for sure. Mother is always giving loaves of bread and stuff to old people in the slums, like in Moore Street.

Everything quietened down for a while after that but

Jack is wrong about my life being boring so, Dear Diary, together we are going to show him! I know one or two secrets about him and presently I may reveal them if he isn't nice to me!

But let me tell you more about myself and my family. I was christened Margaret but everyone calls me Molly. I am tall for my age with reddish hair and a dusting of freckles. My mother says my hair is "Titian" like the women in the pre-Raphaelite paintings. Jack says my hair is like rusty old springs and I look like I have the measles – that I am so ugly no one will want to marry me. But I don't care. There IS someone who wants to marry me – even if it's only Anto. Though I don't want to marry him. So Jack is wrong!

Jack is also wrong about me playing nurses with my dolls. I'm practising being a doctor like my grandfather, a Surgeon Major in the Army in India who died before we could meet him. Or my mother's friend, Dr Ella Webb, who lives in Hatch Street. She even has a husband and four children. So I hope to be a doctor like her.

My father tells Jack he won't amount to much. But even if he is not one for book learning and gets his words all jumbled up, Jack is very clever. He knows how to fix watches and bicycles. He repaired my music box when no one else could. It belonged to my grandmother in India and plays "The Last Rose of Summer" by Thomas Moore. Father told me that the music reminded her of home when she felt lonely.

Jack can also climb anything. He scales the roofs all over Dublin (this is a secret!). His friends call him "Jack the Cat" for he would make a great cat burglar and can land on his feet from any height.

We play this game where I dare Jack to put one of his tin soldiers in a difficult place. You should see where those soldiers get to! The chimney of the Provost's House, Trinity College. On the shoulder of the statue of Daniel O'Connell. Even the roof of the GPO between the statues of Fidelity and Hibernia!

Jack is golden. His hair is an unusual amber-gold that glows in the light, a prettier shade than mine, his skin is tanned and he has brown eyes. Lots of girls like him. Like Hyacinth O'Hare who lives a few houses down who is thirteen and has fat sausage curls like a spaniel. I've looked out the window just now and, yes, she is standing outside on the pavement hoping to see him on her way to her dancing class. How pathetic! She's supposed to be my friend but she's always mooning over Jack, making googly eyes at him.

My father's job at the General Post Office was specially created for him, as he knows so much about telephones and telegraphs. He has even been to America to visit Mr Edison who invented them. They have been rebuilding the Dublin Post Office and my father made sure they had all the best equipment in the world. It opened six weeks ago and Mr Norway, the head of the Post Office, and the Lord Lieutenant gave a special thanks to my father. We were all very proud.

We even have our own telephone that stands on its own table in the sitting room like a statue to be adored. It is like a big brass candlestick with a mouthpiece on top with a listening device attached by a wire. Truth be told, it is almost never used as the only people we know with telephones are mother's friend Dr Ella Webb and Great-aunt Bessie in Belfast. Father is usually at work so makes all his calls from the GPO. And the higher-ups and staff always send a messenger to fetch him if there is an emergency, which is often – too often, says my mother. But my, when that telephone rings it's like the bell of a ship and we all jump to attention!

How I love to look out our window at the General Post Office! You see, Dublin is the second city of the British Empire which is so mighty the sun never sets on it. That makes our GPO the second most important, after London, in the whole world!

As I said, Sackville Street is the widest street in Europe. It hums like a hive with shoeblacks outside calling out to polish shoes, the flower-sellers around Nelson's Pillar singing, "Get your daffs – a penny a bunch!" and the paper-sellers shouting out the news: "Battle of Verdun still raging on the Western Front!" The telegram boys skitter past on foot or whizz by on their bikes and all day long the deep-red mail cars come and go with the royal insignia, GR for Georgius Rex (King George), on the side. They carry sackfuls of letters, postcards and parcels destined for all over. It's the very navel of the world!

I have to stop writing now as Miss Nosy Nugent is coming for half an hour to teach English grammar and stuff. *Groan.* I don't go to school because we have moved around so much. We have lived in London, Manchester, Belfast, Birmingham and Dublin. But I love Dublin best.

My mother wants me to learn Latin and improve my Mathematics so I can sit the scholarship exams for Alexandra College for Girls in Sandymount and the Dominican Convent in Eccles Street. Those schools believe in educating girls to be the same as men. My father says my mother should not be encouraging me in such notions. But Mother will bring him round. She believes in votes for women.

Miss Nugent says I will fail every exam on account of being so lazy. I don't care because school is probably full of very stuck-up young ladies – and I am not exactly a young lady. (This is a secret. Sometimes I pick my nose when no one is looking. And Jack and I have "passing wind" competitions. This is something we both excel in. Shame it is not a proper subject. We would be professors! But now that I am twelve I won't do those babyish things any more.)

I've peeked in his room and Jack has already sneaked out his window. I bet as I've been writing he has scrambled over the rooftops and is laughing at the people in bathrobes visiting the Hamman Turkish Baths, or he's larking around the Pagoda roof of the Dublin Bread Company and stealing a bun.

Or maybe something worse! When we were on holiday in the Lake District he learned how to climb with ropes and grappling irons, and now he practises all over Dublin's parapets. The rascal is planning to scale bridges next. He secretly plots dangerous forays. I found maps and drawings in his room of different routes around Dublin by rooftop. There are sketches of bridges: the Loopline Railway Bridge, a viaduct crossing the Liffey by the Customs House, Butt Bridge over to Tara Street, O'Connell Bridge, the Ha'penny footbridge and so on up to the Bridge at Knightsbridge Station on the way to the Phoenix Park. Miss Nugent would be amazed how carefully he plots his escapades! I told you he was clever.

My parents fear he has taken to drinking and gambling, sneaking out at all hours, and that that's why he's always hanging around Tom Clarke's tobacco shop in Little Britain Street. But, Dear Diary, as promised it's time for me to tell you a big secret . . . the truth is he really has joined Countess Markievicz's Boy Scouts . . . and as Tom Clarke is not just a tobacconist with a long droopy mustache like a walrus but, as Nancy says, a Fenian bomber who spent fifteen years in jail, well, all I can say is the sparks would be flying if my parents put two and two together!

Once I ran into Mr Clarke's shop for a dare. It is quite a fancy shop on the outside with big gold lettering and a swinging sign for "Titbits" magazine. It has a hugely high counter and leaning on it was a portly young gentleman in an overcoat. He was talking to Mr Clarke's wife, who is a sharp little woman and a bit scary, and he didn't see me come in.

I recognised him as Mr Pearse, the schoolmaster who wants everyone to talk Irish and writes poems. His first name is Patrick but lots of people call him by the Irish version of it which is Pádraig. My mother went to see him about Jack going to his school, Saint Enda's in Rathfarmham, when he was thrown out of Belvedere College. They would have taken him and she thought Mr Pearse has some very good ideas about education. But he was too romantic about ideas of blood sacrifice, she said. I thought this meant Jack would have to kill a goat or something, like Abraham in the bible, but my mother explained it meant dying for your country in a fight. Mr Pearse wants Ireland to be free of English rule even if we all have to die. But who will live in the country then, asks Nancy.

When Mother heard from Nancy that even some of the Irish nationalists had taken their children from the school, that put paid to that scheme.

Pearse looked very solemn and a bit squinty-eyed that day in the shop.

"It is a sacred duty," he was saying to Mr Clarke's wife. "The wives and dependents will be in good hands with you."

Mrs Clarke looked a bit sad when he said this, so perhaps she has a lot of things to worry about.

He then noticed that I was standing there like a gobdaw, so he smiled at me, bade Mrs Clarke good day and left.

Mrs Clarke was arranging the little tricolour badges she sells for a penny that the bakery boy, Tommy, was wearing this morning.

"Can I help you?" she said smartly.

"I-I-I was looking for my brother Jack," I stammered.

She visibly relaxed. "You're in the wrong place."

I didn't dare ever go back in again.

Anto swears all the Clarkes are able to shoot guns, including the children. And they even have a secret hidey-hole in the back of their privy. Anto talks such arrant nonsense, I'm amazed his nose isn't as long as Pinnochio's!

I am sworn not to tell my parents about Jack. Miss Nugent doesn't know how to control him – or me!

Dear Diary, I confess I sometimes join him – hitching up my skirts to shimmy up drainpipes and scramble on the roof of the Pillar Café and the Imperial Hotel. It is a bit scary but great fun. I am not as nimble or courageous as Jack and wouldn't dare do it without him, but now that I am twelve I will try to be braver.

My mother says I am too devoted to my brother and that I am like his shadow, that if he put his hand in the fire I would too. Alas, that is no longer true. Now he only wants to be with Anto and I am very sad.

But, in truth, Jack is as important to me as my own heartbeat. If anything ever happened to him, I fear I would pine so much I would die. I think I would do anything for him. I know it is silly but sometimes I dream he gets into trouble, and that only I can save him.

Miss Nugent has just come in downstairs. She has a face like a fish, bulging eyes, no chin and a mouth clamped shut in disapproval of everything. She has just come back from being a governess in India. That's why my father employed her – to give her a start, he said. Her real aim, Nancy says, is to trap someone into marrying her. She met some horrid old colonel on the boat who is staying in the same hotel as she is and she is laying siege to him.

"I would rather teach all the heathens in Asia than even one O'Donovan in this filthy godforsaken backwater," she says a thousand times a day.

I'd better go. Miss Nugent is calling me. But I only have to stand her for half an hour for an English lesson.

Twenty minutes later . . . 10.50 a.m. Saturday morning. My bedroom.

I have a confession to make. I have really upset Miss Nugent even though I promised my mother I'd behave. She kept calling us nasty names and I was nearly in tears because it is my birthday and I want it to be a happy day. I made a hames of my Shakespeare quotations.

"Now complete," she instructed, "'Cry havoc and let slip the . . .'"

"Cup of tea?" I said.

"'Dogs of war', Miss Idle," she growled at me and frowned at Jack. ' "'Time and the hour runs through the roughest . . .'"

"Trousers," said Jack, in a devil-may-care voice.

"Does it now?" her eyes bulged at him. "'Roughest day', Mr Dunce! Roughest trousers indeed!" And her stomach growled.

She suffers from the dyspepsia and her stomach makes all manner of growling noises as if she has swallowed a small dog.

I thought her stomach was making her cross. So I tried to be kind to her and fetched her a glass of liver salts.

Well, she nearly choked when she tasted it. Her face turned bright red and she roared at me: "You stupid booby! Are you trying to kill me?"

"But I read it in my First Aid book," I said, fighting back the tears.

She rushed into the kitchen. I followed her and saw to my horror that I had used the salt instead of the 'liver salts'. She held it up and shoved it near my face.

"You did that on purpose! Or else you can't even read."

"I was just trying to nurse you – it said it in my First Aid Book . . ." My voice was trembling and I could hardly say the words properly.

"Nurse my foot! I hope you never get near real patients, for you will kill them all," she cried.

She grabbed her coat and things and ran out the door, saying I had made her ill, and went home in a dreadful temper.

I was distraught. Not just because she thought I had tried to poison her, but also because I'd been careless and didn't pay attention and make sure I was giving her the right medicine. Perhaps she is right and I would be a terrible nurse, never mind a doctor. Even Mother says I am a bit slapdash.

Jack dried my tears. "Don't worry," he said. "She didn't sound that sick to me. She was just looking for an excuse to make a quick exit."

We were all alone then, Jack and I, Mother having nipped out on another mission of mercy. He went up to the attic to tinker with his tin soldiers and I came up to my room to write this.

11.45 a.m. – still Saturday 22nd April and my birthday! My bedroom.

Because Jack was being nice to me again, I went up to his large attic bedroom and asked him to explain to me who all the different armies were.

He smiled at me and pulled my pigtail in a friendly way. Then he dragged the counterpane off his bed. It was the beige tasselled one with our faint footprints from the time we'd jumped on the bed in muddy boots. There are marks all over the grey rug too. Nancy could never quite get the stains out!

"Imagine this is Great Britain," he said, laying it on the floor. Then he took off his pillowcase and placed it to the left of the counterpane, "and this is little Ireland." He put a pile of soldiers in England, then the group he'd been tinkering with on the pillowcase. I noticed they were larger than the others and he had painted their uniforms green.

"And the rug over there is Europe, where the Kaiser is fighting everyone," I said.

Jack laughed and put some of his German tin soldiers on the rug. "Look, they're just invading France." France was a faint footprint of Jack's. "And there is little Catholic Belgium which has been invaded by the Germans." He pointed to another smaller stain above and to the right of France. Then he picked up some of his redcoat English soldiers. "Now the English are going to help the Frenchies and little Catholic Belgium." He made the Germans and the English bash into each other.

"Ah, but there aren't enough English soldiers," I said. "They need some of the Irish ones."

"Well spotted," he said and walked over on his hands to the pillowcase of Ireland and did a belly-flop down, nosing some of his soldiers.

He has so many of them: Napoleonic, English cavalry,

Grenadier Guards, American Revolution. Most are about three inches high but his Prussian infantry are bigger. I think these are the ones he has turned into an Irish army.

"But not so fast," he said in a funny voice. "It's a little bit more complicated in Ireland." He juggled soldiers in the air and, catching them nimbly, positioned three different groups on the pillowcase.

He stood upright again and pointed to the first group at the top. "These are the Ulster Volunteers. They want to fight in the war because they want to stay in the United Kingdom." He made them jump over to Europe.

I drummed on the floor and hummed a marching tune, "The Minstrel Boy", as he skipped them along.

He pointed to a pile in the middle of Ireland. "These are the Irish Volunteers who believed in Ireland's right to independence. But at the start of the war against Germany, most of them decided that they would help the Empire, if they would get Home Rule after the war and those were then called the National Volunteers."

"And what is Home Rule exactly?" I asked.

"It means the Irish will get their own parliament, like they had in the eighteenth century."

He marched them away in a line over to the counterpane, leaving behind a few of the larger-sized ones whose uniforms he had painted green.

"So this left a small group of *Irish* Volunteers who said: 'We are not going to fight your war, Mr King. In fact, we want nothing to do with you and your imperialist ways. Up the Republic!'" He formed them into a triangular squadron on the pillowcase with a flourish. "Now the Irish Volunteers aren't the only ones not too keen on the Empire. The Irish Citizen Army don't want to fight for England either because they were formed by the trade unions to fight for the rights of the workers and the poor. Now where are they hiding?"

He pretended to search his pockets, then magicked another two green soldiers from behind my ear and put them down on the Irish pillowcase. It's a magic trick he's been trying to perfect for a while. And it was thrilling to see him pull it off. He gave me a conspiratorial wink.

"They're the ones from Liberty Hall, who will fight for neither King nor Kaiser," I said.

"Good girl," he said.

"But where are the Fenians?" I asked.

He took his old teddy down from a shelf. "Why, the Fenians are a group of old fellows, like Tom Clarke, who have held the flame for a free Ireland. By force if necessary." Teddy too was plonked down on the pillowcase and I propped Jack's slide rule against him, so he is armed to the paws! I saw a little tricolour badge on Jack's dressing table and made him smile when I pinned it on Teddy's ear.

"And the Fianna Boy Scouts?"

"They are the youths of Ireland who are learning the ideals of a glorious future," he said.

I ran to my mother's room and returned with a couple

of little bisque baby dolls of porcelain that she collects, about three inches high. I added them to his soldiers.

"They are the little baby soldiers," I said.

"Waah, waah, waah!" Jack cried. "Give us our own country or we'll grow up to fight you!"

We laughed and laughed. I was so pleased to have made him happy that it made me forget my worries. I didn't want to spoil the mood by questioning him too closely about what he gets up to himself.

"Now put Mother's dolls back, Molly dear," he said to me, turning all serious. "There is something I have to do." He ushered me to the door but, before he closed it, he looked me straight in the eye. "If I asked you to do something for me, without asking any questions, would you do it, Molly?"

I nodded eagerly, but then bit my lip. "It depends. I'm twelve now and Mother say I'm not to run around after you any more."

"I just want you to check the names of some of the equipment Father has in the Instrument Room," he said casually.

"Why?" I asked.

"Father is always trying to interest me and I'd like to learn them and surprise him," he said. "And I'm not very good at writing or spelling, so you'd make a much better job of writing them down."

I embraced him. "Of course," I said, pleased that he wanted to impress Father and had asked my help. He handed me a piece of paper with the names on, all ink-stained and crossed out.

But then he pushed me out of the room gently, and I felt all alone again.

So on a fresh piece of paper I corrected his shockingly bad spelling and wrote out some of the names of the equipment in the Instrument Room: fast-speed duplex repeaters, duplex Wheatstones, line concentrators and so on. I'm not sure I got the spellings completely right but certainly my attempt was better than Jack's.

Jack's door was locked so I shoved the note under his door.

It makes me a bit sad that he has secrets from me, but I have to learn to be more grown up, as Mother says.

Besides, I can have my own secrets now, in my very own diary. And I have cheered up, looking at all the bustle out the window.

Our skinny house of four stories is above Richard Allen Tailors, next door to O'Farrell's Tobacco Importers. Mr Allen provides outfits for all the servants and so I know every maid in Dublin from meeting them coming in and out. We are in the same block as Noblett's Confectionary (yum!) on the corner, then Dunn's Hatters and Clerys department store and the Imperial Hotel above it. Clerys has enormous plate-glass windows.

The rooftop of our terrace block is another world. It frightens me when Jack leaps from chimney to parapet, the low wall at the side. There is a small pitched roof and raised stone capping at the front of the building so you don't fall off, and quite a lot of space at the back for lounging about. There are several big chimneys with rows of pots. One of them bears an advert for Will's Tobacco. Further along our terrace, the Imperial Hotel is as fancy as a giant iced cake and is much grander than its neighbours. But you can climb a metal fire escape to get up there. Once on the roof, it is quite a large flat expanse with several more tall rows of chimney pots where we like to play hide and seek. Then we can see the copper dome of the DBC on the next block quite easily.

My father likes to live near his work but that is not the only reason my parents like the city. They say it is easier for couples of "mixed marriages" – that is when two people of different faiths marry each other. I have heard my mother discuss it with her Catholic dressmaker friend who is married to a Protestant tea-traveller. They say how sad it is that some so-called Christians disapprove and bicker over what religion the children are brought up in. That it's worse in the suburbs because people are all in each other's pockets. At least in the city people don't know your business and there's more intermarriage. My father is also a Catholic. His people are from Cork, but he was born in Goa in India. People think that is strange enough, never mind my mother being a Quaker, where they don't even have priests! Jack and I are being brought up in both religions because my mother says it's all the one God.

I have never met my parents' families as they were both cut off when they eloped. How romantic! She was training to be a nurse and he was in the army, Royal Engineers Corps, then. My father says Mother is a frustrated nurse, which is why she looks after all the poor people and is so active in the First Aid training. She is a trainer for the Saint John's Ambulance Brigade,

But, truth be told, we all love Dublin city. It is teeming with life even though it is noisy and messy and some of the people who live here are poor and unfortunate.

I don't miss not knowing most of our relatives, because there is so much going on under our noses! Nelson's Pillar is the very centre and Dublin spins around it like a wheel around an axle. It has 138 steps inside and is 135 feet high, almost as high as the width of the street and more than twice the height of the surrounding buildings, according to Jack. From the top you can see all the rooftops that Jack likes to dance across, and the Georgian Squares, the green dome of Rathmines church, the roof of the 'Pepper Canister' church, the spires of Saint Patrick's and Christchurch Cathedrals, the green of the Phoenix Park, the biggest park in Europe. All set against the purple backdrop of the Dublin Mountains to the south. And, dividing the city, the broad stinky River Liffey that flows at the bottom of Sackville Street to the Irish Sea.

There is all manner of diversion here. Like on Henry Street, there is the Waxworks where the displays are as good as Madame Tussaud's in London. They have the Prime Minister David Lloyd George and King George the Fourth. Also some old fusty ones like Wolfe Tone, whoever he was. And not just wax but also visiting real-life curiosities. Here I have seen Anita the Living Doll – just twenty-six inches tall – and Marcella the Midget Queen who sings all kinds of songs.

WORLD'S FAIR VARIETIES AND WAXWORKS,
30 HENRY STREET, DUBLIN.

SPECIAL COSTLY ENGAGEMENT
FOR A FEW DAYS ONLY,
COMMENCING TO-DAY (Monday), June 9,
THE BIG SUCCESS AND MOST INTERESTING
FEATURE OF THE OVADA BAZAAR—
Charming ! Dainty ! Fascinating !
ANITA, "The Living Doll,"
THE TINIEST ADULT LADY THAT EVER
LIVED.
30 YEARS OLD ! 26 INCHES HIGH !
PERFECT IN FIGURE, FACE AND FORM.
AN ASTONISHMENT TO EVERY BEHOLDER.
RECEPTIONS IN THE THEATRE DAILY AT
SHORT INTERVALS from 12.30 till 10.30 p.m.,
In addition to a Specially-selected Superior
Programme of the Latest Moving Pictures,
without extra charge.

Real people, I'm telling you, not waxworks! Just last month I saw the one-hundred-year-old Bushmen who were wild and dancing. My mother does not approve of this. But I am great friends with Mr James the manager who lets me in free. Normally it would cost a penny, so I am saving my mother and father a great deal of money every time I visit.

Sometimes Jack and I sneak into the Coliseum, with

three thousand velveteen seats and plush walls inside. The safety curtain is enormous! We have seen some gymnastics. There was a man from Barnum and Bailey Circus and when he saw Jack walk on his hands, he gave him his card. I think Jack secretly dreams of running away to the circus. He could probably teach them a thing or two when it comes to climbing. He's shown me some of his climbing tricks, like distributing your weight between your hands and toes and he's a much more patient teacher than Miss Nugent!

There is also Lemon's sweet shop. I absolutely love their pineapple rock and butterscotch even if it sticks to my teeth. Jack's favourites are bull's eyes and bonbons. Another wonderful place is Lawrence's Toy Shop and Photographic Emporium up near Cathedral Place that has everything from tricycle horses to beautiful China dolls. Beside them is Tyler's Boots and also Cables shoe shop. In fact, there are loads of shoe shops around here – Saxone, Trueform Boots, Mansfield's – which is quite surprising because I often see children without any shoes. My mother says they are poor people with no money. Not even to buy food. She says Dublin is the poorest city in Europe with the biggest slums. That is not so nice a thing to be best in.

Jack and I have often peeked through the skylight of the Hamman Turkish Bath in Upper Sackville Street. The visitors look most peculiar wrapped in their towels, lying on deck chairs and sweating like pigs. Then they jump in a freezing cold plunge pool! But they get to drink from a soda fountain. One of the maids there told us it has

EIGHT different kinds of cooling drinks. Imagine that!

I will have to stop writing soon as we are off to Howth Head to collect sphagnum moss for the war effort, with only a quick bite to eat before. We are to catch a tram.

You have to be very careful not to get run over by all the trams going up and down Sackville Street. Nelson's Pillar is also the centre of a spider's web leading out to all parts of the city. Because many people can't read, the trams have signs – a red triangle for Terenure, a brown diamond for Rialto and Glasnevin, a brown oval for Inchicore and Westland Row and a shamrock if you are going all the way to Dalkey. I like the green crescent on the side of the one for Sandymount, like a smiling mouth. The hoarse Dublin United Tramways Company timekeeper bawls out the names of trams as the single and double-deckers swerve down the line. "Rathmines! Terenure! Rialto!"

The Cars on the Several Routes are distinguished, in addition to the Name Boards on each side and the Destination Indicators at either end, by the Following Signs above the destination Indicators:-

NELSON'S PILLAR AND TERENURE (VIA RATHMINES)	▲	RATHFARNHAM AND DRUMCONDRA (VIA HAROLD'S CROSS)	⊠
NELSON'S PILLAR AND DARTRY ROAD (VIA UPPER RATHMINES)	◬	RIALTO AND GLASNEVIN (VIA DOLPHIN'S BARN)	◆
DONNYBROOK AND PHŒNIX PARK (VIA MERRION SQUARE)	◈	NELSON'S PILLAR AND DALKEY	❀
DONNYBROOK AND PHŒNIX PARK (VIA STEPHEN'S GREEN)	⬌	NELSON'S PILLAR AND CLONSKEA (VIA LEESON STREET)	◯◯
KINGSBRIDGE AND HATCH STREET (VIA SOUTHERN QUAYS & WESTLAND ROW)	☐	NELSON'S PILLAR & SANDYMOUNT (VIA RINGSEND)	◡
PARK GATE AND BALLYBOUGH	◆◆	NELSON'S PILLAR & DOLLYMOUNT	▼
INCHICORE AND WESTLAND ROW	●	COLLEGE GREEN & WHITEHALL (VIA CAPEL ST. & DRUMCONDRA)	♡
O'CONNELL BRIDGE & PARK GATE (VIA NORTHERN QUAYS)	☐	KENILWORTH ROAD AND LANSDOWNE ROAD	☐
NELSON'S PILLAR & PALMERSTON PARK	○		

Dollymount then walk to Sutton Railway station for the Hill of Howth tramway. I'd better wear my galoshes. It will be very boggy on Howth Head as it has been raining cats and dogs for the last twelve days!

4.30 p.m. Saturday April 22nd – back home after a busy trip!

We spent a lively time in the Bog of Frogs on Howth Head collecting bog moss for the war effort. Mother says we have to help the unfortunates caught up in the war. I am proud to be the youngest girl in the whole country trained in First Aid. They even gave me a certificate, though Mother said my bandages were a bit of a mess! But I try to practise on my dolls and teddies when I can.

It is through the training that I know women can be doctors. We are taught by my mother's old friend Dr Ella Webb, whose father is the Dean of Saint Patrick's Cathedral, and Dr Kathleen Lynn of the Irish Citizen Army (the boss-haters that Jack magicked out of my ear!).

Among us today was Miss Huxley who runs the Volunteer Aid Detachment hospital in Mountjoy Square with the Trinity College graduates – or the 'Very Adorable Darlings' as they are known! They look after the wounded men who come to Dublin from the front.

My mother says Miss Huxley is trying to improve nursing and make it more scientific in Ireland. Jack says her uncle was a famous scientist who insists we are all descended from the apes. Not Mr Darwin with the big beard but another one with an even bigger beard who they called Darwin's Bulldog. Jack says she wants to turn us all into monkeys who are our cousins. But I don't think this can be right. Except in his case. At least it explains his climbing skills!

As the tram rattled through North Dublin, Mother confided in Miss Huxley about Jack as I pretended to concentrate on looking out the window.

"He is sharp as anything," said Mother, "but he gets all his letters jumbled and cannot read well."

Miss Huxley, who is kind and sweet, said she had heard of such "word blindness". Some doctors thought it was to do with the eyes and the brain not connecting properly and she promised to look into it. It has nothing to do with intelligence in her experience. I dearly hope she can help Jack because he flies into such rages when he cannot understand.

They also had a conversation about wound-cleaning. Miss Huxley told Mother that, if stuck, sugar and honey could be good for treating wounds. I found this very curious and interesting.

We had a competition to see who could collect the most moss and Jack and I collected twenty mail sacks! But at one stage he snuck off. I followed him for a little way but I was worried about falling into a bog. I am not as surefooted as Jack. I thought I saw him conceal something in one of the sacks. I will have to investigate.

Let me tell you about bog moss because I find that very interesting. Not like what Miss Nugent teaches me!

With so many poor men being injured in the war, the army needs a great quantity of bandages and there is not enough cotton. So they are using bog moss, also called sphagnum moss, instead. Its leaf and stalk quickly absorb up to twenty-five times their own weight in liquid. That would be a lot of blood!

We have spent many a cold afternoon in the Dublin Mountains collecting bog moss, I can tell you! My mother prepares as much as she can before we drop it over to Merrion Square Supply Depot. First we pick through it to remove grass and twigs and small insects, then we sew it into muslin bags – two ounces of moss into each bag which Mother insists must be precisely ten inches by fourteen or half that again at five by seven inches. At the laboratory at Merrion Street, the bags are passed through a solution. Jack pretends it is a secret potion but one of the laboratory workers there told me it is made from mixing mercury and chloride. In small doses it is an antiseptic but otherwise it is a powerful poison. The lab worker also told me they have sent over half a million bags of dressings to help poor soldiers in Flanders or even Gallipoli in Turkey. Imagine, a stalk of bog moss collected by me might save someone's life! One of these could be Nancy's husband or son. I have now all those bags to prepare. Groan! The moss is moist and green and gold now but when dry it becomes crisp and springy and the colour of hay. We dry it in the basement of the GPO because there are many hot pipes there. At first my father was reluctant in case we dropped mud on his shiny new instruments. But my mother talked him around.

As we were coming back up Sackville Street, who should pull my pigtail but Anto Maguire on his bike, delivering groceries for Findlater's. Mother and Jack got all tied up in dropping off the bags of moss at the GPO and left me talking to Anto.

"Gi's a kiss," he winked. "Tá tú mahogany gas pipe, O'Donnell Abú!" Anto pretends to speak Irish but I know it is pure gibberish.

I stuck my tongue out at him. "Even your own mother calls you 'a good-for-nuthin' lazy article'!"

"You wait 'til we fight for Ireland's freedom," he insisted. "Me an' Jack will be runnin' the Republic."

"And, pray, what will you be – Minister for Groceries?"

"I've even written a poem about our leaders an' all," Anto said, sticking his chest out like a crowing cock.

"Pádraig Pearse is not so fierce
And has a squinty eye,
But he has a dream for Ireland free,
And is prepared to die!"

"Why then, you can be Ireland's national bard," I said,

laughing so hard I nearly fell over. "Good luck rhyming 'Countess Markievicz'."

"That's easy," he said, all puffed up. "'With the Fianna she flits.'"

"Why, even Mr Yeats couldn't better that," I mocked. "What about: 'Countess Markievicz and her Fianna nitwits'?"

"You'll see," he said, trying to sound all mysterious.

"You'll see even further if I tell on the Countess's noble Fianna Boy Scouts gambling on the roof at the back of our house!"

"There's no way you'd rat on Jack." He shoved a note in my pocket and, before I could box his ears, he disappeared.

I pulled out the note and had a look at it. This is what it said: "Two tins of peaches, a pound of sugar, five rashers of bacon . . ." Our future national bard has given me a Findlater's grocer's list! How very funny, I don't think! I crumpled it up and shoved it back in my pocket.

But now I am so excited because I am going in my new birthday clothes to Bewley's Oriental Café in Westmoreland Street for high tea!

I am so happy to have something swanky to wear, for my one-piece velveteen frock is so patched it cannot be said to be the original garment at all.

I am now wearing the height of fashion from Roberts' in Grafton Street. A cream coat teamed with a mushroom-shaped hat and pink ribbon, a pleated brown kilt (which Mother says won't show the dirt) and a lovely cream Viyella blouse. Best of all, I got a new dress for Easter of snow-white cambric lace with a tiered skirt and a V-shape detail in the front panel.

I also got some new "unmentionables" – some camiknickers and drawers that go down to the knee. I do so hate these garments. My mother bought herself a liberty bodice, which is a one-piece. She says I am lucky, that when she was a girl her grandmother made her wear her old whalebone corsets and it was like being locked in a suit of armour.

We will walk across the Liffey, to the café in Westmoreland Street. We pass by Clerys Department Store where you can buy EVERYTHING: silk hats, baby carriages, woven rugs all the way from Arabia. We pass by the DBC and Reis's Wireless Repair shop on the corner of Abbey Street but that is closed because of the war. My favourite shop is further down on Eden Quay on the banks of the Liffey: in Hopkins and Hopkins, beautiful ticking watches and chronometers keep the time for the whole of Dublin. On the opposite side of Sackville Street, at the corner with Bachelors Walk is Kelly's Fishing Tackle and Gunpowder shop. I always get the shivers passing by for fear someone will light a match! No doubt bought from Mr Tom Clarke. I bet he puts dynamite in them!

📖　📖　📖

7 p.m. Saturday 22nd April.
My bedroom.

Well, I was so excited to have my first proper cup of tea that I nearly scalded my mouth and had to splutter into my handkerchief. Normally I am only allowed milk as my mother thinks tea is too stimulating for children's stomachs. So I am not used to being a fine lady taking high tea. The Bewleys are Quaker friends of hers so she would have been vexed to see my bad manners. Luckily she was too busy, waving to friends all the time.

Many people wished me Happy Birthday including Skeffy, a friend of my mother's, who is quite eccentric in his tweed knickerbockers. He hates war but loves quarrels, including disagreeing with his wife Hannah Sheehy whose name he took (and won't give back, ha, ha!). My mother told me that she supports the Fenians who want a republic and he wants Home Rule peacefully. He causes a sensation wherever he goes. Some bad people beat him, which must be very hard for a peace-loving man – even if he could start an argument in an empty room, as Nancy says.

"The bould Molly!" When he embraced me, his badge 'Votes for Women' caught my face.

He gave me a big bear hug and a penny whistle which is a hard-striped candy that you can actually blow. He had probably bought it for his own boy who is seven. But that's Skeffy – would give you the shirt off his back, as Nancy says.

He set to whispering with my father and mother. I pretended to suck on my penny whistle while listening for any interesting news for my diary.

"A friend at the paper told me Eoin MacNeill will cancel any Irish Volunteer marching tomorrow with adverts in the Sunday Independent," he said.

"Does Professor MacNeill actually know what's going on?" my mother asked. "I know he's Chief of Staff of the Irish Volunteers, but he's always struck me as being out of touch."

"You have a point." Skeffy frowned. "Connolly's Irish Citizen Army and some of the Irish Volunteers have become very close recently. And you never know what the old Fenians might be stirring up in the background."

I thought of Jack's old teddy bear and it made me smile to myself.

But, oh dear, it's all confusing again, as if someone had pulled up Jack's counterpane and mixed all the soldiers up!

"I hope there will be no trouble," said my mother.

"What about the Fianna Boy Scouts?" I asked, forgetting I wasn't supposed to be earwigging.

"Countess Markievicz is their leader, but she of course is very pally with James Connolly of the Irish Citizen Army," said Skeffy.

"Some members of the government think there is a lot

of playacting involved but others are beginning to share your suspicions," said my father in a low voice. "Pearse is always going on about being a martyr to the cause and it's making the English nervous – they already think Liberty Hall is a hotbed of revolution."

"There are too many people willing to die for Ireland," said Skeffy. "Why can't more people just live for it?"

"The government won't act until they actually break the law," my father said.

"It's well your family are all out of it," said Skeffy. "I wish Hannah wasn't tied up in it."

"The extremists who want to take up arms are only a small group," said my father. "I'd be surprised if they're still at liberty next week."

"But there are many gifted people among them," sighed my Mother. "Pearse the patriot, Connolly who has fought so much for Dublin's poor, the glamorous Countess – all those flowers of Ireland in love with the idea of dying a glorious death for Irish freedom. It is sad."

"I agree with the idea of a united Ireland," Skeffy said, "but I hate violence of any kind. Wars and armies are organized murder and lead to chaos."

"I dislike politics," my father said emphatically. "We should embrace progress in the twentieth century. Modern communications will bring us closer together."

"If Danny has his way, we'll be off to America on the next boat to live under Mr Edison's light-bulb!" joked my mother.

They all laughed but I got a bit worried. For my family isn't all out of it. That is, of course, Jack's secret!

9 p.m. Saturday 22nd April.
My bedroom.

Someone gave my mother free tickets to see Yeats's play 'Cathleen ni Houlihan' at the Abbey Theatre next Tuesday. It's about Ireland as an old woman or something. I have to confess it sounds a bit yawny. Mr Yeats is a poet who believes in ghosts and my Mother says is a terrible snob though probably a genius. He has a Ouija board and has séances with the dead, Nancy says. (Probably summoning his audience.) I would prefer to go and see the Gilbert and Sullivan musical in the Gaiety. Their panto last Christmas was wonderful! Addy, Mother's friend, knows one of the Gaiety Girls, Louisa Nolan. She sang like an angel!

When I was getting changed for bed, as I pulled out my tea-stained handkerchief, Anto's crumpled grocery list came tumbling out with it and I saw there was more writing on the other side.

It read: "Dir Bootyfool Muly, wil u b my sweethart? I may soon go into battle for thee, your secrit admiyerur, AM"

So much for being my secret admirer! Signing it with his initials! His spelling is even worse than Jack's. I would rather become a nun in Eccles Street Convent than marry him.

But what is that battle he talks about? Skeffy said all the marching will be cancelled. Anto must be behind the times as usual!

11 p.m. Saturday 22nd of April – still my birthday! My bedroom.

I am writing with the moonlight coming in through my curtains because I am eavesdropping on Jack up on the back roof above, smoking and playing cards with his friends. I have opened the window a crack to listen to them. One cheeky beggar is whistling an Irish air and I hear Jack hiss.

"Would you keep it down, Martin! If Father catches me I'll be packed off to Belfast and miss all the action."

Parp! Parp!

I don't believe it. The sound of a bugle!

"Matthew Connolly! You madman!" Jack is laughing so much he can barely speak.

They are being shocking unruly. I know Matthew Connolly from First Aid training. He is fifteen, a year older than Jack and rather good-looking. His even better-looking brother Seán, the actor, is going to be in that dreary play we're seeing on Tuesday. But they aren't related to James Connolly who is the boss of the Irish Citizen Army.

"I hope I get the chance to sound the fall-in tomorrow," says Matthew. "If we're joining ranks with the Volunteers it might go to one of their boyos."

"Janey Mac, are you sure it's not all off?" says Anto's little reedy voice. "I can't keep up with all the changes."

I can hear from the catch in his words that he's smoking as well.

"The brother, Seán, says Pearse and Connolly are determined about getting the boys out. No matter what MacNeill puts in the papers," says Matthew.

What a lot of intrigue about a march! Anto was just being dramatic in his note when he boasted about a battle.

"My da says he's going to take the air out of my bicycle tires so I can't leave," says Martin.

"You can always walk, you lazy galoot," jokes Anto.

Now they're quiet for a bit as Jack deals their cards.

"Come on, Jack, you have to raise me a stake," says another voice that I recognise as Gerald Keogh's. He is older than the others, maybe twenty-two and also very handsome. His father used to own a shirt and glove factory in Sackville Street. He now lives in Cullenwood in Ranelagh and is from a most respectable family.

"But I'm clean out of money," moans Jack.

"Let's play for your new Sam Browne belt," says Gerald.

"Get up the yard!" jeers Anto. "That's Jack's pride and joy. He's saved up all his gambling winnings to pay for it."

"You don't have to tell me it's a beauty," says Gerald. "I was apprenticed to a draper."

A cart rattles by and they all stay quiet for a minute.

"Go on then, Gerald, double or quits," says my brother.

I hear the faint rattle of a dice and then my brother groan, followed by Gerald Keogh's laugh.

"Hey, do you want to hear me poem about our leaders?" Anto says and goes on without waiting for a reply.

"Pádraig Pearse is not so fierce

And has a squinty eye,

But he has a dream of Ireland free –"

He is interrupted by a loud cheer and a whistle. Mercy! It is his "national bard" poem he was boasting about earlier. I can barely hear it with all the clapping and "Go on, boy!"

He's going on now about being prepared to die. Then more guff about "Old Fenian Clarke" lighting the spark from his tobacco shop and Mac Diarmada having a gammy leg. Now it's brave Connolly and history, and hark, he's on to Countess Markievicz but I cannot hear how he resolved the rhyme with all the caterwauling and "Hear, hear!" I don't know why because it sounds like the worst poem ever written.

There's more! About Joseph Plunkett being born to a life of leisure and Thomas MacDonagh wanting to revive the Gaelic and Ceannt being a piper and rooting out tyranny. Does he mean to go through every single one of the leaders?

No, he's finishing . . . with being slaves of empire no more. That's set off the most shocking rowdy hullabaloo. I fear one of them will fall off the roof!

Well, upon my life! Anto couldn't have had a more appreciative audience if he'd performed it at the Abbey Theatre itself! But they would wake the very dead with their hooplas and whistles. I can hear a noise on the stairs so I'd better stop.

**11.30 p.m. Saturday 22nd April.
My bedroom.**

It was my mother on the stairs earlier.

"Molly, Molly, what's all that racket?" she called up to me. "I could have sworn I heard a bugle!"

I stuck my head out the back window and whistled. Five startled boys stared down at me over the parapet – Jack, Anto, Gerald Keogh, Matthew Connolly and Martin Walton, who is about fifteen and has a shock of black hair like a gypsy. The surprised look on each face was frozen like Mr James's waxworks.

"You lot better leg it and, Jack, get into bed while I put her off the scent," I hissed. Jack's bedroom is in the attic, so it's easy for him to get in through his window.

I pulled the curtains shut and ran out to the landing.

"Mama, I just had a funny dream. The ghost of Ireland banged the window, saying: '*Ochone, ochone*! We are in terrible trouble!' It must be because we're going to see Yeats's play . . ."

"A likely story, Miss Molly O'Donovan. Now go back to bed and tell the ghost of Ireland to be a bit more quiet!"

Midnight, Saturday 22nd April.
My bedroom.

I've just had the most terrible fright! There was a rustle and I really did think the ghost of Ireland was coming to get me! But I had left a gap in the curtains and after my nerves calmed down I saw in a shaft of moonlight that there was a note pushed under my door. I was almost too afraid to get out of bed but my curiosity got the better of me. So I dashed out to retrieve it.

With great excitement I lit a candle and saw it was written on paper from the Imperial Hotel. But I was sorely disappointed to see it was only Anto's poem, dedicated to "dear bootyful Molly". At least he got my name spelt right this time. He must have got the notepaper from May, his sister who works there as a scullery maid. And someone must have helped him with the rest of the spelling, because it is much improved – in fact, it is good. Not Jack obviously!

This is what he wrote.

"Pádraig Pearse is not so fierce
And has a squinty eye,
But he has a dream of Ireland free,
And is prepared to die.
Old Fenian Clarke,
Has lit the spark, from his tobacco shop,
Mac Diarmada has a gammy leg,
But has the British on the hop.
Brave Connolly,
Believes history,
Says no more masters and slaves,
He founded the Citizen Army,
And now the Republic is his craze.
Countess Markievicz around Ireland flits,
With her noble Fianna Boy Scouts,
Now the boot is on the other foot,
And we'll kick the British out.
Son of a Count, Joseph Plunkett,
Is very sick with the T.B.
He was born to a life of leisure.
But will fight for his dear country.
Poet and scholar, Thomas MacDonagh,
Wants the Gaelic to revive,
He too will fight and die,
To keep the dream of free Ireland alive.
Then there's Ceannt the piper,
All sons of Erin's shore,
We will join them to root out tyranny,

And be slaves of Empire no more."

Well, perhaps it is a little bit good. Except Countess Markievicz is a daughter not a son of Erin's shore. Lively certainly, though I will never tell him that. Anto is too full of himself already and if he thought I admired his poem, well, his head would swell so much he'd never get through the door!

10 p.m. Sunday morning, 23rd April 1916.
Our house.

It is Easter Sunday! The day the Lord is risen and also the O'Donovan family, up and out bright and early even though it is a holiday. Mother told me Jack left to go to the mountains at the crack of dawn with his pals. That's the first I've heard about a trip to the mountains. I wonder if that is true or if there is going to be some sort of march after all, and that's his excuse.

Mother and I set off at seven o'clock with baskets of eggs for some of the families in the slums around us. The blind basket-makers up the road had given us some dear little baskets, which we had decorated with ribbons, and we had painted the boiled eggs.

We didn't have time for breakfast, so my mother gave me a sticky bun as a special treat from the Dublin Bread Company (saints don't have much time for cooking). I ate half and put the other half in my hankie in my pocket beside my tin of humbugs.

We were out so early I saw the milkman for the hotels come rattling his scooper against the churn.

"No rest for the wicked!" he called out.

"Nor the good neither," my mother replied.

First, we called into Henry Place to our char Nancy. Their hallway was open as it is a tenement where many people live in different rooms. I was relieved we didn't have to step over any drunks, who sometimes take refuge in such doorways. I have seen them when passing by other Dublin tenement houses and they scare me with their unfocused eyes and clumsy movements.

We only meant to leave the gifts outside Nancy's door without disturbing the family. Nancy usually rushes out to meet us at the front door, as if she has been watching out for us – Mother says she is probably embarrassed about her poor living quarters and doesn't want us to see them. But this morning we were earlier than usual and there was no sign of her. So we climbed to the second floor and met her daughter May just as she was coming out their door on her way to her work as a scullery maid at the Imperial.

We did not go in but I could see into their poor room as May stood in the doorway and I must admit I was shocked. Poor is a cold, damp room with peeling paintwork and sagging ceiling in a dingy street. A room that smells of potato peel and smoke. I understand now why my parents are so kind to Nancy and pay her even when she doesn't turn up, which is often. I saw three of the younger boys asleep on a mattress on the floor. The room was almost bare with a few tea chests for furniture. One upturned box was used as a table and had our old chipped cups and jam jars with cold tea on it. A line was hung across the room draped with a filthy cloth and the boys slept on one side and the girls on the other. They had no curtains but old newspapers over the windows to keep out the light. There was a glow of embers in the fire grate so May who is quiet and kind must have lit a fire before she went out.

Her eyes filled with tears when my mother handed her the basket of eggs, a loaf of bread and a pound of butter.

"Me ma will be thrilled," she whispered. "She's fast asleep. She was up all night with the babby."

I confess, I was surprised that Nancy has a new baby. She seems to me to be already an old woman. Her three-year-old, Alice, who is small for her age, peeked out from behind the curtain and cried to see May leave. I felt so sad when I saw her worn little nightdress, all patched and frayed, that I gave her the rest of my sticky bun. Well, you'd think I had given her a hundred pounds!

"Can I eat all of it?" she asked.

"Just for you," I whispered. "Now be a good girl and go back to bed." She crept back in behind the curtain.

"Is Anto gone to the mountains with Jack?" I asked May as we went down the stairs.

"I wouldn't put anything past that little bowsie since he fell in with them eejits with their Irish Republic," said May quietly to me. "Ma needs the money that comes from Da and Jemsie fightin' in the army in Flanders."

"I think he wants to be a hero," I said.

"He's not a bad lad. Gives my mother most of his earnin's. But he's got some quare notions in his head."

"I know," I said. "He's even written a poem about our 'leaders'."

May smiled at this. "Is that the one about Mac Diarmada with the gammy leg and the Countess flitting around Ireland with her Boy Scouts?"

We shared a little laugh at this.

"I gave him the paper, and helped with his spelling," she continued. "I'd be happy if he sticks to writin' the poems. Our poor ould Anto hardly ever went to school because he had to go to out to work so young. So maybe it'll encourage him to get a bit of educatin'."

I felt bad for always being mean to Anto, so I gave May my tin of humbugs for him.

We visited Mr Hanrahan, an old man of over eighty. His room was in an attic with barely enough space for a bed. It had no fire and it's a mercy he doesn't freeze to death. He was so happy to see us, he gripped my hands in his old worn ones. My mother also gave him Father's old tweed jacket that is frayed and patched.

"Mrs Bessie," he said to my mother, "you may be a Cracker but you're the best class of Christian I know."

They both laughed.

I was about to ask what was so funny when Mother silenced me with a look. She thinks it impolite when I pepper her with questions in front of people. But she explained the joke as we strolled back home.

"He mixed up 'Quaker' with 'cracker'!" I said.

"No, he didn't," said my mother in her soft Northern Irish accent. "The Dublin people are great wags so they are. Cream Crackers are made by a Quaker family, the Jacobs, in Bishop's Street, so he was pulling my wee leg."

"The Jacobs don't make the crackers by themselves, do they?" I said. "Don't they have that big factory up near Saint Patrick's Cathedral? Daddy and I cycled by it last week and it must make a million crackers a day!"

"True for you. There's two thousand women and over a thousand men there," laughed my mother. "They are better employers now but there was a strike in 1913 led by little Rosie Hackett – you know her from the First Aid. The women workers weren't paid much more than seven shillings a week."

My new kilt at eight shillings and eleven pennies cost more than that. My new coat was thirty shillings! No wonder the poor have to wear rags.

My mother is going to Belfast today to see her Great-aunt Bessie. She is the only relative who has kept in contact with her, because she too 'married out' – outside her own religion, that is. Some people really don't like this, the "so-called Christians" that my mother talked about. But I think

Jesus wouldn't mind because he thought everyone should love one another – even Great-aunt Bessie!

Aunt Bessie bewitched a very rich Protestant factory owner to marry her (for she does indeed look like an old witch) and is a staunch Unionist who believes Ireland should still be part of England. My father jokes that even her unmentionables are red, white and blue – the colours of the Union Jack! The Ulster Protestants also have their own army as Jack explained. They are so keen on being part of the United Kingdom that they are prepared to fight the government to stay in! But they too have gone to fight the Germans. So the only ones who like the Germans are the Irish Volunteers who want to kick the British out by force. I think I have got that right.

My father was reassured when he saw in the Sunday Independent the notice from Eoin MacNeill for the Irish Volunteers. It said no marches were to take place. There was also news that arms had been seized in Kerry! Along with some fellow called Roger Casement who was bringing them in from Germany. So they can't fight if they have no guns.

After Mass, Father and I accompanied Mother to Amiens Street Station. When we got back home, there were several messages for Father to go straight into the GPO to run some maintenance checks. Our own telephone line wasn't working either. So he sent one of his boys to fetch Miss Nugent to mind me and left straight away. But she sent a message that she had a headache even though she had promised my mother she would be on hand to help out if an emergency arose.

My father had already gone out and I was on my own. Not that I minded. I looked out the window and saw Jack's shadow, Hyacinth, pretending to window-shop in Dunn's Hatters. Since it was Easter I felt sorry for her wasting her time.

"Jack's gone to the mountains since the crack of dawn," I called out the window.

"I've just seen him go down by the Quays with Anto," she said, saucy as you please.

So he was lying about the mountains! Since Father has already gone out and Miss Nugent isn't here, I'm going to look for Jack with his new friends at Liberty Hall. This is being a bit daring – I don't normally go so far afield on my own without Jack or my parents. But I really must find out what is going on and I am a big girl now.

9 p.m. Easter Sunday.
My bedroom, after a busy day in Dublin.

Well, I came to no harm even though I went into the Lion's Den and didn't have Jack to guide my steps. Liberty Hall is on the River Liffey on the north side of the quays, just beside the Custom House. It used to be a hotel, Jack told me, but now that it is the headquarters of the Irish Trade and General Union it is more like a fortress. They have the Irish Citizen Army because the police beat them all up in 1913 when they went on strike. The bosses sacked all the workers who were in the Union, and wouldn't let them back to work, which is why it was called "the Lockout". Now the government say it is a hotbed of revolution my father says!

I was surprised to see a great many people coming and going on a Holy Day. I snuck in the door when no one was looking. There are always so many children about that nobody pays much attention to us.

Goodness! What a commotion there was inside! Their leader James Connolly was running around like his trousers were on fire! He once patted my head when I was in the Post Office, so I think he is a kind man.

I ducked under the stairs when he stopped to talk to young Martin King, who is a cable joiner in the Post Office. He has called to see my father sometimes. I didn't know that he was a member of the Irish Citizen Army.

"So cutting all the cables will cut off communication with England?" said James Connolly.

Martin King handed Connolly a piece of paper. Connolly glanced at it quickly.

Then King lowered his voice. "There may be other secret cables so you'd have to cut off the underground wires to the Telegraph Room to make sure. The Instrument Room on the first floor has an armed guard."

My ears pricked up. But I would not be able to tell my father because I was not meant to be here. And Jack would never ever speak to me again if I did.

"But it doesn't matter as we are not to do anything," said Martin King.

I was happy to hear that, for then I didn't have to feel guilty.

"When the time comes we will find out who is for Ireland," said Mr Connolly.

As I crouched under the stairway, I saw the Countess rush in. She was dressed as if for a play, in a uniform of green with gold buttons, a black velvet hat with a heavy plume of cock feathers, men's knee breeches and heavy boots. Around her waist was a cartridge belt and over her shoulder a bandolier, which is a belt with bullets in it. She is a handsome woman, very aristocratic. Jack says she doesn't really like girls, so her Fianna scouts is only for lads.

She was distraught.

"I was all ready to go at half past six this evening!"

"MacNeill has cut the ground from under our feet. But it will only mean a little delay," Connolly said.

"I have made the flags," she said proudly.

She shook out a rectangle of green, white and orange, which is the tricolour flag for the Irish Republic. Then she took out another green cloth that looked like a tatty old bedspread with words written on it.

"That's the green bedspread from Larry's bed. I cut it out on the drawing-room floor. The gold paint had dried out, so I moistened it with a tin of mustard. It's just barely dry."

I hoped Larry wouldn't get cold, whoever Larry was!
"There's a bit missing," said Connolly.

"Poppet my spaniel took a chunk out of it," she said.

As she smoothed it out, I saw the words "Irish Republic" in old-fashioned Irish writing, with a bit of the 'C' missing where the dog tore it. 'Republic' means they don't want to have a king. The last people who had a republic were the French and they cut their royals' and aristocrats' heads off. So I wonder would the Countess Marzipan, as Nancy calls her, have to cut her own head off if Ireland became a republic?

At first, I thought the Countess was being very silly making a huge fuss about cancelling something small like a parade. But then I felt a cold pang in the pit of my stomach. I still feel it. It was like a heavy sky before a storm, something threatening in the air, though it hasn't happened yet. Or maybe it's just because it's the time for April showers despite sunny days. Perhaps because I am writing a diary, I am getting fanciful.

As I left, Rosie Hackett, the tiny little woman Mother told me had organized the women's strike in Jacob's, dashed in clutching a document. She was in a state of excited panic.

"Hurry! The proclamation! Be careful, Jim, the ink is still wet!"

I waited until she was gone, then wandered about looking for Jack but got lost in the maze of rooms. I passed a music room where lots of people were practising as if for a concert. I recognized the man playing the flute, but I didn't know from where. Blundering about, I spied Mr Pearse through a doorway talking to a lot of other gentlemen. He glanced out but as his eyes go in different directions, I wasn't sure if he saw me or not.

I left with a creepy feeling of dread, suddenly desperate to find out what Jack had hidden in the mail bag of sphagnum moss during our trip to Howth Head. I had a bad feeling about it. So I ran in a panic back to Sackville Street.

Father was still at work. He almost never takes a day off, as he says the communication links always have to be kept running. And since the Post Office has just reopened, it still has teething problems.

I dashed over to the GPO and the sentries let me in, thinking I was looking for Father. They told me there had been a few problems with the wires around the country and he was in the Instrument Room so I just nodded and went into the lift – but instead of going up to the first floor I went down to the basement. I felt very brave going down to the rabbit warren of rooms and vaults like a secret world. But unlike the unfamiliar Liberty Hall, at least in the GPO I had my bearings and I thought I could find my way blindfold through its labyrinth.

I found the pile of mail sacks which had been left there and, making sure nobody was coming, began to search frantically in the five bags that still needed to be dried out. But all I gripped were handfuls of still damp sphagnum moss.

I was feeling very downhearted by the time I came to the last bag. It was much heavier than the others. With a heavy heart, I rustled through it and to my horror my hand touched cold hard steel. I took the object out, my hands shaking.

It was a gun! "Automatic Colt – Calibre .32 Rimless Smokeless" was printed on one side. It bore a little medal of a rearing-up colt on the handle, like something a cowboy or a gangster would have. It didn't weigh much and could easily be concealed in a coat pocket.

I panicked. A year and a half ago, there was major gun-running in Howth by the Nationalists bringing in German guns. I'd heard Jack and Anto going on about it before. This one looked American but it must have been hidden in the Bog of Frogs and Jack had retrieved it.

I wanted to hurl it into the Liffey to rust for all eternity. But my brother would never speak to me again for sure if I did, so I resolved to at least get rid of the bullets. I was terrified in case I shot my foot off but I managed to slide open the safety catch and empty out the bullets. I put the gun back. I weighed the bullets in my hand for an instant, sickened by the cold clink of steel. Then I ran as fast as I could, out of the GPO, down to O'Connell Bridge, past the blind beggar rattling his tin, and flung the bullets in the water. A Guinness barge came under the bridge and a plume of smoke rose up. A couple of bullets rattled off the boat and then plopped in the water.

Now at least Jack will not rot in hell for shooting someone dead.

I dashed back home and, feeling like a spy, I set about searching Jack's bedroom in case he has any other concealed weapons. I did find something new laid out under the mattress. A green soldier's jacket and a crusher hat, which has one side of the brim turned up – a Fianna Boy Scout uniform! Maybe he had been planning to wear it but they cancelled the march. There was also a beautiful new Sam Browne belt with a cross strap for the shoulder, just like the soldiers wear. It had his initials carved on it: JFO'D, Jack Fitzgerald O'Donovan. So that was the one he'd saved all his money for and was gambling over. He must have won it back from Gerald Keogh when they played double or quits. The sight filled me with dread. Jack's defiance of Father is definitely going up a notch.

As I pushed the belt back under the mattress, who should burst in but Jack! He ran at me and hastily checked I hadn't disturbed anything.

"I'm sorry, Jack," I cried. "I didn't mean . . ."

He pushed me roughly then grabbed me by the arm, twisting it behind my back. "If you so much as breathe a word!"

Tears pricked the back of my eyes but I tried not to cry. "But why do you have this, Jack?"

"They're for Anto," he mumbled.

"You're not mixed up in anything?" I asked him anxiously. "Only I don't want you to die for Ireland or any place else."

He dropped my arm and, screwing up my courage, I faced him. But when I looked him in the eye, his face crumpled like a small boy's. Then he tried to harden his features but looked sad and yearning.

"We have to shake off England's yoke one way or other. Ireland needs to be free."

"It's one thing trying to impress boys on a street corner. Another picking a fight with the British Empire that rules half the world," I said. "Even if they are all fighting the Germans, England still has millions more soldiers and loads of them are Irish. It's not just tin soldiers on a counterpane."

"Sometimes you have to take a stand. Anyway, what would you know about it? You're just a girl."

"I know it is wrong to take a life," I said.

"All of us young men are doomed to die in any case. Soon they will make us join the British Army by conscription," he said. "We might as well choose the cause we want to give our lives for. I can be cannon fodder in the British Army or sacrifice myself for something I believe in."

"But it's not just about dying," I said. "It's also about killing. Shooting someone dead with that gun –"

Jack gave me a sharp look that cut through me like a knife. I had said too much.

"What do you know about a gun, you stupid girl? If you dare breathe a word about anything, I will cut you dead."

Something suddenly struck me and I wondered why I hadn't realized it before. "Why did you ask me to check the names of the equipment at the Post Office? I was at Liberty Hall looking for you and I saw Martin King giving a note to James Connolly – was it the one with the list of machines I wrote out for you? Are you spying on Father?"

"Shut your mouth!"

"And all those sketches of bridges and rooftops?" I asked desperately. "Jack, please, tell me there is nothing amiss!"

"None of your business. I'm warning you!"

He stormed out. I am very much afraid and worried sick.

Father came home at lunchtime and to my relief showed no sign that he knew I'd been over to the GPO. Nor did he enquire about Miss Nugent. But I was still a bag of nerves. I tried to eat the boiled ham and potatoes my mother had prepared earlier but my stomach felt sick after my fight with Jack. I couldn't even manage a DBC currant bun.

After raining non-stop for the last thirteen days, there was a small break in the weather and Father decided to take me out on a bicycle ride to cheer me up. Often my father is so busy and distracted he doesn't notice me, but sometimes he surprises me by a sudden attentiveness. Jack had disappeared again and I was glad of the diversion. I changed into my new dress of cambric lace. Mother wouldn't have let me wear it cycling but Father doesn't care about such things.

Outside Trinity College Miss Mahaffey was just going out. She bid us good day and enquired after my mother. I was surprised she talked to us at all as she looks down on you as if you were a smell under her long pointy nose. Just because her father is a famous professor or something and head of Trinity, doesn't mean they are better than anyone else.

There was a lovely holiday air about Dublin. Many people had taken the tram into the city to go window-shopping. We cycled up to Dublin Castle, the centre of government, with its grey stone and impressive archways. It looked very quiet and brooding.

At Stephen's Green, we peeked into the Shelbourne Hotel where "the Quality" stay, as Dublin people call the rich. The hotel was heaving as the races are on in Fairyhouse tomorrow and the Spring Show, which is full of bulls and sheep and farmers, is due to start in Ballsbridge next week. My father advised the hotel on their telephone lines so we are always made welcome by the manager, Mr Olden, who invited us in for a cup of tea, his treat, and we sat in the front lounge. I felt just like a lady as I ate the finger sandwiches.

I kept trying to pluck up my courage to say something

to Father about Jack but he looked so careworn I didn't have the heart. I soon got distracted staring at the "the Quality". One fashionable Miss was wearing a yellow silk dress with a tiered skirt which was very daringly mid-calf length, with flesh-coloured tights and high shoes crisscrossed at the ankle. She caused quite a sensation and a couple of old ladies muttered under their breaths when she swished past. The stylish young woman winked at me. She was also wearing a jolly panama hat with a peacock feather and her hair was bobbed underneath.

But the highlight for me was seeing a woman wearing a Lanvin gown from Paris – Mother and I had admired it in the paper and it was a thrill to see it for real. It was beige silk with a little bouquet of artificial flowers at the cinched waist. The material was draped over the hips in folds and she looked like a doll. I was glad I was wearing my new white dress and didn't stick out like a scarecrow.

After that we cycled on up by Boland's Mill, the forbidding-looking large hulk of a building where they grind the flour, and stopped at the bridge into Ringsend to watch the boats docking. Several fishing boats pulled into the quayside and small groups of fishermen loaded barrels. No wonder the locals call it "Raytown" after the flat bony ray fish.

As we stood on the bridge, my father spied Mother O'Brien down on the quayside. She is the fishmonger my mother always buys from. She's still in her thirties, a handsome woman, but everyone calls her "Mother". She was inspecting ropes of mussels and a bucket of cockles brought to her by some fishermen.

"Happy Easter!" my father called out.

"The same to you!" She gestured to the bucket. "I'm sendin' these over to Gleeson's pub for the Waxies' Dargle tomorrow. All the aul' wans will be comin' for their annual outing."

"Ah, the annual cobbler's holiday," said my father. "Good luck to them. The cobblers deserve to rest their feet too."

"I'll be goin' off to Fairyhouse myself for the Irish Grand National. Bridie, my little one, loves the gee-gees."

"Put an each-way bet for me on Civil War," laughed my father.

"You're on! Though I fancy Allsorts myself," cried Mother, giving him a thumbs-up. "Hope it's worth the thirty-mile round trip."

What a strange name to call a holiday – the Waxies' Dargle! Father explained to me it's because the cobblers use wax to preserve the thread they use in stitching shoes – and in Dublin slang 'Dargle' means a holiday resort because the Quality go to picnic by the River Dargle in County Wicklow.

It sounds like the whole of Dublin will be betting on horses tomorrow! Hyacinth's family, the O'Hares, also plan to go to Fairyhouse. Her father is a photographer with Lawrence's, so he will be busy photographing the horses and jockeys. I wish Father would take me to the races. But he won't because he loves to work so. We don't have a motor car but he learned to drive when he was in America working for Mr Edison. I think he would go back to work for Mr Edison tomorrow but my mother still has hopes of being reconciled with her family here.

There is another reason. My mother lost two babies after me and they are buried in the Quaker Temple Hill Graveyard that is between Blackrock and Monkstown. They have but a simple stone saying, PATIENCE O'DONOVAN AGED THREE MONTHS 1905 and TERENCE O'DONOVAN 1913. I think my mother still sorrows for her lost babies and does not want to leave them. That is why she also collects those tiny porcelain dolls. Sometimes I think if I was still a baby she would pay more attention to me. But she is kept very busy being a saint.

We cycled back by the quays and passed by Liberty Hall. I was very anxious in case my father saw Jack inside and there would be a great to-do. But it seemed quiet.

We also called in to visit Father's youngest brother Edward and his wife Elizabeth who live in Oriel Street on the north side of the docks. Edward is a seaman and sails a pilot boat for ships coming into Dublin Harbour when he isn't on long voyages. He and Father enjoy speaking Hindi together on account of them being raised by *nyahs*,

Indian nurses, when they were little. Edward and Elizabeth too have been cut off by their parents, though Elizabeth is attempting a reconciliation. As well as "marrying out", Edward also disappointed his parents by leaving the Merchant Navy before he finished his training, as he was so desperate to have adventures. And Elizabeth's family is Presbyterian who didn't like her marrying a Catholic. In fact, her grandfather is a Minister of the Church. My aunt and uncle are very poor now but proud.

Elizabeth is kindly and was fretting over her baby Josephine who is just nine months old and sickly. William who is ten and seven-year-old Dan Junior were playing ball in the back yard. Dan is very skillful with a ball and very quick at everything. He is excellent at the mathematics and a firm of accountants, Craig Gardiner & Co in Dawson Street that he runs a few messages for, has offered him an apprenticeship when he is older. But Uncle Edward is not too keen because he says many of the clerks there are Irish extremists. He is happier that his older boy is being considered for a scholarship to his old school Blackrock College and is to visit there this week.

When I was practising the sailor's knots Edward teaches me, I heard my father say very quietly to him, "The Viceroy has sent to England for permission to arrest them all next week."

I saw little Dan's ears prick up at this, though he is but a small boy.

"Dan is all for a united Ireland," laughed Edward.

"He wants to fight the English but he's not even in long trousers yet. There's a fellow at the accountants called Michael Collins, a Corkman, who also works for another extremist, Count Plunkett, and Dan admires him very much."

Afterwards, we nipped over to the Post Office to collect more bags of sphagnum moss, for I shall spend tomorrow sewing, stuffing, sewing . . . *yawwwwnnnnn*!

We entered the vaults by the Prince's Street entrance. Father was glad to see all the wires humming. To him it is like music.

It is a most splendid building, like a palace. The roof is a large glass dome with elaborate plasterwork. There are beautiful white pillars and a mosaic floor, with counters all of red teak wood and bright brass fittings everywhere. Father is very proud of it, as if he designed it himself!

We took the lift up to the Instrument Room on the first floor that directly looks out over Sackville Street.

Father repeated to me the names and numbers of some of the equipment – *four fast-speed duplex repeaters – twenty and forty line concentrators* and so on – all the names I had heard so often before. I confess it just all looked like boxes of wires and "circuitry" to me. I might as well have been looking at the innards of a goat. But it gave me a cold sick feeling to think I'd revealed something I shouldn't have.

"Behold the beating heart of the Post Office," Father

said proudly. "Jack is getting very interested in it too. Maybe he wants to follow in my footsteps."

The mention of Jack unnerved me.

Father pointed to a bunch of red and yellow wires. "Without those cables, the Lord Lieutenant of Ireland couldn't talk to the Prime Minister. The whole government of Ireland would come crashing down."

I felt another pang as I wondered why Jack had really asked me to copy out those names. Maybe it was just my imagination that he had passed the note to Connolly through Martin King. But then I told myself they said they weren't going to do anything so it was of no consequence. I crossed my fingers and hoped so!

But then Father has been pleased that Jack has shown an interest recently, asking him what lines were connected to where. I truly hope that Jack really is interested and is not some sort of spy for the extremists. And I his foolish, unwitting accomplice. Father would be devastated!

Especially as I love it all for Father's sake, even if I don't understand it, most of all the Telegraph Room. Here there are about fifty desks, each with a phone and a bank of wires. The Telegraph Officers interpret the electronic pulses of dots and dashes called Morse code into meaningful words and sentences. My father sees it all as terribly modern, but to me they are like magicians, interpreting signals from beyond like Mr Yeats and his Ouija board.

Both Jack and I have learned Morse code from Daddy and for our amusement we have developed our own tapping system, using knocks like prisoners use instead of dashes and dots. We sometimes communicate with it through our bedroom walls. "God Bless You" for example is G-B-U – two knocks pause two knocks, two knocks pause one, then five pause four. It's gas fun.

I spent a watchful evening sewing muslin bags for the moss.

I don't know what to do about Jack, and it gives me a feeling like I'm teetering on the roof.

In any event Father was so tired and dozed so peacefully in his armchair by the fire, I didn't have the heart to add to his cares by saying anything about Jack. I tried to put it out of my mind. Perhaps it is best if I sleep on it and see what tomorrow brings.

Then Jack came home briefly and said he was going out to the Dublin Mountains again, tomorrow. I bet he's up to something.

"You cannot go!" I cried. "You will have to stay with me when Father goes to work."

"Molly, dear, Miss Nugent will come."

"But her headache," I said very loudly.

"What headache?" my father laughed. "Unless you are planning to give her one with your shouting!"

Jack smirked at me. I could say nothing, or I would be caught out in not owning up that Miss Nugent was sick today.

All I have to do is say Jack is in the Fianna and there will be skin and hair flying! But if I do he will never forgive me and I don't want to lose Jack.

7.45 a.m. Monday 24th April 1916
My bedroom.

I awoke sweating from a troubling dream. I saw fires, all scarlet and leaping flames, and Jack lost in a burning forest. I ran in to see if he was in bed, but there was only the faint imprint of his head on the pillow. I looked under his mattress and his uniform was gone! So I think he does mean to go on some practice with the Countess and the Fianna Boy Scouts in their game of soldiers.

I had my breakfast of porridge with honey, lining up all the husks around the rim of the bowl. My father had a boiled egg and toast. When I put on my shoes, I found a little white rosebud inside one. I smiled and admired it in the palm of my hand. Jack must have picked it up somewhere and left it as a peace offering. I put it in my locket behind his little portrait, opposite the one of my parents. But I am anxious to see him and settle the peace between us properly. For I cannot bear to be out of sorts with him!

11.30 a.m. Easter Monday 24th April

Father and I went for a walk up to the Green to feed the ducks at 9 o'clock. It was a lovely warm spring day for the bank holiday with daffodils and crocuses out in the parks. I could see buds on the trees, including the cherry blossoms that are wearing white for Eastertide. But I felt uneasy about my dream and all the mystery surrounding Jack's actions. My conscience was troubling me about the list of GPO machines and equipment I'd written out for Jack. So I resolved to say something to Father about my fears.

But just as I opened my mouth, we bumped into the Killikellys on Sackville Street – the grandfather, the aunts, Addy and her younger sister Jane, and their glum nephews who live on Upper Gloucester Street. I thanked Addy most kindly for my wonderful diary.

"It is her constant companion," my father joked. "No doubt it is full of secrets."

I blushed, for he was nearer the mark than he guessed.

"We are taking a special excursion to Athlone to visit my granddaughters Annie and Fanny who are at Our Lady's Bower Boarding School," Mr Killikelly informed us. "The nuns have kindly told us we can board with them for the week." With his upright bearing, he looked every inch the retired Royal Irish Constabulary Officer. His two grandsons Christopher and Gerard are both in the Fianna and they didn't look very happy to be carted off to Athlone to stay with a bunch of nuns!

"I have to hurry," said Jane. "I'm on duty at Crown Alley Telephone Exchange all over the holiday."

"Just like Father," I said.

Most of the shops were shut for the holiday. Even the Dublin Bread Company café, which is normally full of chess players, was closed.

We stopped at the bridge over the swift-flowing Liffey to gaze out to sea. I noticed a good many people in uniform cycling up to Liberty Hall, so perhaps they are starting a cycling club instead of marching everywhere! I hope the Countess will be happy and get to wave her flags.

As we walked by Trinity College, we met a jolly group of British soldiers in uniform.

"G'day, mate," a man said in jaunty tones. "Is this here Trinity College?"

"It is indeed, sir," my father said. "And where do you hail from?"

"Australia, mate. The name's Private Michael John McHugh." He shook my father's hand. "We're off-duty Anzacs – ya know, Australian and New Zealand soldiers – and just taking in the sights. Have been with the 9th Battalion in Gallipoli in Turkey."

"You are brave men," my father said.

"I'm on sick leave, had influenza – but I'm fine now. My mate here is another wild colonial – from South Africa." He pointed to one of his companions who was wearing a kilt.

"Always glad to take the Irish Air," the South African said, swirling his skirts and pretending to dance a jig.

"Have you ever seen a kangaroo?" I asked eagerly of Private McHugh.

The man mussed up my hair. "Not only have I seen one, I've eaten one!" he laughed. "Tough old critters. Not for young ladies." He jumped up and down to show me how they bounce around.

"You can be sure that kanga didn't get away from McHugh," laughed one of the other Anzacs. "He's the best damn shot in the whole army. Whole world I'd wager."

"Not today, I'm off duty. G'day to you. We'll make our way up Sackville Street?"

All McHugh's sentences sounded like questions so I answered him just in case.

"It's up there across the bridge," I replied. "The widest street in Europe." With much laughter they continued on their way.

We sauntered up to Stephen's Green. I fed the ducks with a great many other children, some with their nannies gossiping on park benches. My father got talking with the park keeper, Mr Carney, and they remarked that there weren't many men about – they must have all gone to Fairyhouse for the day.

There was such a holiday air abroad that I felt quite relaxed again and was glad I had not spoiled the mood by opening my big mouth about Jack. It's probably best if I wait until Mother is home before disturbing the hornet's nest.

Back home, I was wearing my mother's Red Cross apron and pretending to be a doctor when Miss Nugent came to sit with me again. In between scolding my poor arithmetic and calling me a booby, she embroidered her big tapestry of Dublin city, with Nelson's Pillar at the centre. She is such a poor needlewoman and always in such a temper, I expected her to stab herself. She said she'd much rather be going to Fairyhouse with her beau, Colonel Foster, who has also hired a motor car. Her "beau" is about a hundred and has a red face like a baboon's bottom and a yellow mustache like an old sweeping brush. I am not being rude but "stating the facts" as she instructs me to do.

"Still playing doctors and nurses at your age," she said nastily, glancing at my aprons and my teddies and dolls. "At least you have little chance of killing them."

She made me so cross again, I confess now, Dear Diary, to doing something unkind. Not on purpose exactly.

I went to the privy at the bottom of our backyard, and when I came back she noticed something clinging to the top of my head.

"Child, you are a disgrace. There is a big black piece of dust in your hair." She cruelly grabbed at the hair on the crown of my head and swept something off that landed in her workbox. But she didn't notice it.

Straight away, I saw it was a spider as big as the palm of your hand and all twitchy and black. I tried to say something, but she told me to stay quiet and attend to my English lesson, which explained the difference between "paradox" and "irony". So, for once, I did as I was told.

Well, it was very funny and just like a re-enactment of "Miss Muffet"! She went back to her needlework and when she reached for her scissors, her hand brushed the massive creepy spider and it scurried onto her embroidery cloth. As she leapt onto her chair, her shrieks would have woken the very devil!

I said, "Why, what can be the matter?" Knowing full well.

She pointed with a terrible face like thunder.

I regarded her embroidery of wavy streets and said, all calm, "I see you have stitched a strange large straggly spider. It is most lifelike. Your best work yet." I was being pert but then I did something naughty. I picked up the cloth and made to bring it to her.

"Why, it's real!" I said.

"Go away, horrible unnatural child! Tell your parents I am not coming back! To think I nearly missed Fairyhouse because of you!" She ran from the house.

I felt a tiny bit guilty but then laughed and laughed.

I was free, hurrah! I decided to crawl out on the roof. I took Father's spyglass with me. It is brass and leather and extends out in four sections to just over a foot and a half. It helps you see stuff miles away as if it's under your nose.

As I looked down Abbey Street, I saw the marchers from Liberty Hall and strained to see if Jack might be among them.

I saw Matthew Connolly, the bugler, at the front, sounding the fall-in as a group including his brother Seán the actor headed over Butt Bridge by the Customs House. They were quite a raggle-taggle army of about sixty. I spotted the leader, James Connolly, in his dark green uniform with a gun with a bayonet. On his right, Patrick Pearse the teacher with his large pale face, in the darker green of the Volunteers. Beside him, the man who looks half dead, Joseph Plunkett the Count's son, with a bandage around his throat. He was beautifully dressed in high tan leather boots with spurs and wore a pince-nez eyepiece. They were marching together, just like in Anto's poem.

Some of the small army were in green uniforms. But many had made up their uniform as if for a play, with leggings and tunics and those bandoliers that make them look like bandits. Some had no uniforms, just armbands. At the back I thought I spied the old bomber tobacconist in normal clothing, Tom Clarke himself.

Two dray horses rumbled along in the rear and pulled an assortment of equipment, including guns. I also saw a pile of cauliflowers on the back of the cart.

As I gazed at the marchers and thought how sad it

was that so many people want to fight each other, I felt very guilty for frightening poor old Nosy Nugent. I vowed to make an apology. So I raced downstairs to take her embroidery to the Metropole Hotel across the street where she boards, forgetting for the moment that she had probably gone to Fairyhouse.

I noticed that my father had left behind his sandwiches, as he was in such a rush for a meeting with the Post Office Head, Mr Hamilton Norway. I decided to take them to Father as the GPO is just beside the Metropole. After that, I knew I would have a boring day doing Latin as penance.

9 p.m. Monday evening 24th April.
My bedroom.

Mercy! The events I now have to describe are most extraordinary and terrible and I am out of my mind with worry!

As I ran out the door today I saw the tin-pot army turn into Sackville Street. Another small group split off and crossed the bridge towards Westmoreland Street. I made haste, as I didn't want to get caught up with them, though I nearly tripped up scanning their ranks for a sight of Jack.

A group of British Officers were gathered on the pavement outside the Metropole Hotel and laughed to see their junk-shop weapons.

"Will these bloody fools never tire of marching up and down the street?" sneered one.

"Here comes the Citizen Army with their pop-guns!" jeered another.

I bolted into the main entrance of the GPO and enquired after my father. One of the counter staff said he might have left with Mr Hamilton Norway who had an urgent meeting at the Castle. But another said he might still be in the Instrument Room, as there were a few problems with the wires. I joked with the clerk that some people have nothing better to do than buy stamps on a holiday.

I was one of them! I quickly purchased a postcard and stamp for my mother and wrote a brief message saying how much I missed her.

The clerk was ushering me towards the lift when the marchers from outside suddenly surged in.

"Everybody out!" shouted a tall good-looking man. It was "The Big Fella", Michael Collins.

Several people looked with amusement, as if it was a joke or some kind of game.

The woman in front of me, a large lady in a colourful hat, sighed in annoyance. "I'm sorry but my daughter is getting married in six weeks and these are the wedding invitations," she insisted. "I am not leaving here without my stamps!"

She got the message when a rebel poked her gently in the backside with his pike. Then the clerk vaulted over the counter and ran for the door. That was like a signal. A sudden understanding swept through the room and it was bedlam! People rushed towards the main doors in a frenzy, coats flying, bodies bumping into each other.

A British Lieutenant was held on the end of a pike as Michael Collins searched him. It was the officer who had earlier sneered at them.

"Stop this nonsense at once! I am Lieutenant Chalmers!" he shouted.

Collins looked at him coldly.

"Am I to be killed?" said the officer.

"You are being held as a prisoner of war," said Collins.

They tied him up with telephone cord and put him in the tall wooden telephone cabinet with the clock on top, the centerpiece of the new public area. I thought the soldier would die of fright!

There was so much turmoil that some of the rebels were nearly pushed out the doors themselves. I got the impression that some of them didn't realize themselves what was going on. At first it was comical but then, as guns were brandished, fear gripped me like ice in my veins. I felt my legs glued to the floor by the counter.

"Smash the windows!"

The yell broke through my stupor. There was a hellish racket as axes, rifle-butts and hammers smashed into the beautiful big glass panes all around the building. Shards of glass flew up into the air like icicles.

A woman outside shouted, "Glory be to God! Would

you look at them divils smashin' all the lovely windows!"

A young boy rebel gashed his hand and his comrade wearing a Red Cross on his chest shouted, "Damn those windows – they're more dangerous than the British army!"

The sight of scarlet blood on the boy's tunic shook me to the core. Nothing in the First Aid manuals prepared me for the shock of real injury and, to my shame, I shrank back, relived to see the rebel with the Red Cross armband come to his aid. In the confusion, nobody saw me scuttle around and press open the lift on the Henry Street side of the building.

How long those few seconds felt, reaching the first floor! My stomach clenched into a knot. "Please let us all be safe!" I prayed. But it gave me time to regain my composure and think of a plan.

I would warn my father and then immediately try to find Jack. If he was caught up in this it was my fault. If I had betrayed information about the GPO, I was just as guilty. I should have spoken sooner.

The doors of the lift opened, and all seemed weirdly normal on the first floor. I realized the rebels had yet to come here. But it wasn't calm for long. A telegraphist flew by the glass panels between the offices that lined both sides of the corridors, into the Comptroller's office.

"All the telegraph connections are down!" she cried.

There was such a hubbub in the Instrument Room, with people checking connections, that nobody noticed me.

"All the cross-channel wires are disconnected!" a man called out.

A man ran in breathless. "There's nothing wrong with the heat coil frame. O'Donovan is checking it now. But he thinks all telegraph wires have been cut."

My father was in the basement! I had to try to get to him.

Someone else called out, "It's armed insurrection! The Shinners have occupied downstairs."

The Shinners is what everyone calls the rebels, even though I've heard my father say that the Republican Sinn Féin party ('sinn féin' means 'ourselves' in Irish) doesn't have its own army. So I'm not the only one who gets them all mixed up.

An older man, Samuel Guthrie the Superintendent, called out,

"Kelly, phone to Army Command HQ, the Police at the Castle and to Marlboro Barracks!"

He ran to the windows to look out at the glass being smashed.

"Glory be, they're piling up all the Post Office ledgers to barricade the windows!" a man called out in the street.

Now I understood why they had smashed the windows. To house the barricades and in case they got shot at in an attack.

Nobody noticed me. So I tucked in behind a stationery cupboard, as I tried to figure out a way to get to the basement.

It felt like hours in that cramped space, but I could only have been there for little more than ten minutes.

Around twelve thirty, a Sergeant of the Guard rushed in with four men.

"They are forcing the stairs entrance leading from Henry Street to the Instrument Room!"

At once the Post Office staff started to barricade the passage leading from the head of the stairs, filling it with chairs, wastepaper baskets, and boxes.

"We have no ammunition in our damn guns," called out another one of the guards. All four of them and the sergeant stayed outside the door to guard the Instrument Room.

"Ladies, go to the retiring room on the southern corridor," Mr Guthrie instructed. "Put on your outdoor apparel in case you have to leave the building."

I came out of my hiding place, gambling that he would take me for one of the telegraphists. His eyes glanced over me and, in the tumult, I think he did not notice that I was but a child.

But before the women could leave, several shots rang out close by!

"The sergeant is wounded!" called out a man. "The rebels are coming up through the southern entrance!"

All at once a group of rebels burst through from the dining room next door.

"Everybody out!" ordered a rebel, fixing us with his bayonet. He was a fine-looking man in a beautifully cut uniform, better quality than the others. "I'm very sorry to disturb you, gentlemen and ladies. This is the first and last act."

"You came, The O'Rahilly!" another rebel who had just come in greeted him.

I thought it was funny that his first name was "The" but I found out later that the chiefs of the old Irish clans were called like that.

"I was going around the country cancelling the Rising on Eoin McNeill's orders," The O'Rahilly said. "Nobody bothered to tell me it was happening anyway. I drove straight here. I helped to wind the clock, so I have come to hear it strike."

"Everybody out now!" his comrade shouted.

"I will not leave without this sergeant who needs to see a doctor at Jervis Street Hospital," rang out a clear Scottish voice. It was Miss Gordon, the Assistant Supervisor of Telegraphs. She was trembling but fixed them with a resolute look.

The O'Rahilly looked horrified when he saw that the sergeant's right upper arm was bleeding profusely from a gunshot wound.

"But I must take him prisoner," he said. "That is my instruction. Anyone here know First Aid?" Then he noticed me. "You there, attend to the man."

I looked down. I had forgotten I was wearing Mother's Red Cross apron. I froze but the injured sergeant let out a cry and I knew I had to do something.

With trembling hands, I cleaned out his wound with water from his flask. I had in the large front pocket of the apron a couple of bags of muslin filled with sphagnum moss. So, suddenly remembering my training, I applied the dressing and told him to be brave. Having no other bandages, I tore Miss Nugent's embroidered cloth that I was still carrying. I hoped she would not mind but it was in a good cause and it was very ugly anyhow. But blood continued to seep through Miss Nugent's embroidery, staining the straggly embroidered streets with crimson, and the sergeant grew pale.

"He needs a doctor," I said, terrified my poorly executed bandage would make him worse. I dearly wished I had listened to my mother and paid more attention to the basic instructions.

"Allow me, good sir," said Miss Graham. "When he has received professional attention at the hospital, I will return with your prisoner. No one will think much of you if your prisoners die for want of a doctor." She was nervous but firm.

To their credit, they allowed her to leave with the injured man. I breathed a sigh of relief that at least the poor sergeant would get a proper dressing for his wound at the hospital.

Still shaking, I looked out the window and saw rebels distributing pamphlets to astonished onlookers. I wondered if it was the same notice I saw little Rosie Hackett running in with yesterday at Liberty Hall. The "proclamation", whatever that is.

"One of them is going to read something," I called out. "It's Patrick Pearse!"

Everything stopped in the Instrument Room. We gazed down below at Patrick Pearse surrounded by broken glass. He held a paper in his hand and twitched with nerves. But he read out his "proclamation" in a clear voice.

"Irishmen and Irishwomen, in the name of God and of the dead generations . . ."

There were a few shouts of "Hear hear!"

Then one person called "Traitor!"

"Let the man speak," called out the flower-seller at Nelson's Pillar.

"We hereby proclaim the Irish Republic as a Sovereign Independent State, and we pledge our lives, and the lives of our comrades-in-arms, to the cause of its freedom."

Several people walked off but the flower-seller was weeping.

"The Republic guarantees religious and civil liberty, equal rights and equal opportunities to all its citizens . . . cherishing all the children of the nation equally . . ."

There was now a chilling silence and I felt sorry for Mr Pearse that his great speech was met with so little enthusiasm.

"Until our arms have brought the opportune moment for the establishment of a permanent National Government . . . elected by the suffrages of all her men and women, the Provisional Government, hereby constituted, will administer the civil and military affairs of the Republic in trust for the people."

So this was no playacting. The extremists were rebelling and were seizing control of the country!

There was something very moving in the pale poet speaking from his heart. Even if one did not agree with him. But then I noticed the armed guard near him and saw they meant to win the argument by force.

I heard some of the names of the signatories and it was just like Anto's poem. As well as Mr Patrick Pearse, there was old Thomas Clarke the tobacconist, his friend Seán Mac Diarmada who has a gammy leg, Eamonn Ceannt the piper, James Connolly who hates all the bosses, Joseph Plunkett who looks half dead already and Thomas MacDonagh who writes poems and teaches at a university. They must be the most unlikely bunch of revolutionaries ever. No wonder the government didn't bother arresting them. Though they may feel differently now.

But are all these good things to be achieved down the barrel of a gun? Can you get good things by bad means? I confess I am confused and much troubled by this. What is the word Miss Nugent was trying to drum into me? Paradox. Where two things that are seemingly contradictory can possibly be true. That's what it is. Or is it an irony? Where one thing is said but the opposite is meant? Can you come in peace if armed to the teeth? I really should listen to Miss Nugent and pay more attention to my lessons so I can think about these things properly in my own mind.

The soldier doing First Aid downstairs reported for duty to The O'Rahilly, and said his name was Private Chapman. He asked me where I'd got the bags of bog moss from. I told him I'd made them and asked him if he knew my brother Jack but he just shook his head.

"Most of the Fianna boys will be under the command of the Countess," he said. "She is a roving ambassador and will be travelling to all our occupations."

"Where?" I asked him quickly.

"They don't tell lowly privates," he whispered. "Until an hour ago, I thought we were on parade. This is as much a surprise to me as you."

I tried to fix him with a scowl but tears sprang to my eyes.

"I think they mean to take the Castle and Stephen's Green," he said quietly. "The Countess and Dr Lynn were driving first to the Castle, I heard them say it."

In all the confusion no one saw me make my way down to the basement. As I inched along the corridor towards the lift, I heard James Connolly call out to a young man.

"O'Kelly, would you ever go back to Liberty Hall and fetch the flags out of the room at the back where we keep the brushes?"

I suppose he meant the Countess's flags.

Down in the basement, the wires had been hacked to bits. I prayed Jack had at least played no part in this. There was no sign of Father. I made my way out of the GPO by clambering over the barricade to the Henry Street exit that had been hastily erected by the staff, mercifully still unguarded. As I looked up the street, by good fortune I caught sight of my father by Arnotts' drapers, with Mr Gommershall the Superintending Engineer.

"Father!" I ran to them.

"Molly!" he said, grabbing me tightly. "I sent a messenger to find you but told him to go around by Moore Street." In the strangeness of the situation he did not question what I was doing there but was relieved that I had saved him a journey.

He gave me twenty pounds! A fortune.

"Get Miss Nugent to take you to my cousin Elizabeth who will get you all to Kingstown to her parents. Edward is sailing to New York and won't be back for some months. Willie, their older boy, is on trial for a scholarship to Blackrock College so is away for the week. So you will be a help for Elizabeth. Stay there until we send for you. I will telephone the ticket office at Poulaphouca to hold on to Jack when he comes from his trek in the mountains for his tram and also telephone your mother to stay in Belfast until further notice."

I blushed at the mention of Jack at the mountains but I couldn't say anything.

"Miss Nugent has gone to Fairyhouse, I think," I admitted.

"Damn that woman! Be my good brave Molly and get your bicycle and go over to Oriel Street by the back routes. With any luck all this trouble will be over by tonight. Lancers might come to Sackville Street on horseback. So hurry."

"We must get to Crown Alley to the Telephone Exchange now," urged Mr Gommershall quietly to my father. "The rebels haven't cut the private telephone lines yet."

"Then we can reroute the telegraphs," my father said. Then he turned to me. "If you cannot get to Oriel Street, make your way to Dr Ella Webb on Hatch Street. She will take care of you."

Mr Gommershall touched my father's sleeve and I knew he had to go and it might be to some danger.

"I would take you with me, Molly, but it might not be safe to be with a GPO official."

I embraced Father tightly, afraid that it might be the last time I saw him. I didn't dare linger as I know I am in a whole heap of trouble.

It was only as I rushed down Henry Street that I realized I had lost his sandwiches somewhere in all the confusion.

I ran on and noticed a crowd of onlookers had gathered outside the GPO. I saw a copy of the proclamation weighted down with stones so it wouldn't blow away at Nelson's Pillar. I picked it up and stuffed it in my big front pocket. There was a strange atmosphere abroad – almost like a show was being put on in the capital. But then I noticed rebel snipers posted on the corners of the GPO.

"They've taken the Daily Express and City Hall, but not the Castle!" someone called out.

My mind was churning as I ran for my bicycle at the back of our house. I felt bad that I couldn't confess to my father that Jack was one of Countess Markievicz's Boy Scouts. But I was going to stick to my plan for good or ill. I would find Jack – that was my main goal. We would go together to Cousin Elizabeth and head for Kingstown. If he wouldn't come willingly, I would drag him. But I had to find him, either way.

At home, I got busy and loaded a stock of sphagnum-moss bags into my knapsack and some pannier bags. I also took my First Aid kitbag and my Saint John's Ambulance armband with the white eight-pointed star. I put my mother's Red Cross tabard apron over my new coat and a little Red Cross flag on my knapsack. I also packed my father's spyglass in its little leather case. I already had a photograph of Jack in my locket. And I took my Dear Diary in case I wanted to note down anything interesting. Even mother would have been impressed at how neatly I packed it all in. I also checked in Jack's room and noticed there was no sign of his climbing gear. His bike was gone too, and that made me think he was most likely to be around the city as he would have taken the tram to the mountains.

As I wheeled my bicycle around from the back yard, I noticed flags being hoisted over the GPO. One of green, white and orange at the Henry Street Corner and at the opposite end the Countess's bedspread with the words "Irish Republic" picked out in gold. Only I know the gold is also mustard!

I hurried across the road and, as I looked up towards the Parnell monument at the top of Sackville Street, I saw a troop of lancers on horseback coming down from the Rotunda, all feathers and plumes like cockatoos.

Shots rang out! Two horses dropped dead, one near the Pillar and the other much further back along the street, and the whole unit turned tail and charged back down Parnell Street. A soldier fell down, his arms outstretched in the shape of a cross. His poor horse nosed him, waiting for his master to get up. It was the saddest sight. My legs took over and I pelted with my bike from the scene. Now I felt truly unnerved.

I was going to look for the Countess at Dublin Castle first. I raced across the city, pedalling like fury, going down the quays, across Ha'penny Bridge, through Temple Bar and over to Dublin Castle by the bottom of Dame Street.

As I cycled through Dame Street, I saw the familiar figure of Skeffy. His face was white with shock as he looked at a broken shop-front window.

At Dublin Castle, I was met with a very different scene. Hostile crowds had gathered and were jeering at the Green Fenian uniforms of some fellows on the roofs of City Hall. Against the blinding sun, they were like a line of cutouts we make for our scrapbooks.

A policeman lay in the road. I shuddered. He did not look alive.

"They burst through the Castle gates. It was all them actors from the Abbey Theatre," a dairyman said. "Constable James O'Brien tried to bar them, so he did, and they shot him in the head. That pretty actress woman, what's her name – Helena Moloney – fired her revolver into the air and the rest of the police ran like blazes. Imagine they have women fightin' and all. Then a soldier on duty fired at the gate before runnin' for cover and the rebels all scattered like mice."

"But then they didn't go into the Castle, that's the strange thing – there are hardly any soldiers there," said a young woman office worker in a smart suit. "They've gone into City Hall instead," she pointed to the City Hall which is right next to the Castle, "and the offices of the Mail and Express newspapers. They're posting snipers on all the roofs."

"That Mr Sheehy Skeffington nearly got shot himself rescuing a British soldier," said the dairyman.

I knew then why Skeffy had looked so shocked and pale.

As we spoke a heavy rat-a-tat rang out. It was raining bullets down on the Castle. My hands flew to my ears and panic gripped my stomach. But it also felt unreal, like a pageant was unfolding, and at any moment the curtain would come down.

"Girl, you should go home!" said the dairyman as we crouched in a doorway.

"That's Seán Connolly on the City Hall roof, I'd swear it!" said the young office worker, Eileen, who'd told me she was a typist in the Castle. "He works at City Hall, in the driving-license division, so he must have got them in. He's a great actor. I have tickets to see him in Yeats's play tomorrow."

I told her we also had tickets.

"I go to everything he's in. He should be in the pictures." Her eyes shone when she spoke of him.

I looked up and saw several people moving about on the ramparts. I took out my spyglass and, flickering on the edge of my field of vision, I thought I saw a youth with red-gold hair blazing in the sun.

"Jack!" I cried out.

If Seán Connolly was up there, his brother Matthew and Jack might be also!

There was a lull in the shooting and, without thinking, I ran towards the City Hall gates and somehow, I don't know how, I scaled them. No shots rang out. Perhaps because they saw I was wearing medical insignia and carrying my First Aid kit.

I rushed into the building and the young man guarding the entrance let me through. I ran, my breath ragged in my throat, up the wide marble staircase and heard the hail of bullets as it ricocheted off the building. It sounded different to the rifle fire – more constant.

Shards of glass flew by as I ran up those stairs. Bullets splintered wood and raised clouds of plaster and stone dust.

I passed two women, one in Citizen Army dress, the other in plain clothes, who were looking out the window on the second floor.

"There's been a change in the weather, looks like a hail shower," one called.

"That's not hail, that's bullets!" her comrade replied.

I glanced back. Sheets of bullets were streaming past the window.

I gained the roof and saw about ten Citizen Army rebels up there. The city flag of Dublin, with three gates on green with a blue corner, was lying limp. Up the slope, behind the roof gable facing Parliament Street, I saw a roof ladder, and on it Matthew Connolly! He was on lookout duty, his bugle still around his shoulder. As more volleys of shots rang out, the roof slating near him was becoming cracked and chipped.

"Get down from there, you eejit!" I called out.

Matthew glanced back and nearly fell off his ladder.

"Are you one of us?" he asked.

I pointed to my Saint John's Ambulance armband.

"No, I'm looking for Jack."

"Haven't seen him since this morning," he said.

"But he's in it, isn't he?" I asked.

He nodded.

Another volley of fire rang out. The slating became perforated with holes and slid into the valley beside him.

As Matthew came down the ladder, another rebel shouted out, "For God's sake, Matthew, get over to the Dame Street end!"

He obeyed, moving to the far corner of the roof obscured by chimneystacks.

I saw a First Aid Instructor, Dr Kathleen Lynn, who was one of the Citizen Army. She had taught us how to make a tourniquet to stop bleeding and how to do artificial respiration.

"You have the supplies?" she said to me.

So, I had been let in because they were expecting some First Aid kit.

I handed her a bag of dressings. "They have yet to be purified," I said. "But they are cleaned and packed."

She scanned the rooftop. I saw a strikingly handsome man coming towards us, walking upright as if he was taking the boards at the theatre.

He raised a flag over the balustrades. The green flag unfurled and blew in the breeze.

"Get down, Seán Connolly!" called out Dr Kathleen. "Crouch and take cover!"

He gave us a slow smile. It was his last act. A shot rang out like the crack of a whip and he fell like a tree. Immediately a woman rebel ran to him and cradled his head in her lap. Her tears fell on his face. It was the actress Helena Moloney. She whispered the Act of Contrition into his ear. Dr Kathleen crawled across the bullet-pocked roof and felt his pulse.

"There is no need for First Aid."

He must have died instantly. I was too shocked to take it in.

A cry rang out. Then a burst of wracking sobs. It was Matthew over on the other side of the roof. He must have been told about his brother.

"Stay at your post! There are snipers on the Castle Roof! That's an order!" another rebel called to him.

But Matthew tried to stand again to get to his brother.

Dr Kathleen crawled over to him and pulled him down.

"Matthew, get off the roof! I don't want your mother to lose all her sons."

But he refused to move now. "I will defend the position," he insisted.

Beneath the next crack of bullets, I heard a whimpering sound. Someone with a shock of red-gold hair was slumped behind the opposite side of the dome, the hair all the more brilliant for being reflected in the glass. I panicked that it was Jack.

I crawled over, my heartbeat drowning out the bullets

in my ears. He was just a boy, of my own age, holding his right shoulder, his hair a redder shade than Jack's. I saw the blood seep on his green, homespun jersey. My heart was in my mouth, pleased it wasn't Jack, yet guilty for feeling relieved that it was someone else.

Immediately Dr Kathleen was at my side. She tore open his clothing and exposed the pulsating flesh at the top of his shoulder, checking the back for an exit wound.

"It's superficial," she said, and immediately applied one of the dressings I had just handed her. She reached into her bag and brought out a spool of bandages.

"You're going to be okay, Arthur," she said to the boy as she handed me the roll of bandages to fix the dressing.

My fingers were trembling, but I concentrated with all my might to pass the bandage over his shoulder, under his arm and across the chest to fix the dressing in place. I secured it with a pin. My only practice was on a woman in class and on my doll. I had no time to wonder at what I was doing.

The boy was shaking and saying his Hail Mary.

"Oh Mother of God, will I die?" he asked me. "Don't let them leave me here."

"Let's get Arthur downstairs," Dr Lynn instructed.

I helped her drag him to the rooftop entrance.

"Do you know if there are any more Fianna here – or the Countess?" I dared to ask.

"Constance is at Stephen's Green with her boys," she

said. "Tell someone to give that boy a tot of whiskey, as his nerves are shook. But he will be okay if the wound doesn't become infected. Throw some whiskey on it if there's no iodine."

I helped the boy down the wide marble stairs and left him in the care of the Citizen Army Women.

"Don't leave me behind!" the boy called out as I left.

"You stay here, Arthur," said one of the women, giving him a swig from a flask. "Your legs won't carry you."

"Tell me ma I won't be home for me tae!" he called after me in a shaky voice.

I ran down the stairs, determined now to get over to Stephen's Green as soon as possible. Dr Lynn's words had given me a clue, and I intended to find Jack and drag him bodily with me if I had to. This was no game of tin soldiers. Death was all around me.

I reached the bottom and the door was wide open. The earlier rebel sentry was nowhere to be seen, but further up the street British soldiers were pinned to the sides of buildings, guns at the ready. More snipers were dotted on the roof.

"Hold fire!" I called and, summoning my courage, raised my Red Cross flag.

"Halt!" roared a voice.

There was a break in the gunshot, and I ran around to the doorway where I'd left my bike. The dairyman and the office girl were gone. My hands shook when I first mounted but the soldiers and rebels let me clear the scene. But as soon as I passed, gunshot ran out behind me, sparking off the granite paving stones. I cycled away up Dame Street, pedalling like fury.

Knots of onlookers blurred at every corner. It was like the flickering silent films at the Masquerade Picture Cinema on Talbot Street. People gathered in doorways, gawping, as if waiting for a parade to pass by.

"Go home, child!" a woman shouted to me from a window.

"Go by the back of Trinity Street!" one man roared to me as I came opposite the tall columns of the Bank of Ireland. "There are snipers on the roof of Trinity. They've shot at some cyclists already."

The great gates were closed and barricaded, the windows filled with sandbags, over which peeped the barrels of the defenders' rifles. I prayed to God Jack wasn't one of those shot.

As I pedalled up Grafton Street, all the shops barred and shut, I began to see makeshift barriers: then along Stephen's Green and towards the Shelbourne Hotel. Every kind of vehicle you could think of was pulled together to make the barricade as if giants were playing a game. I saw a splendid motor car with a holy medal in the front, a lorry, a dray cart and countless bicycles. Behind one barricade was an empty halted tram. I hid my bicycle out of sight in a doorway.

Rifle fire suddenly rang out from the park. The gated entrance facing Grafton Street was closed but a man in a civilian suit ran up with packages in his hand and gained admittance. I guessed he was a rebel carrying ammunition.

I saw the writer Mr James Stephens. He often comes to the GPO to send messages to newspapers in England. He is not very tall and jokes that he is Ireland's tallest leprechaun, which is rather funny as he is famous for writing books on Irish mythology for children.

The gates opened and three men ran out, two with rifles and fixed bayonets. The third man gripped a heavy revolver. They charged towards a motor car that had just come up Dawson Street, driven by a chauffeur. The man with the revolver saluted and addressed the occupants while his comrades fixed their bayonets on the chauffeur.

"I beg your pardon, but you need to get out by order of the Irish Republic." The rebel was polite but nervous.

A terrified woman and a bewildered middle-aged man got out.

"I want to get to Armagh today," the man said, to no one in particular.

The Volunteers directed the chauffeur to wedge his car into the barricade. I could see his legs were shaking through the open door at the front of the car, although his big tanned face was composed. He froze in fear when he finally managed to get it where they wanted.

"Out, sir," the man with the revolver ordered.

The two passengers and the chauffeur staggered into the Shelbourne, supporting each other on shaky legs. There were several knots of curious onlookers, men, women and children, who refused to move.

Mr Stephens approached the boy rebel with the revolver, who was about twenty. He had curly red hair and a kind face but he was constantly scanning the area, jittery and tense.

"What is the meaning of all this? What is going on?" demanded Mr Stephens.

"We have taken the city," said the young man. "But these people won't go home for me. We're expecting an attack from the military at any moment. We have the Post Office, the railways, the Castle. We have everything."

The onlookers seemed to be taking it all as a joke. One little boy ran around with his hoop. "But who will feed the ducks?" he cried out.

Much of the rebels' activity in the Green was obscured by shrubbery, but I peered through the gates. Women were laying out picnic teas and men were digging holes in the warm summer sunshine. Daffodils and crocuses swayed in the breeze.

There were so many youths, the rebels looked to be an army of boys – and it gave me hope I might find Jack among them. There were also lots of young girls, some only a little older than me, wearing knapsacks, and singing rebel songs. I saw behind a bush a black hat with a cockade of feathers. The Countess, I guessed.

I realized if I found Jack, it might not be so easy for me to persuade him to leave. His comrades all had guns.

I was trying to think of a way in when who should I

see trying to climb over the gates but young Dan O'Donovan, my cousin. He was just like my brother, as limber as a monkey.

"What are you doing up here?"

"Ma sent me out for some bread and milk and I just came to see," he said.

"Is Jack in there?"

"I saw Madame Markievicz with a dead bird on her head and dressed like a man. She has a Mauser and an automatic pistol. They have a British Officer prisoner. There are only about twenty of them."

"I'm going to go in," I said.

Dan jumped down beside me. "I'm coming with you."

At that moment, a Boland's bread van turned into the Green. The gates flew open for an instant and two young girls ran out brandishing revolvers. They halted the van and demanded that the driver hand over his supplies.

"Take whatever you want," the man said, taken aback by the youth of the rebels. "But let me keep me van."

One of the girls wrote him a note. "Please put the car in the barricade. The note says you can redeem it, by order of the Irish Republic."

"The Irish Republic, my foot," said the man, but did it quick enough when the girl waved the revolver wildly.

They unloaded trays of loaves from the back. Quick-thinking Dan ran to help out and I too picked up a tray of loaves.

"We are here from St John's Ambulance," I told one of the girls.

When we came to the gate, we were waved in and went to the summerhouse. There was a First Aid shelter in the glass conservatory and a little field hospital in the bandstand, a few wounded there already. Rosie Hackett was there, wearing a white nurse's overall that came down to her toes. As I approached the First Aid station, Dan announced he would search the park and ran off before I could stop him.

"I'm looking for my brother, Jack. He's tall with red-gold hair," I told Rosie.

"You're Bessie's girl, aren't you?" she said.

"I think he might be on his bicycle," I added.

"Ah, if he's a dispatch rider on courier duty, he might be working with Margaret Skinnider. She's from Glasgow but all for Ireland. She smuggled our detonators for the bombs from Scotland into Ireland under her hat."

"What is a dispatch rider?" I asked.

"They carry messages by bike between the various posts," she said. "We even have two fellas who were in the Olympics doing it – but the women and young boys are doing it mostly. Commander Mallin said we're to make sure we keep our lines of communication open for food, reinforcements and ammunition."

At that very moment, a woman cycled up wearing a uniform of green moleskin, knee breeches, a belted coat and the leggings known as puttees.

"I need to speak to the Countess urgently," she said in a Scottish accent. Margaret Skinnider, I guessed.

"McCormick and the men have abandoned the attempt to occupy Harcourt Street Railway Station. They are falling back."

At that moment the commander, Michael Mallin, arrived with the Countess. I had seen him only yesterday – playing the flute in Liberty Hall! And I remembered that he was a silk weaver and Mother had once bought a shawl from him.

The Countess was smoking a cigarette and putting her revolver back in her belt. She was tall and dashing like someone out of an adventure story. Her strong face must have been beautiful when she was young and even now she was arresting. She moved like a panther stalking prey.

"I've been dealing with the objectionable snipers," she said casually, as if she was out fox-hunting.

Her companion, Mr Mallin, was tense and nervous. "There are at least sixty guns held at the College of Surgeons, belonging to the Trinity College Officer Training Corp," he said. "We need to occupy the building."

"This open ground is not safe," said the Countess. "We need a back-up position."

Mallin looked up and saw a party of men approaching.

"Robbins, why aren't you at Davy's pub on Portabello Bridge?"

"We had to abandon, sir," said the young rebel.

"Take a dozen over to the College of Surgeons and establish it as our headquarter position. The Green is too large and exposed. Mary and Lily, the Kempson girl, will go with you."

They began to form into a unit.

Dan and another young boy of about twelve – Tommy, the delivery boy from the Dublin Bread Company – attached themselves to the straggling column of fighters. Margaret the cyclist dismounted and made to join them but the Countess called her over and whispered something in her ear.

I seized my chance. I stepped close to them.

"Do you know my brother Jack O'Donovan? Is he a dispatch rider?" I said quickly, a bundle of nerves.

They both looked at me, in surprise at my audacity.

"My boys are doing me proud! Some are on reconnaissance around the boundaries," the Countess said.

"Is Jack, tall with red-gold hair, among them?" I asked.

"He and another boy might have been sent to liaise with the Fairview men and deliver a message to Tom Clarke's wife Kathleen who lives there. They are to report to the GPO tomorrow."

I was crestfallen at her words. Fairview was the other side of the city, I wasn't sure where.

"And Anto Maguire?"

"Child, he is on a military mission. You cannot just

chase him around." The Countess waved her hand to indicate I was dismissed.

The column marched off. Dan tagged along with the DBC bakery boy, Tommy.

I caught my cousin by the scruff of his neck. "You're going home to your mother!" I said.

"You can sneak back out," laughed Tommie Keenan, his tricolour badge glinting. "Me da locked me in and I jus' climbed out the winder!"

"Go home, you eejit. Or you might lose your job at the DBC," I said.

"I'm twelve, nearly thirteen," he said. "The Countess says we're old enough to fight."

Another group of very young people arrived, including a girl I knew from North King Street, Mary McLoughlin, who was fifteen. Her brother Seán was in the Irish Citizen Army but she had another brother fighting in the Great War.

"What are you doing here?" I asked.

"I'm a member of Clann na Gael, attached to the Hibernian Rifles," she said. "The Fianna doesn't let girls in but I want to fight for Ireland."

I looked at the group, in their green uniforms – a bunch of children like me.

"We were on a route march with our captain, May Kelly," she said. "There was no train from Dundrum station because of the Rising, so we walked back. This is the first military post we've reached."

"The Rising?" I said. "Is that what this is called? But you're just young girls!"

"The Countess let us in," she said stubbornly.

The Countess and Mr Mallin came striding up.

"What are all these children doing here?" demanded Mallin.

"If they're old enough to work in Ireland, they are old enough to fight," said the Countess. She pronounced it 'Ah-land' in her grand voice.

"Dead children will discredit us. Get them out of here," said Mallin.

I remembered that he himself had five young children and that's why mother had bought his shawl.

"Everyone under sixteen please leave," said the Countess, not exactly pleased.

"But we want to fight," persisted Tommie Keenan.

"Your day will come," said Mallin. "Now out of here before I box your ears."

Dan and I were swept up in the crowd of departing children. Some of them were very frightened and it was a mercy that some of their parents had started to turn up to take them home. I held tight onto Dan's hand in case he ran off again.

But, as she remounted her bicycle, I asked Margaret Skinnider again exactly where Anto Maguire had been sent. He might have more information about Jack.

"He's a messenger boy with Findlater's Grocers," I added. "He knows Dublin well."

She ignored me.

"Anto and Jack are scarcely fifteen," I said. "Mallin would send them home. I'll go ask him, will I?"

"Anto is on food-procurement duty," she admitted. "He's moving between South Dublin Union and Jacob's Factory over near St Patrick's."

She broke off abruptly and rode off.

"Are you off home now?" I asked Mary McLoughlin as we skirted the shrubbery and left the park.

"I am not! Me ma won't let me out again. I'm going to the GPO."

I showed her Jack's photograph in my locket and asked her to look out for him – and to give him a message that he must head to Oriel Street to see Aunt Elizabeth and we were planning to go to Kingstown. Or if that proved difficult, to go to Hatch Street to Dr Ella Webb.

As Dan and I hurried past the Shelbourne by Kildare Street, there was a break in hostilities and, when we looked back, the park seemed deserted.

Mr Stephens was at the corner talking to another gentleman, William Smith, a Saint John's Ambulance organizer and acquaintance of my mother.

An elderly man stepped on the footpath and walked directly up to the barricade where he gripped the shafts of a wooden cart with a canvas hood, which was lodged near the centre. At that instant, the park exploded into life and from nowhere armed men appeared at the railings, shouting.

"Put down that cart at once!"

The old man ignored them and continued to drag the cart out.

The shouts became, menacing. "Leave it be, or die!"

"It's his cart!" a voice rang out.

There was dead silence as the man slowly drew his cart out. Suddenly, like the crack of a whip, three shots rang out, fired over his head, to frighten him. But he walked straight over to the rebels.

"He has a nerve," someone said.

Ten guns were aimed at him. But the man walked slowly, his finger raised.

"Put that cart back, or you are a dead man! One – two – three – four!"

A rifle spat out. The man sank in on himself and crumpled to the ground.

We ran to him.

It was a most dreadful sight. The man's brains were blown out and his hair clotted with blood. I handed a cloth from my bag to Mr Smith, who draped it around the poor man's head.

"We cannot leave him here," said Mr Smith urgently, directing a group of men to pick up the poor unfortunate. "Dr Ella Webb has turned the War Supply Depot at 40 Merrion Square into a field hospital – up past the Arts Club. Better take him there."

A woman fell to her knees in the street and keened at the top of her voice. It was a noise like you'd hear in hell.

"He was one of our own!" she cried. "A loyal Sinn Féiner! He was part of the theatre and the set was in his cart!"

The mood turned against the Volunteers among the onlookers. At that moment, they were hated.

Young Dan was white with shock. It was getting towards dusk. There was no point in me going to Fairview now to find Jack and I wasn't sure I knew the way. I needed to get my cousin to safety first and think what to do.

"There are no more trams from Westland Row. They've torn up the track," I heard a man say as we hurried down the street. It would be difficult to get to Kingstown.

We got back to my bicycle which mercifully, being out of sight on Grafton Street, hadn't been taken to put on a barricade. More and more people thronged in bewildered groups, wondering how they were going to get home, with no trams or taxis.

"Is that man dead?" Dan asked me as I cycled, with him sitting on my crossbar.

"I think so," I said truthfully. "He couldn't survive that."

"I would like a free Ireland," said Dan, "but I am afraid. They shot a policeman too, you know. They took him away to the hospital."

I felt guilty for my cousin, little more than an infant, seeing such sights. I should have got him home sooner.

We crossed Butt Bridge without incident and hurried to Oriel Street. My Aunt Elizabeth wept with relief when she saw us at the door and she smothered Dan in an embrace.

"I'm very sorry, Mam. I didn't get any milk."

Elizabeth wept through her smiles. "I have been listening to the sound of guns all day, but couldn't leave the house what with poor Josephine."

"My father has telephoned your family, Aunt Elizabeth, and we are to go to Kingstown." I showed her the twenty pounds. She shook her head.

"You won't find a cab for love nor money. And it's too late for young girls to be wandering around. Stay here with us. You mind Josephine for a while and I'll see if I can find some food."

Elizabeth looked anxiously out the window of their first floor flat. The sky was darkening with heavy rain clouds. Bad weather was on the way.

As Elizabeth put on her coat, I looked out the window and a small miracle occurred. On a horse and cart below was the Ringsend fishmonger. She looked up at the exact same moment I looked out.

"Mother O'Brien!" I cried out in delight.

Her little three-year-old daughter Bridie waved to me – a raven-haired beauty with dark eyes who was always dressed in white.

I ran down from the upstairs flat to see her on the street and explained how my father had instructed us all to go to Kingstown but Jack was out in the rebellion.

"There are no trams now," said Mother O'Brien. "We were in Fairyhouse all day and when I heard about the trouble I resolved to get a horse and cart. It's taken me two hours to get back into the city. But I did get my consignment of salmon from the last train out of Killarney. Beautiful plump and silver they are. And some fine speckled brown trout from Killorglin. I've picked up some other provisions as well."

I didn't doubt it. Mother O'Brien was a resourceful widow who knew everybody and had a network of contacts. She was known for supplying the best fish to all the fancy chefs in town.

"Tell Elizabeth she's welcome to spend the night with me and my sister Nanny who has the shop so we're well provided," said Mother O'Brien. "And in the morning I'll take you all out to Kingstown myself."

I could have cried with relief. Just then Elizabeth came down to join us with Josephine in her arms and Dan trailing her, but she did not seem inclined to accept the offer as she is very polite.

"You are very kind, but we would not like to inconvenience you. Have you seen any trouble?" she asked.

"Merciful hour," said Mother O'Brien, "I saw some injured going into the Mater Hospital on the north side. I heard they blew up the magazine fort in Phoenix Park and shot the poor youth that was tryin' to raise the alarm. I saw a few of them about in Cabra but they let me pass. Asked me if Civil War won the Grand National. I told them he came in third. My horse Allsorts won! They're in the South Dublin Union, I've heard, as well as the GPO."

"The South Dublin Union, a hospital and workhouse that has three thousand paupers!" said Elizabeth, amazed. "What use is that?"

"It commands a street where troops would come by. They've taken Knightsbridge Station. There are all kinds of quare rumours flyin' about. That the Germans are invading and the Pope has committed suicide in fright. Dublin people say more than their prayers, that's for sure!"

"What's the world coming to!" said Elizabeth, cuddling little Josephine.

"If they just ate more fish, we wouldn't have these carry-ons," said Mother O'Brien. "And if there were more women sortin' tings out, there would be a great deal less trouble!"

"But there are quite a few women alongside the men," I said. "Like Dr Lynn and other nurses I know from First Aid training. Some are even bearing arms, like Helena Moloney the actress and the Countess."

"They ought to have more sense," Mother O'Brien said. She held out her arms to take Josephine. "Come with me now and we'll give you all a good feed and we'll set off first thing for Kingstown. I saw a few bowsies lootin' shops on me travels, and there's no police, so you don't want to stay round here."

Little Bridie patted the seat and smiled so sweetly that Dan jumped up beside her.

"Would you like to see my picture book?" Bridie asked him, showing him a beautifully illustrated book of Mr Stephens' fairytales!

"Mr Stephens is one of my customers and he gave it to her," Mother O'Brien said. "She's already readin' a few words."

Within seconds Dan and Bridie were chatting happily as children do, as if nothing was going on.

"The little fella's comin' anyway," Mother O'Brien joked as I shot my aunt pleading looks, but Elizabeth still hesitated.

Mother O'Brien handed the baby back to Elizabeth and reorganized the seating by clearing away some sacking.

"Ah, come on!" she coaxed. "I was goin' to give the salmon to the chef at the Shelborne but we'll hang on to it. With any luck all this disturbance will blow over by tonight and you'll be home tomorrow." She dug out from the tarpaulin a jug of fresh milk and poured us all a cup each in little tins. "Got it from a dairy farm off the Navan Road."

I drank, then smiled and licked the creamy milk moustache from my lips. My mother always joked to Mother O'Brien that she never had a wasted journey – she always came back with more than she left with. It was clear Elizabeth could have kissed her as she gave some to Josephine who is a poor feeder.

111

"We could pay you something for the food and lodging when my husband comes back," said Elizabeth.

"I have twenty pounds," I said, remembering the money my father had given me.

"Ah, get away out a that!" said Mother O'Brien kindly. "We'll enjoy the company."

"We would be much obliged to you," Elizabeth told her, "and then tomorrow we can set out for Kingstown."

It was decided. I put my bike up on the cart. Elizabeth packed a few things, locked up the house and we set off.

Just as we came along the docks, as Elizabeth was explaining that her family lived in the manse in Kingstown, I took out my father's spyglass and scanned the city. There was a sudden flare of gold down the lens. My stomach flipped as I focused.

I saw a red-gold head over the parapet of a building near the Customs House along Eden Quay. As I tried to follow the figure with the spyglass, the rain clouds were pierced by a sunburst. The figure became a black outline against the setting sun. In a heartbeat, I knew it was Jack, the King of Dublin's rooftops.

"It's Jack!" I exclaimed.

I jumped down before they could protest and dragged my bike off the cart.

"I'll meet him at the end of the street and we'll catch you up," I said.

There was nothing they could do. I was gone in pursuit.

I tracked him as far as the corner opposite Amiens Street Station. Then the figure disappeared into thin air. Scores of British soldiers were pouring out of the railway station and I didn't dare go any further.

But as I passed the corner into Talbot Street moments later, I jumped out of my skin. Something landed in the basket of my bicycle. A little tin soldier painted green. I looked up but Jack was nowhere to be seen. I searched around but all I saw was my own lengthening shadow. Jack had eluded me, as usual. Leaving only his little green soldier as a calling card.

📖   📖   📖

I'm too tired to write any more now . . .

2 a.m. Tuesday morning 25th April.
Our house.

I cannot sleep now, even though I fell into a dead stupor last night. The shooting goes on for hours. Then there is a lull. The silence is almost more dreadful than the sound.

Mother O'Brien was right about the looting on our doorstep. Coming back I saw a street urchin with five hats on his head from Dunn's Hatters, in our block, including a panama, a straw boater and a bowler hat. Then someone else knocked them off him. People were

113

swarming all over Clerys next door like in an ant heap – the windows smashed. I saw a woman pushing a children's pram loaded with gowns and vases. I was very frightened.

Up by the Pillar the dead horse was beginning to smell rank. I bumped into Laurence Eustace who lives on Eden Quay near Liberty Hall. He was with his aunt and they'd come out to gawp. They scurried on home after that.

I got into my house through the back yard, not daring to open my front door.

The rebels have a post in the Imperial Hotel a few doors down. I tried to peer over the wall of our yard into theirs, but all I could see were some of the staff taking food stores out under the command of a rebel. I wondered if May, Anto's sister who works there, was trapped inside.

I crept out onto the roof and scanned the scene on the streets with my spyglass. There were lots of people milling about, many of them drunk under the blaze of electric light. At one stage a crowd surged into Mansfield Shoes on the opposite corner. Someone turned on the light to reveal a scene of mayhem as people grabbed boxes of shoes and boots. The noise was disturbing, shouts and catcalling punctuated with gunfire, so I crept back in. The GPO was dark and I thought I saw the flicker of candles through my spyglass. But the streetlights bathed Sackvil le Street in strange shades of blue and green and scarlet, not like anything I'd ever noticed before.

I couldn't sleep so I have spent the hours preparing my First Aid kit. I made up a list and have collected needles, the red iodine that cleans wounds, lint and cotton wool from my mother's supply.

At first I found stitching the bog moss into linen bags calmed my nerves but I started to tremble when I remembered the poor sergeant and his stark red blood on Miss Nugent's embroidered cloth.

So I tried to concentrate on my "First Aid to the Injured Manual" by James Cantlie. I realize now I should have paid more attention at the classes.

I read that you must make sure the patient can breathe, is in a restful position and warm. When the skin is broken you must check there is no sign of poison such as an odd smell, or burning, and cover it promptly. There are also instructions about removal of clothing – mostly by cutting the seams. So I fetched my mother's scissors from her sewing basket.

After my poor performance at the GPO, I read up the chapter on hemorrhages. The book says they must receive the most attention, taking care to find the pressure points for arteries and veins.

To make a tourniquet, you have to remember so many things at the same time you'd have to be a magician! This is what I should have done with the sergeant at the GPO. First you apply a pad on the pressure point. Then you put a bandage around it and tie a knot, like the beginning of a shoelace, on the other side of the wound.

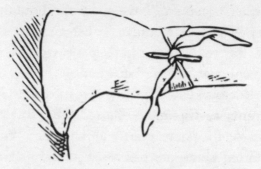

Then you place a stick on that knot and secure it with another knot, twisting the stick to stop the blood flow. If that works you secure it in position with yet another knot. I'm not sure I'll be able to do it in the heat of battle. I will most certainly tie myself up in knots!

As for splints, I will just have to improvise with an umbrella, a billiard cue, or anything that can remain firm – even a rifle.

I can also improvise bandages from straps, ties, braces or string – as well as embroidery cloths!

It is so curious. There is advice on frostbite, electric shock and drowning but I cannot find any information on gunshot wounds. I suppose the VAD's or 'Very Adorable Darlings' know all about that. I remembered my mother's conversation with Miss Huxley and I have put in a bag of sugar and a jar of honey, as they are supposed to be helpful in treating wounds. You just never know!

I wish I could find some courage to put in my kit. I need to show that I deserved that First Aid Certificate and it wasn't given to me because of my mother. Maybe I'll just pop that in instead!

4. a. m. Tuesday 25th April.
My parents' bedroom.

I am curled up on my parents' bed as I miss them so! I awoke from a nightmare of bleeding people in tattered rags and I have decided on a good use for my horrible old unmentionables. I am going to make bandages out of all the undergarments I can find! Mother cannot then say that I am not prepared.

I am making such a mess of the triangular bandage for an arm sling, I could cry. It has a special name – an Esmarch bandage – and it looks so easy when Mother does it. You cut a piece of fabric along the diagonal into two triangles. And with different folds, you are supposed to be able to make broad, narrow or medium bandages. I just have to hope I meet nobody with a broken arm!

8.30 a.m. Tuesday 24th April.
My house, after coming down from the roof.

This morning, I have been holding vigil on the roof. Hoping to see Jack if he returns to the GPO with any messages. There is no sign of him. Instead, I have witnessed the most remarkable scenes though my spyglass.

Sackville Street at first was eerily quiet in the grey dawn with little groups of the Citizen Army patrolling. The rebels have erected a barrier of barbed wire circling around the GPO and across the street to Clerys. The dead horse still lay among broken glass around Nelson's Pillar, and beyond it an abandoned tram at the corner of Earl Street.

But within minutes of the pale spring sun rising in the sky, it turned into a carnival with all of the slums turning out to loot.

As I ate the last of my sticky buns, Anto Maguire's little brother and sister passed by, dressed like jesters in a motley collection of clothing. Little Liam was wearing two odd boots on his feet and was pushing three-year-old Alice on a hobby horse on wheels that I'd admired in the window of Lawrence's.

"You better hurry yourself!" shouted Liam up to me, a too-big silk hat sliding over his eyes. "It's all going fast! Now that we are a 'public, we can take what we want!"

"Liam says we are all kings and queens now," lisped little Alice.

I was relieved to see that May ran out of the Imperial, and tore off the hats and silk scarves that trailed behind them like bunting. She forced them to lay aside their spoils and marched them home to their loud complaints. Others soon quickly grabbed the discarded clothes and toys.

I saw a hard-faced woman clutching an apronful of shoes. "Dem bowsies have only left me with the left feet!" she cried. She must have raided them from the Saxone window display

Two other women fought over garters and corsets, ripping them to shreds. A woman climbed into the abandoned tram near Nelson's Pillar and took off her clothes to try on a new silk dress. Another one, laden with stolen goods, roared out at her. "Would you look at the state of her, naked as a broomstick, wearing nothing but her mortal sins!"

Suddenly, sweeping down the road came a black line of priests, all arm in arm, pushing the looters off the street. But as soon as they passed, the looters scurried back to the shops. I saw a man fire a rock and shatter the window of Lemon's Sweetshop. Within seconds a horde was barrelling in.

"Free sweets, free sweets! Up the Republic!" roared one little urchin, clutching a lollipop the size of his head. He was soon joined by a swarm of little boys all gorging on buttercreams, pineapple rocks, sherbet fizz and bonbons. I must admit I was sorely tempted to join them. Until I saw the hammer – used to break up the block of toffee – come whizzing out the window and nearly take out someone's eye!

A team of rebels flung chairs, desks and tables to build a blockade across North Earl Street at the Pillar Café. But no sooner had they finished than a gang of shawlies – the poor women of Dublin who wear shawls – came running, screaming with joy.

"They're givin' away free furniture! God Save Ireland!"

"They will discredit us!" I heard a rebel say.

Shots were fired overhead and the shawlies were forced to bring back their pickings. But one woman made off with a piano from Cramer's on a truck!

A dirty-faced little boy wearing golfing plus fours much too large for him drove a golf ball up the street, then watched it with shaded eyes.

"By Jove!" he cried out, playing the swell.

Then fireworks really did start. A group of kids brought them out from Lawrence's. Catherine Wheels and Roman candles exploded and mixed with the sound of gunfire. Things were getting out of hand.

I noticed a line strung up overhead on a diagonal between the GPO and Reis's wireless shop on the corner of Lower Abbey Street. Messages went back and forth on a tin can. So I figured my father and his colleagues had so far failed to restore communication to the GPO. Our phone line was also dead when I'd checked earlier.

Rebels darted in and out like shadows, taking

possession of buildings. I clambered up the metal ladder from our roof and moved along the expanse of roof over the Imperial and Clerys. I had to keep a keen eye out, as I saw snipers posted on some neighbouring roofs. Then I shimmied down a drainpipe and crossed over Abbey Street. I went up the next terrace by the fire escape ladder at the back yard of Wynn's Hotel on Abbey Street. Peering through a skylight over the stairwell at the back of Reis's I heard the rebels talking.

"We proclaim the Irish Republic," one of them intoned.

They were trying to get a message out over the radio transmitters.

I figured it out. The rebels were tunneling between the buildings in the street. I reckoned by lunchtime they would have the run of the houses between Lower Abbey Street and Sackville Place. I bet they were doing the same on the opposite side.

But why were they doing this? It could not be good. Maybe they expected British soldiers to come down the street and this was their escape route.

My watch on the GPO for my brother was exhausting. Vans and dispatch riders were coming and going in a steady stream. But no sign of Jack.

The mayhem of the street made me nervous. Booty lay strewn on the ground . . . a silk scarf, a cardboard shoebox, a patchwork of photographs trodden underfoot.

I had to get back inside the GPO. That was the nerve

centre of the rebellion. If I found out where they were sending dispatches that day, I might be able to track my brother. I was desperate to see him. Even though he had thrown me the soldier, the last time I spoke to him there was discord. I must make peace, settle things between us. To never again . . . I cannot bear the thought.

But how? If I ventured out onto the street they might take me for one of the looters. And the idea of going back inside the GPO filled me with terror.

It was starting to get dangerous up on the roof. When a bullet whizzed past my ears, I realized that with my extended spyglass I'd been taken for a sniper. My survival instinct took over and in a flurry of skirts I got back down the nearest drainpipe.

Middle of the night, Tuesday 25th April.
Merrion Square Field Hospital.

About an hour later, sick with worry about Jack, as looters still milled about, I crept under the barbed wire and walked up to the GPO. The windows were lined with thousands of Post Office leather ledgers that detailed all the stamps bought and all the parcels and letters sent.

"I need to find my brother, Jack O'Donovan," I said in a shaking voice to the large, hulking sentry at the Prince's Street entrance.

"Go home to your mother, little girl. If your brother is here, I'll pass on your message."

He gazed at me so sternly under his beetle brows that I ran away at once, and stood at the corner of Abbey Street, quaking. Sentries were posted everywhere.

Barricades made of large paper rolls, filled with type from the newspaper offices that they'd seized on Abbey Street, blocked the road.

I was frozen, unsure what to do, too frightened to go back to the GPO. Then the arresting figure of Cesca Trench came down from O'Connell Bridge, cutting through the crowd on her bicycle. I knew her from the First Aid training. She looked so beautiful and glamorous in her emerald cloak fastened with a Celtic brooch. Even though she is a Protestant born in Kent, to an Anglo-Irish family, and trained as an artist in Paris, she is a passionate Irish nationalist and has changed her name to Sive (pronounced to rhyme with "hive").

"Sive, Sive!" I called.

She cycled up to me and dismounted from her bike.

"Is Pearse really leading the rebellion in the GPO?" she asked.

"Yes, he's one of the leaders. I saw him."

"Many nationalists think it is an act of criminal lunacy," she said. "I have brought my First Aid things. Everyone thinks I am mad, but I have to see for myself."

As we zigzagged across, Sive pushing her bike, a shot suddenly rang out from Trinity College and pinged off the tin can carrying messages from one side to another. We bolted to safety.

"Wow, what a great shot!" I declared as we ducked down Princes Street. "I bet it's that Australian soldier, McHugh, who I met on Monday. He's the best shot in the army." I gabbled to cover my nerves but Sive seemed very cool-headed.

"You should see some of the barricades!" Sive said. "I've seen one of grandfather and carriage clocks from a jeweller's and look at that one of Keating's finest cycles!" She pointed back in the direction of a barricade further down across Abbey Street. "But I am very annoyed about this rebellion. I am going to give Mr Pearse a piece of my mind!"

We crossed under the barbed wire surrounding the entrance.

"Let us through," Sive said in a commanding voice as we got to the door. "I have come to deliver vital First Aid equipment."

The sentry was so busy staring at the beautiful Sive, he barely noticed me shrinking at her side.

It was a very strange sensation walking into the GPO under armed occupation. The telegraph wires were no longer buzzing. There was an uneasy calm and the men were busy and distracted. Curiously, I began to relax, now that I was at the eye of the storm.

I saw two British soldiers happily washing up and in the dining room upstairs a man was eating a full salmon.

I asked after Officer Chalmers who had been trussed up in the phone box yesterday and was told that he was now in the basement – and also that Miss Gordon had returned with the sergeant who was shot in the arm. She had gone home. The sergeant's wound was superficial and he too was quite comfortable in the basement. I breathed a sigh of relief that I hadn't killed my first patient!

Sive saw Pearse among a cluster of men. We joined the queue of women who were cross with Pearse. The O'Rahilly's sister Margaret even pinched him on the arm.

"This is all your fault," she said fiercely. "And now you've taken my motor car!"

"It is for the freedom of Ireland," he said.

She just harrumphed and left.

Another member of Cumann na mBan, the women's part of the Volunteers, called Louise Gavan Duffy, who is a teacher, told him the rebellion was wrong and it would fail. She would help but wouldn't do any active service. Pearse dispatched her to the kitchen.

Then it was Sive's turn. "You don't seriously think you'll succeed, do you?" she asked.

"We would have if it had been on Sunday. Eoin Mac Neill spoiled it with the cancellation."

"It's madness any day of the week!" she cried.

"When we are all wiped out, people will blame us," Pearse said with a glow in his voice, "but in a few years they will see the meaning of what we tried to do for Irish freedom."

The words felt like a chill in my heart. They mean to fight unto the death, God save us all, I thought. I had to find Jack as soon as I could and drag him away if necessary.

"As you are going out, would you mind taking a note to my mother?" Pearse asked Sive.

Sive nodded assent and we looked at each other, both realizing at the same time that these men in here might not live to tell the tale. The troops were bound to come and annihilate their puny force of a few hundred.

Pearse turned to me. "And you, girl? Have you something to say?"

"I-I'm just looking for my brother Jack O'Donovan," I said, hoping he didn't remember me as the ninny in Clarke's shop.

A few shots rang out – sharp and shrill.

"Go and tell that young fella on the roof to stop shooting at Nelson's nose," shouted James Connolly, exasperated. He was running around like a mad thing, issuing orders, shouting instructions.

"I will go to encourage the men and perhaps Jack is among them," Pearse said to me.

My hope soared.

We passed a row of young men waiting for two priests to hear their confessions. The men seemed cheered when Pearse passed by with a friendly word. He is a strange man. Painfully shy and awkward to meet and yet lit with such strong conviction it inspires others with awe.

"I wish I was up on the roof. They get all the action," said one soldier who told me his name was Liam Tannam. He was a tall, humorous-looking fellow with a roguish eye and he gave me a wink. "Better than lugging ledger books around."

Even though there were two other trapdoors in other parts of the building, Pearse went up to the roof through a hole in the ceiling in the Instrument Room that had been created by the rebels by tearing slates off the roof. It was accessed by a makeshift ladder of brooms. My father would have cried to see all the plaster dust on his beautiful machines.

I shimmied up the ladder after Pearse and poked my head up. There were about ten men on the roof and it was utterly terrifying. The parapet, the raised stone lip at the front of the building, offered very little protection. The men had to lie and crouch in a space three or four foot wide between it and the sloping roof behind them. I peeped up and saw there were now British snipers on the roofs of several buildings at the top of Sackville Street.

"You are wiping out the stain of Ireland's history," said Pearse encouragingly to the men. It was another sunny day and his hair was ruffled by a gentle breeze.

Some of the men were little older than Jack, still in their teens and early twenties. They smiled as Pearse greeted them familiarly, much more at ease than he usually seemed. One of them said something about their history lessons coming to life and I realized quite a few of them were his pupils from Saint Enda's.

"Tell them downstairs I'm dying for a cup of tea and a slice of bread," whispered a man called Mick Boland to me. "They forget about us up here." He wasn't one of the Saint Enda's crowd.

Nobody had seen Jack.

We went back downstairs.

By this stage I was getting really anxious.

To my surprise Mr Pearse turned to me and spoke. "Tom Clarke says it is vital that we make a protest before the end of the Great War, so that the declaration of a Republic can be presented at the Peace Conference. President Wilson of the United States supports the rights of small nations. Our sacrifice will rouse the national spirit of the Irish people."

As Pearse talked about blood sacrifice, I thought he was like an Old Testament prophet burning with the fires of true belief. As the faces of all the men around me glowed, I could only think of how to apply a tourniquet. If Mr Pearse had learned First Aid and realized how difficult it is to stop blood flowing, he might not be so keen on spilling it.

Suddenly – rat-atat-tat – there was a volley of sniper fire on the street. Connolly ran by us, heading for the main entrance.

I followed him, curious to see what was going on. There was a group of about sixty men, armed with pikes and pistols, crouching down by the barricades and there were some British soldiers in khaki uniforms among them.

"British soldiers coming!" roared a rebel.

"Hold fire! These are our men with prisoners taken!" Connolly shouted, running bravely into the street to stop the rebels firing on their own men. The rebels in the Imperial were shooting at their own troops!

I thought I saw a bullet glance Connolly's shoulder but he scurried in again so quickly it was impossible to tell.

The new arrivals were the Fairview group! Hope leapt in my heart that Jack had come back with them after delivering his message.

They burst in, full of excitement. I was anxious to see if my brother was among the sixty or so men, but they were all so worked up it was hard not to get trampled over.

"We have eggs, bread and cigars!" they cried excitedly as they came in, as though going to a picnic.

I asked eagerly after Jack, but they looked at me blankly, now transfixed by the sight of the Post Office turned into a fortress.

Pearse handed Sive his note and stood on the table. He was like someone anointed by a special power and I saw then why men would follow him. You could hear a pin drop as he spoke.

"You have wiped out the blackest stain in Irish history," he said. He must have been rehearsing his speech when he spoke to the men on the roof. "In the course of a few hours we will all be fighting for our freedom in the streets of our city. Victory will be ours, even though it might be that victory will be found in death."

There was a rousing cheer but my blood ran cold. As Pearse said the terrible word, I tried not to think of poor Seán Connolly on the roof of City Hall or the man shot at Stephen's Green.

When Pearse finished his fine speech, James Connolly organized the new arrivals into different groups. Some were dispatched to create a new outpost in the Hotel Metropole, others to fortify the positions in Henry Street and the Imperial Hotel. The last group was told to set up barricades on either side of Moore Street, then bore holes in buildings as far as Arnott's, including Bewley's and the Coliseum Theatre in Henry Street. I thought they'd be lucky to keep anything in a barricade with the mob on the rampage looking for loot.

I moved among them, questioning about Jack to no avail, showing them the picture in my locket.

Finally I spoke to a nervous lad of about seventeen who knew Jack from the Fianna.

"Jack went on to Richmond Avenue to give a message to Mrs Clarke, the old Fenian's wife. His message to us was wrapped around this tin soldier." He showed me a tin soldier painted green, another of Jack's.

"So how come you have it?" I asked.

"He said to put it through the letter box of Number 9 Sackville Street if I was passing."

"It's the other side of the street," I smiled. "I'm his sister and he meant to give it to me."

"Yes, right enough. He said his sister Molly might be looking for him and to hand it on if I bumped into you." The fellow was relieved to pass the soldier over and not have to trouble himself any longer with what must have seemed a foolish errand.

I could have almost kissed it and held it tight. A link with Jack. It was like his signature. But I was still puzzled about what he was up to. I took a close look at the soldier, which was about four inches tall maybe. But apart from the expertly applied green coat of paint, it didn't seem any different from the usual. I put it with the other one in my knapsack.

I needed to ask Mr Clarke if Jack had come back with a message from his wife.

All around us people were milling around with supplies, bags of flour, cutlery from the hotels, churns of milk and water. Someone said they had enough provisions for a three-week fight. In the kitchen women, including Louise Gavan Duffy, were carving giant joints of meat. The captured British Tommies were whistling cheerfully, washing up the mounds of plates.

I searched in vain for Mr Clarke.

"Talk to the Big Fella, Michael Collins, upstairs in the Operations Room," a kind, pretty woman who told me her name was Min Ryan said. "He has a finger on the pulse."

In the Operations Room the leaders, including Pearse, Connolly, Tom Clarke and Plunkett were deep in discussion. I didn't dare enter.

"I hope you're not a spy!"

A hand touched me lightly on the shoulder. I jumped out of my standing as a large presence overshadowed me. I cowered into the door-jamb but my accoster let out a large booming laugh.

I relaxed. It was Michael Collins, the Big Fella, and there was something reassuring about him. He had a leather-bound Post Office ledger tucked under his arm.

"My brother Jack," I said with urgency. "He was dispatched to Fairview. He was sent to Mrs Clarke there. I need to find him."

The Big Fella thumbed through the ledger book. "I've listed all the names and addresses of combatants." He tapped Jack's name and showed me. Then he screwed up his eyes. "Yes. He came back here. He was sent off to the Green to go via Jacob's. He should have been back here hours ago."

My heart skipped a beat. "He's missing!"

A shadow passed over his face. "We don't know that. No intelligence has reached us. But three of our riders have failed to come back."

"I have to find him!"

As I turned heel, he restrained me.

"Don't go by Trinity College. It's sniper's alley." He looked at me closely. "I know your father, Molly. A fine man. If he ever has a mind to switch sides he would be valuable for the future of Ireland."

"Not if he dies," I said.

He smiled grimly. "You're a smart girl," he said and then whispered, "There's too many poets running this revolution. Too many panicky decisions and bungled operations costing many a good life."

Pearse looked up and saw us at that moment.

"I'm just telling her to let my girl know I won't be able to take her to the Abbey Theatre tonight," Collins said lightly.

His joke was lost on Mr Pearse, who is not the joking kind.

Could one of the missing dispatch riders be Jack? My first call would be to Jacob's, south of the Liffey.

On Sackville Street, the wild looting continued all around. It frightened me almost as much as the bullets. People were becoming mad with greed. I saw a boy sell off pocket watches for sixpence each, shawlies scratching each other's eyes out over bonnets and petticoats. It was unreal, unearthly. A revolution inside the Post Office and a crazy crazy carnival outside, with men women and children wild with excitement at the absence of police. Respectable citizens looked on, tut-tutting, but did nothing to intervene. Some of them even lost control and joined in.

As I made my way up one side of the street, Skeffy was pinning a notice at O'Connell Bridge while Hannah his wife was hauling a massive bag of flour from the GPO.

"Skeffy!" I cried, running to join him.

He was frowning as he pinned his notice to the lamppost, but his face lit up when he saw me.

"Hannah is helping them with supplies. But we've got to stop this looting," he said, scratching his head under his deerstalker cap. "Run across the road, there's a good girl, and tell her I'll still see her for tea at half past five. She and the whole city have gone bonkers mad!"

I did as he asked and Hannah nodded, then continued to haul a great sack of flour with Mary McLoughlin who I'd met at the Green.

"Connolly gave me eighty pounds to buy food, but I couldn't get any," Mary said. "They're very short of food up at the Green."

"I thought Anto Maguire was dispatched to look for food," I said, worried.

"Yes, Mallin sent me because nothing came back from an earlier message," she said.

"Maybe Anto didn't make it."

Mary just shrugged her shoulders. "People get delayed with all the shooting and have to take different routes. I delivered ammunition earlier but I lost Julia Grennan and Nurse O'Farrell from Cumann na mBan in Dame Street. It's hard to keep track."

But her words filled me with dread.

I went back to read Skeffy's notice for a meeting to set up a Citizen's Militia Force to stop the looting.

A golf ball came flying up the street and Skeffy ducked just in time.

"It's mostly just kids robbing sweets and old ladies grabbing shoes," I said. "They're just poor."

"Molly, dear, I believe in equal rights for all. But this is chaos!"

"Mr Pearse says they are wiping out the stain of Irish history with their blood, and victory will be in death," I said.

"Mr Pearse is a fine man but obsessed with blood sacrifice," said Skeffy, his face white with strong emotions.

"I don't quite see how you can wipe out a stain with another one of blood," I said, thinking of Nancy doing the laundry. "Don't you then just have two stains?"

Skeffy laughed for a moment. "He doesn't mean it literally. I would like nothing more than an Irish republic, but not like this. Good cannot come by bad means." A Catherine Wheel came spinning up the street. "When will the men of Ireland no longer be hypnotized by the glamour of arms? We are falling into an abyss!"

He looked grimly down the street. A stream of refugees were leaving buildings all along Bachelors Walk and Eden Quay and making their way towards to the Customs House. I noticed the Eustaces among them and, further down, a line of blind boys from the home, all tapping their white sticks. I wondered if they had been told to leave.

"Do you know where all the outposts of the rebels are?" I asked Skeffy.

"They have occupied Boland's Bakery and the Mill south of the city near Ringsend. They are in the Mendicity Institute in Usher's Island and the Dublin Union, a hospital for God's sake, to the west. Then there is Jacob's biscuit factory and Saint Stephen's Green and the College of Surgeons. They are establishing smaller outposts as they go."

I hastily drew a map on the back of one of his fly posters, while he suggested additions to it to help me out.

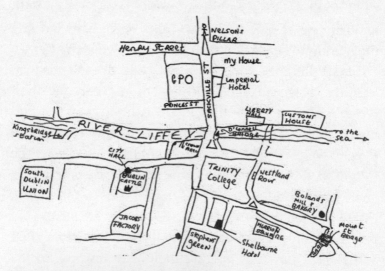

"I must find Jack," I confided in him. "He is in grave peril."

Skeffy embraced me. "The British will not let the second city of the Empire be occupied for long. Troops and guns will be on their way. Go and find Jack if you must. But don't come back here."

I hugged him tight and went on my way. Even if everyone thinks him mad, Skeffy is the sanest and kindest man in Dublin.

As I was about to cross the bridge a tall young man ran to join me.

"Could you tell me the way to Jacob's?" he asked me.

I looked at him in surprise. It was Jack's friend, musical Martin from the Fianna.

We crossed the bridge quickly, hugging the sides. A shot rang out from near the Ballast Office between Aston Quay and Westmoreland Street just across the bridge. We crouched down in a doorway of the Carlisle Building on Burgh Quay.

"Why do you ask about Jacob's?" I asked once I'd caught my breath.

"I mean to join my comrades," he told me. "My father took the air out of my bicycle wheels this morning. But I told him I'd lose my job if I didn't go to work."

"It's that way," I said, pointing out to sea in the hope of sending him to safety rather than doom.

He laughed. "That's a lie. I know it's not that direction."

"I won't send you to your death," I said.

"If you don't tell me, someone else will."

Before I could stop him, he raced towards Aston Quay, bullets snapping at his heels as he ran raggedly. He had a pronounced limp. I breathed a sigh of relief as he dodged into the alley before MacBirney's.

I headed left on Burgh Quay, then cut through Hawkins Street. I heard shots ring out from the direction of Trinity College and I ran full pelt, cursing that I hadn't taken my bike and had left it at home in my haste to get into the GPO. At least on foot, I wouldn't get taken for a dispatch rider, I reasoned. Raising my Red Cross flag, I dashed across Westmoreland Street into Lower Fleet Street, then down to Fishamble Street, to go the back way around Dublin Castle. It was just as well I was on foot as there were so many barricades now.

I paused breathless in the doorway of a pub, which was closed, though you could smell the drink from the very stones. But moments later Martin Walton came limping in front of me. He was shaken but exhilarated.

"Are you shot?" I called out in fear.

"They didn't get me! Trinity College is full of soldiers. I nearly got shot down by the Castle gates!"

"That's because you are wearing a green uniform, you eejit," I said.

I felt bad because I should have warned him to avoid going by Trinity College Entrance.

He grabbed me gently by the arm. "I mean to join my company, C Battalion, in Jacob's Biscuit Factory in Bishop Street – even if it kills me."

He was very handsome under his wild dark hair.

"Please help me, Molly, for Jack's sake," he said. "The

Big Fella himself has sent me and I didn't dare say I'm from Drumcondra and I've hardly ever been south of the Liffey. If you guide me there, I'll check inside for your brother."

"You have to get me inside Jacob's," I insisted.

We set off and I noticed he was rubbing his cheek as well as limping.

"Fine soldier you are," I said mockingly.

"I had a toothache all day yesterday," he explained. "My father put whiskey on it for me. But it's bothering me more than the soldiers."

I reached into my haversack and gave him some oil of cloves on a piece of cotton wool, which he put in his breast pocket saying he would save it for later. He wouldn't tell me what was wrong with his leg.

We rounded a corner over near Christchurch to take us on a route around the back of the Castle. In truth, I do not know this part of the city so well and was getting a bit lost myself in the back alleys. With a start, I saw British troops on the opposite side of the road. I told Martin to hang back. If they saw his uniform, they would arrest or shoot him.

I was right to be cautious.

A soldier called out. "Freeze, you there!"

Martin's face turned white. I stepped back. I quickly took my Saint John's Ambulance armband from my knapsack and put it on Martin's arm.

"Pretend to be injured and put your arm over my shoulder," I hissed.

He groaned and gurned like he was on the stage.

"He hurt his leg, sir," I said to the soldier, as I staggered under Martin's weight. I dug Martin in the ribs and hissed, "Don't lean on me so much!"

"Are you sure you're not a pair of Fenian rebels?" jeered the soldier, who had a Northern Irish accent. "Boy, what's wrong with your leg?"

Martin got flustered and began to speak but I kicked him so hard he really did go "Ow!" in pain.

"He's not from here. He's from Drum – France! " I improvised. "I'm taking him back to his aunty. He's in the Saint John's Ambulance and fell over a barricade."

Martin started to chunter in random French. "Oui, oui, non, non, merci."

A fusillade of gunshot rang out and the soldier lost interest in us.

"Stay at home," he said menacingly, then more tolerantly, "Bunch of kids!"

We cut through a laneway running near to the back of Dublin Castle and I felt a pang about the poor policeman shot yesterday and poor Seán Connolly. I wondered if Matthew the Bugler was still alive. The Castle was quieter today, but not in a peaceful way, more like the lull before a storm.

Martin had to stop to catch his breath and control his shakes.

"You picked a good time for one of your first visits south of the Liffey," I said. "Though are you sure you're from Drumcondra? You spoke French like a native!"

He laughed, and pretended to cuff my ear for my cheekiness.

We continued down the back of Saint Patrick's Cathedral and rested briefly in the little park beside it. Martin was very sad when I told him about Seán Connolly dying on the roof of City Hall in the hope it would scare him off joining the rebels in Jacob's.

We sat in silence for a few minutes and I hoped he was going to change his mind.

"It's a bit hard for a lad with a toothache to go into a biscuit factory," I said, trying to lighten the mood. "Would you not consider going home and living for Ireland instead of dying for it?"

"We have to be free," he said with passion and then winced with the pain in his jaw.

I had not succeeded in frightening some sense into him. He hummed to calm himself – 'The Last Rose of Summer' just like my music box!

"I play the violin," he said. "Won first prize in the Feis Ceoil, the Irish Music competition."

"Play music for Ireland instead," I said lightly.

"I will," he replied, with sudden determination. "You'll see. The new Ireland will be a grand place."

The labyrinth of streets was eerily quiet and we hugged the buildings and crept onwards, stealthy as thieves. The tenements, even the small cottages, seemed empty. We soon learned why.

We heard the mob before we saw them, gathered at the railings of the large hulking Jacob's factory that occupied the triangle of Bishop Street and Peter Street and loomed like a fortress, its two tall towers no doubt useful for look-out.

A howling mob of rough-looking women was screaming at the balustrades.

"Come out, ye so and so's! Ye're too yellow to fight, ye slackers!"

"Get over to France, ye bowsies, and die alongside our husbands and sons!"

"The Tommies are comin' and will bate the hell outa ye!"

It was going to be impossible to get in.

"Let me in, let me in!" Martin shouted suddenly, desperate to find sanctuary.

The mob turned on him. I thought he would be torn limb from limb. They were like French revolution furies, spitting and screaming all manner of abuse. A massive woman wearing a great big coat and with a face like thunder raised a frying pan to strike him down. A shot rang out. The woman collapsed like a sack, her legs going from under her. Shot, I feared, though there was no sign of blood.

The door flew open and, in the split second while the mob took it in, Martin was pulled inside. He grabbed on to me and I was swept up in his wake. The doors banged shut.

Martin and I huddled together in shock.

"I would give the pope, me granny, and even Patrick Pearse not to be here now," he whispered to me.

"I should go out to tend to the poor woman," I said. "They're angry because they can't get their separation money for their men fighting in France. They have nothing to eat."

"They'll tear you apart," said a man's voice.

"Peadar!" exclaimed Martin, embracing his friend. "We are friends through the music, Molly. Peadar wrote our 'Soldier's Song!'"

They began to sing a song that was like an anthem for the rebels.

"Soldiers are we, whose lives are pledged for Ireland . . ."

I soon learned the reason for Martin's limp. He pulled out a murderous-looking shotgun from his trouser leg. I grew very afraid to look at it. The barrels had been sawn in half.

"It's a sawn-off shotgun," he said proudly. "Father O'Shea over in Beggar's Bush showed us how to do it."

"Give me that here or you'll be killing yourself and all of us with it," said Peadar. "Go and report to Commander McDonagh who is on the roof, by the tall chimney towers."

The factory was badly lit with its vast machinery shrouded with dust-wraps, carefully placed by the workers before they'd left on the previous Saturday. There was an overwhelming, cloying sweet smell, as if we were inhaling sugar.

Rebels carrying sacks of sugar to use as barricades passed us on the stairs. I showed them all Jack's photograph with not one flicker of recognition from them.

Martin's ears pricked up as we passed one room. We pushed open a door and heard the distinct sounds of a gramophone playing "God Save the King". A group of young Fianna boys and Cumann na mBan girls were gathered round, giggling. They were in a beautiful library lined with leather books behind glass cases and leather sofas and armchairs. There were special artifacts in glass cases, now covered with biscuit crumbs.

"We're going to put it on when the leaders make their tour of inspection to get a rise out of them," laughed one young girl.

"Have you brought your fiddle here?" one lad asked Martin. "We'll have a céilí when it gets dark."

When they had finished listening to the record, I showed them Jack's photograph in my locket. They promised to keep an eye out for him and pass on the message that I was looking for him. I ripped a page out of my diary and wrote him a note.

"Jack. Father has left instructions for us to go to Aunt Elizabeth's family in the Presbyterian Manse, York Road, Kingstown, or Dr Ella Webb in Hatch Street. If you can't get to either, Mother O'Brien, at Nanny's Shop in Whiskey Row, Ringsend, will look after you or help you get to Kingstown. Your loving sister, Molly."

I gave it to a sensible-looking girl who had a First Aid armband.

It was strange in that library, so full of frivolity and fun, and so different from the chaotic Stephen's Green and the tense atmosphere of the GPO.

A group of lads gathered around a large volume.

"'Friends, Romans, countrymen!'" one intoned, mock theatrical.

"That's 'Julius Caesar' by Shakespeare," I said.

"'Cry "Havoc" and let slip the dogs of war!'" another boy exclaimed. Everyone laughed. Except me. For I had been out on our streets and seen havoc.

We went up on the roof, beside the tall chimney towers. The position commanded a good vantage point over the whole city. Shots were exchanged and I was able to distinguish them. The British soldiers' guns make a higher note than that of the bark of the rebels' Mausers.

I peeked over the balustrade and looked out over Stephen's Green. By the barricades of motor cars and bicycles at the corners, rebels in green darted into the College of Surgeons that is to the west of the Green. Something was up.

I saw a group of men crouching by a chimney tower and realized they were the commanders. One, a small wiry man, was relaxed and smiling as if he didn't have a care in the world.

"That's Thomas MacDonagh," whispered Martin.

I jumped. I'd forgotten he was with me.

"He's a great chap," he added. He pointed to a tall bluff man in a well-cut blue suit casually smoking a cigar and leaning on a cane. He had a military bearing and a cold, steely look.

"That's Major Seán MacBride that was married to Maud Gonne, the Englishwoman who joined our cause. He's an old Fenian and a hero of the Boer War in Africa against the English."

The commanders were talking in low voices and unaware of our presence.

"City Hall has been retaken," Major MacBride said quietly.

My ears pricked up. Dr Kathleen Lynn, Matthew and that young boy Arthur would have been amongst the captured rebels. Seán, God rest his soul, had already gone to meet his Maker. I wondered if the rebellion was beginning to fall apart.

"There is fierce fighting down at the Mendicity Institute under young Con Colbert," MacBride continued. "And Boland's Mill is still occupied. But there is some sort of retreat going on at Stephen's Green into the College of Surgeons. I'll post snipers to cover their positions."

"Our garrison is strong here," said MacDonagh.

"One of our lads shot that troublesome policeman who was taking notes of our position. He refused to move on," said MacBride, drawing on his cigar.

"The police need to know we mean business," said MacDonagh.

I was shocked. He did not seem like he would relish fighting.

"We should take them prisoners," said MacBride.

"Connolly's orders are that we should encourage Irishmen in the British Army to come over to our side. It is up to us to do what we want with the police," MacDonagh said grimly.

I remembered my mother saying that Mr Connolly did not like the Dublin Metropolitan Police. They were very brutal to unarmed workers during the 1913 Lockout. But then I thought of old Mr Killikelly who was a Royal Irish Constable and, Jane said, a very kind and popular person who always helped those who could not read or write in his area. They were not rich or grand people. Nor was Louisa Nolan's father. And they were Catholics.

I thought what an awful business this war was. Irish person against Irish person. It was even difficult to tell whose side anyone was on. Like father and Jack. Would Jack kill Father if he was ordered? Or how would he feel if one of his comrades shot him dead? There are really only two sides: life and death.

"But we must avoid unnecessary bloodshed, even of policemen, particularly if unarmed," continued MacDonagh.

I was glad to hear it.

"We need to let Mallin and the Countess know we are well defended," said MacBride, "and Jacob's is a secure back-up location for withdrawal from their positions around Stephen's Green and the College of Surgeons. Send for a courier."

Martin immediately jumped forward.

"That was quick!" MacDonagh laughed as he wrote out a message. "If all young people are as eager as you, me laddie, we'll be the best country in the world."

I plucked up my courage and thrust the locket with Jack's photograph in front of MacDonagh and MacBride, asking if he'd delivered any messages to them.

"We cannot reveal details of military operations," said MacBride.

I looked up and, wedged in a gap a few feet up the brick tower, I spied a strange object. Another of Jack's soldiers painted in green, its silver face glinting.

"I know he was here," I said. "He even went halfway up that chimneystack."

I saw a brief smile flash across MacDonagh's face.

"Jack the Cat," he said, peering at the photograph and glancing up the tower.

"I saw him scale the rooftops all down Grafton Street," said MacBride in admiration. He knocked the tin soldier down with his rifle butt and passed it to me.

I held it tight. "When was that?" I asked eagerly.

MacBride scrunched up his eyes, scanning his memory. "Day and night is all the one here. That would have been yesterday."

"He was here at dawn today and sent onwards to the

Countess," MacDonagh said. Then he laughed kindly. "I hope you're not a spy!"

"Please, sir, I am Jack's sister and trained in First Aid. I just want to make sure he is well," I said. "We've had no news and are very worried."

"He is working for Ireland," said MacBride.

"Was there another boy here?" I asked. "With freckles and buck teeth – Anto Maguire?" But their blank looks told me they hadn't seen him.

"It is not safe for you to be wandering about. Return to your home and family," said MacDonagh.

I didn't say that my home was no safer, being opposite their headquarters. Nor that my father was, at that very minute, risking his life to repair what they had undone.

Their news was worrying. Jack had not been seen since dawn and riders had been shot.

I slipped back down the stairs and decided to look for another exit in case the wild women of the slums were still raising hell.

At the back gate, there was a young fellow looking for a horse but they were giving him short shrift. I overheard him say the password, which was "Limerick".

"I answered the call-out yesterday and borrowed Gypsy, the brother's horse, to come as fast as I could. I was in so quick, I was here with the fellas that blew off the locks of the main door to get in," he pleaded. "We put Gypsy in the stable. Give him back – me brother's going to scalp me! He doesn't know I took him. I have to take him back home to Fairview for me brother's cab."

"The lookouts have been searching everywhere for you," said the sentry. "We thought you were dead. They'll tan your hide, you big *amadán*! Giving them all that worry!"

At that, the young fellow just ran off, not wanting to face any more trouble.

In the confusion, I slipped down towards York Street, which leads to the College of Surgeons but took a zigzag route down laneways.

I soon realized Martin Walton was on my tail again and I waited for him in a shop doorway. It would be an advantage to be with him, to get access to the Countess.

"You don't know where the college is either, you big galoot," I said. "Come on – I'll show you."

He pulled my hair playfully and pointed upwards towards the corner of a building. A sniper was crouched by a chimney breast, pointing his gun the other way.

Even though I'd intended to question him more about why he was fighting, we soon began to play like children do – hopscotching and playing tag up the streets as we dashed from doorway to doorway.

We made it down York Street and saw small parties of rebels in twos and threes retreating from the Green to the College of Surgeons. Commander Mallin emerged from the park and out of nowhere a big rough-looking shawlie hurled herself at him. She was ready to tear him limb from limb. A young Irish Citizen Army soldier raised his rifle butt to hit her, but Mallin to his credit knocked it away – thus saving her life. Then Mallin and the young soldier ran like maniacs past us to the side door of the College of Surgeons, the furious woman still screaming, "The Tommies will get ye, ye divils and rats!"

We waited for the sentry to let us into the College and saw a curious sight, a white flag raised over the Shelbourne Hotel.

"It's the twice daily ceasefire to allow the keeper to feed the ducks," the sentry explained.

I was happy for park-keeper Carney for he does love those ducks so!

It was but a brief reprieve. Soon the rat-atat-tat of sniper fire resumed. British Troops had occupied the Shelbourne Hotel overnight under cover of darkness. And now the rebels were the sitting ducks.

Martin went inside to deliver his note to the Countess but they wouldn't let me in. So he took my locket. As the seconds, then minutes ticked by, my fear increased and I prayed to God that Jack was safe.

It was ten minutes before Martin returned. I almost embraced him when he came back.

"Jack was sent to the GPO this morning. There were three riders in all and none have come back.'

"But where can he be!" I cried.

"Many of the injured are going to the Merrion Square Field Hospital."

I grabbed the locket and made to dash off but Martin grabbed me by the arm.

"I have to go back to Jacob's. When all this is over, I'll buy you and your brother an ice cream at Matassa's Ice Cream Parlour on Moore Street near Coogan's Grocers. It's the only place I know in town."

I laughed and shook hands, somewhat shyly. "I'll have the raspberry ripple with chocolate sauce."

I felt a pang at our parting. We had become good friends despite the strange nature of the encounter. I wondered if I'd ever see him again.

I cut down through Molesworth Street and via Kildare Street across Leinster Street to get to the Field Hospital. Dr Ella, my mother's friend, might know more.

As I cut across Merrion Square, I was surprised that there were still many people going about. But, taking a leaf out of the rebels' tactics, there were British soldiers' barricades now.

The War Hospital Supply Depot, at 40 Merrion Square, was in an imposing Georgian house and I knew it well because it's where we send the sphagnum moss.

As I came up the steps, an ambulance car drew up and Mr Smith and a woman carried a man out on a stretcher. His hand was bleeding and he was groaning. I immediately ran to help. The woman greeted me warmly.

"That's the spirit, girl. Show the men we can do the same work!"

"The St John's crowd have been great," Mr Smith said. "Dr Lumsden is running a field hospital out of Baggot Street Hospital. And your mother's friend, Dr Webb, is cycling in from Hatch Street, going straight through the line of fire. She put the call out yesterday at midday and within three hours there were twenty women setting up a thirty-bed hospital."

"It's brutal out there," I commented. "Nobody knows who the enemy is so snipers are firing at random."

We carried the injured man in to the ground floor, and helped him onto a bed.

"Doctor will be with you presently," said the nurse as she washed the man's wounds.

"I think his wrist bone is very bad," I said.

"Go and fetch Dr Webb. She's on the first floor," said the nurse.

I ran up the stairs two at a time and entered the makeshift ward. Here, in what had been an office, mattresses were laid on piles of books to elevate them from the floor. There were also some mattresses on a couple on desks, which looked like makeshift operating tables with instruments alongside them.

At one of these, Dr Ella Webb was examining a smartly dressed older man with a leg wound who was wincing with the pain but trying to be brave.

"We'll have you dancing the polka in no time," she assured her patient. The man relaxed and the way in which she steadied his nerves was magnificent to see.

"My dear Molly!" she exclaimed. "You're a bit early for our tea."

She is a small pretty woman with energetic movements, a beautiful voice and kind eyes. As we walked down the stairs I told her of my quest for Jack. She took my hand and looked into my eyes.

"Molly, child, you must stay here with me. But I will be on the look-out for Jack. I am moving between all the positions. We are going to set up an ambulance patrol out of Harcourt Street Railway Station and I will tell them all to keep an eye out for Jack and pass on your message as to where to go. I am the Lady Superintendent of the Ambulance Brigade, so they will oblige me."

"But are the ambulances getting fired on?" I asked.

"The rebels do not fire when they see our red or white crosses," she said. "But both sides make mistakes because so many of the fighters and soldiers are nervous, God help them and us all."

"You are so brave!" I exclaimed, struck by how forgiving and kind she was.

"It's fine for me. I get to do the interesting work," she laughed. "And it's admired."

We passed a well-dressed woman scrubbing the floor and another in a man's overcoat hauling up packages of bandages.

"They're the ones I admire," Dr Webb said. "They're doing the dull, boring work. Do you know, they transformed this house in three hours!"

Women were still carrying in mattresses, blankets, bedding and utensils from neighboring houses.

Dr Ella examined the man's wrist. She carefully scrutinized the bloody mass for any shrapnel. I noticed she kept her features clear and pleasant, not betraying any information to the patient.

The patient mumbled something and I bent down so he could talk into my ear.

"I want a real doctor," he groaned. "I am a clerk. I don't want to risk losing me hand!"

"She is a real doctor!" I said. "And one of the best in Ireland." But the man just groaned some more.

Dr Webb smiled at him. "You are lucky. There is extensive tissue damage but we can save your hand. Molly, go and ask the nurse for some Dakin's solution."

I returned with the solution. She administered it through perforated rubber tubing. I forced myself to look closely at the wound, even though the smell was awful and it made my stomach heave.

"This is an antiseptic solution to clean the wound," she explained. She took out a small instrument like an eyebrow-plucker and removed pieces of dead flesh from the wound. "The most important thing is to clean the wound site and prevent infection. We will reset the bone and then let nature do its work."

I mopped the man's brow.

"You are interested in this, Molly, I can see," Dr Ella said.

"I have a lot to learn," I said.

She let me apply the moss dressing and I handed her the bandage. The sling had been beautifully folded by a nurse, unlike my clumsy attempts. As gently as she could, Dr Ella placed it around the man's neck, all the while talking to him and reassuring him. He winced slightly but relaxed when his arm was in place, all worries about being tended by a woman doctor forgotten.

"Good girl, Molly, thanks for your help," she said. "A bit more practice and you'll be the makings of a medic."

I felt a swell of pride and thought she was very kind to encourage me.

I told her that I could find very little on bullet wounds in my First Aid Manual.

She smiled. "The best book is by a Frenchman – 'War Surgery' by Edmond Delorme. It has just been translated."

I asked her what to look out for.

"The German Mauser ricochets do a lot of damage," she explained. "It can be better to be shot at point-blank range because the wound is cleaner. Or better still, from a distance. Ricochet bullets at short distance are bent out of shape and do more damage to tissue, punching and tearing it."

She told me shrapnel from exploding artillery was like lots of tiny knives stabbing a person and because bits of clothing got attached it, could do a lot of damage by causing infection.

"So what should a First Aid person do?" I asked.

"Keep your hands clean, Molly. Remember infection is the enemy," she advised me. "Don't poke the wound or touch the holes. Check if there is an exit wound as well as an entry. And clean the wound surface with a clean swab wrung out in alcohol or in tincture of iodine. Then apply your dressing and get your patient to a doctor as soon as possible!"

"What if the patient is bleeding a lot?"

"Good question, girl. Stop the bleeding, that's the first thing you must do. Remember what you learned about tourniquets! Now, crash course in medicine over. I must go over to see Dr Lumsden and help with the wounded at Baggot Street Hospital."

A nurse came in to help refill Dr Ella's bag with supplies and dressings and said she'd heard rumours of rebel dispatch riders shot outside Trinity College on the way to the GPO in the early hours of the morning.

I nearly dropped the bottle of iodine I was refilling.

"I know some of the dispatch riders," I said, trying to quell my agitation. "I'm worried it might be Jack. I need to look for him at the GPO and could check in Trinity College. It's on the way."

"It's best if you stay here with me until we get the lie of the land," Dr Ella said.

Tear, unbidden, spilled from my eyes. "But I must find out! What if it's Jack, or Anto or one of his friends?"

She gave me a hug and wiped my tears away.

"Why don't you help me load the supplies to Trinity College into the ambulance. They are taking in a lot of wounded there and running short. We'll tell the ambulance and stretcher-bearer to check about the dispatch rider in Trinity and other places."

I helped her carry the boxes of lint dressings, boric powders, peroxide and iodine down to the front door where the ambulance was parked.

We scanned the square and, checking that the coast was clear, carried the supplies to the back door of the ambulance. It was a motor vehicle with a big red cross painted at the side. Dr Ella frowned at the sound of gunfire from the Green.

"It's only the second day of conflict and already there are scores dead and hundreds wounded. If this goes on for much longer, the casualties will be in the thousands."

"I hope we have enough bandages and iodine," I said.

She set me to arranging the supplies carefully into the pockets and chests in the vehicle, so there would be room for any injured picked up en route. I found it calming to stack the bottles and dressings neatly in their places.

At that moment, an ambulance car drew up and more casualties were ferried in by stretcher.

"Dr Ella!" someone shouted from the doorway.

Quick as a flash Dr Ella ran out. "You'd better finish on your own, Molly – the new shift to take over ambulance duty will be down in a few moments."

I was glad she trusted me and became so absorbed in

the task that it took me a moment to register that the engine was cranking up and the vehicle moving off. I hesitated, not sure what to do as I was flung across the vehicle but we had already roared out of the square. I banged on the window between the driver and the interior of the ambulance, but he misunderstood my intention and just gave me a friendly wave, without turning round. I decided it might be dangerous to halt the driver. I was on my way to Trinity and it was too late to do anything about it. I didn't want Dr Ella to think I had stowed on board. So I would explain the situation to the driver when we arrived

I must confess I got quite a thrill to be conveyed in the ambulance. We passed Westland Row without incident. There was much glass around and we nearly got tangled in a big coil of wires. The rebels had a barricade at either side of the road but they let us through and proceeded round to the small side entrance of Trinity College. We drove by the imposing college railings that surround the several square miles of the playing fields and the large stone buildings of the students' residences.

When we pulled up, the driver, an elderly man in his seventies, didn't seem to notice how young I was. He barely listened to my explanation about being on board by accident as he was preoccupied about securing petrol for the vehicle. He entrusted me to the porter, Mr Massey, who was guarding Trinity's side entrance and hurried off into the college, telling me to attend to the medical supplies.

Mr Massey gave me a little cart for the supplies and led me to the chief porter George Crawford, a large bluff man with an air of authority and friendly personality, who was checking provisions going into the student dining area known as 'The Buttery'. Knowing that I wasn't meant to be here at all, I began to lose confidence about asking about the dispatch riders. As I hung back, waiting for Mr Crawford to finish what he was doing, all my courage seemed to ebb away.

As we walked over the ancient cobblestones through the quadrangle, I was astonished to see that already this lofty place of learning had been transformed into a garrison. There were hundreds of British soldiers in front of the dining hall or lounging in doorways. So many horses and men milled about, Trinity resembled an open-air stable or a horse fair. I felt completely intimidated.

A father ran in with a little boy with a wounded hand.

"We have no food," said the father. "He is very weak."

They took the boy but wouldn't let the father come any further. I looked to the porter to intervene but he said he had no sway now.

"It's military rules, I'm afraid," he said. "We're to have four thousand troops here. They're coming in from all over. Athlone, the Curragh, Belfast. There's a battalion of Sherwood Foresters arriving in Kingstown tomorrow – the Lord knows where we'll put them all! General Maxwell has been put in charge and the rebels won't know what hit them."

"Fall in!" shouted their sergeant as four huge guns were brought through the main entrance.

"The eighteen pounders are here!" an excited student exclaimed.

The sheer size of these weapons nearly made me faint. They were mini-cannons, designed to fire shells, I heard the student tell his friends.

"Amass company!" shouted a corporal and six young Trinity students in civilian clothes stood to attention.

"Proceed to Tara Street to dig gun emplacements," shouted the corporal. "Tell anyone who asks that gas is cut off in Trinity."

"But, sir, we won't be able to dig through the cobblestones," one of them protested.

But the corporal snarled, "You are now a member of His Majesty's forces and not in the debating chamber. Do as you are instructed or face court martial."

The young student turned pale and joined his companions on his no doubt futile task. For it is well nigh impossible to dig up cobblestones.

Now that the big guns were going to be turned against the rebels, I feared for us all.

The porter, George Crawford, took me to the medical centre set up in the music room opposite the dining room. I saw the small boy having his arm bandaged. He was crying for his father. But he looked considerably better after a drink of tea and some toast.

They were most grateful for my supplies. One of the

nurses was another friend from First Aid training and I asked her in a whisper about any rebel casualties – but she'd just come on duty. The only other patients there were ordinary people caught in the crossfire and a couple of British soldiers with superficial injuries.

"It's a wonder the rebels didn't try to take Trinity College," said Porter Crawford as he led me out. "Though I'm glad they didn't."

I saw a group of students emerging from an exam hall, including a couple of women.

"Imagine, they all turned up for their entrance exam!" he laughed.

I thought this a good moment to enquire about any rebel dispatch riders, but just then the porter saw two soldiers come out of a building near the front entrance.

"Why, it's the very man himself! Best damn shot I've ever seen!"

I gasped. It was the Australian private, McHugh, who I'd met just yesterday. The best shot in the army.

The porter called him over.

"Here, tell the girl about the dispatch riders. It was just after dawn and three of them came pelting down from Stephen's Green. But we had fifteen sharpshooters . . ."

McHugh smiled and scratched his head. "I dunno, mate. The shooting was done by the crooked light of the electric lamps, and at a high angle downwards."

"It was wonderful shooting," said the porter. "Four

shots were fired at the three cyclists. Three found their mark in the unfortunate dead victim."

I turned pale and thrust my locket in front of them.

"Was he one of them?" I could barely say the words.

"I couldn't see my own hand up there," McHugh said, not looking me in the eye.

"I brought the body into the Provost's House about quarter past four this morning," said the porter. "Let me fetch Miss Elsie Mahaffy."

"My mother knows her," I said. "I spoke to her only days ago."

My legs turned to jelly as they led me across the cobblestones, to a small room between the Provost's House and the Porter's Lodge at the main gate.

As we reached the door leading to the room, Miss Mahaffy joined us.

"Well, the corner boys, not content with spitting into the Liffey, are trying to murder us all!" she exclaimed.

The porter whispered in her ear.

"How Bessie will be devastated to have a boy disloyal to the crown!" she cried.

"Permit me, young lady, to inspect the body for you," said the porter kindly. "I think it is not circumspect for a young lady to do so."

I was angered at Miss Mahaffy. My mother would be much more put out to have a dead son than a disloyal one. My anger gave me courage.

"I will identify him," I insisted.

But, when I got to the room, my nerves failed me. I froze at the doorway. The porter lifted the cloth from over the face. There was a great deal of dried blood around the head but I recognized the clothes. His hair was so matted with blood it had turned a strange shade of coppery brown. The facial injuries were extensive and I could hardly bear to look.

I saw what remained of a waxen profile covered in blood. The porter saw my face turn pale. He went up to the body and removed the Sam Browne belt and handed it to me.

With shaking hands, I examined it. It was streaked with dried blood and near the buckle were his initials, JFO'D.

My legs were so weak, he had to support me.

"Another of the riders was wounded and escaped on foot. The third abandoned his bicycle and bolted down a side street. No doubt he went back to his headquarters and told them the College was stuffed with armed men," said the porter.

"We captured their three bicycles, five rifles, four hundred rounds of ammunition and their dispatches," said Miss Mahaffy in triumph.

I felt faint but refused their offers of tea. All I wanted to do was get away. Jack was dead. I could never face my parents again.

I gripped the belt tightly to my chest and took some strength from it.

I was hollowed out and lifeless, my own breath ragged in my chest. Yet my duty was clear, as stark as the blood that Jack had shed. I had to confess all to my parents and arrange for the collection of Jack's body. This was the sole thought in my mind. I would go to the Telephone Exchange in Crown Alley and try to speak to them.

Miss Mahaffy wanted me to stay with her but a sudden flurry at the gate distracted her. A new battalion arrived and a messenger accosted both her and the porter. I saw my chance and bolted out the front gate across College Green.

Even though it was now a shooting gallery, I managed to dart around the porticos of the Bank of Ireland. Around me bullets whined and pinged. My mission made me reckless. I didn't care if I was soon to join Jack and was possessed of a mad hectic energy that propelled me like a fury all the way round the back of the bank to Crown Alley.

The windows were barricaded by what looked like the wooden casings of the banks of telephones. There were soldiers' rifles poking out of the top-floor windows.

Suddenly my mad energy deserted me and I collapsed in sobs against the wall. I watched the sun sink in a blood-red sky and felt I could not face another dawn without my darling brother Jack.

"You there from the Ambulance!"

It took me several seconds to realize someone was

shouting at me. It was an elderly gentleman with a long white beard leaning out from a window above my head.

"There's a boy injured in the Store House opposite the Telephone Exchange. He's been there since dawn. I'll let you in by the wooden door."

I roused myself from my stupor. Jack was dead. I'd seen his body. But there were two other riders and one had been shot in the leg. Was it possible one might be Anto? I felt energy flood into my limbs and a tiny bud of hope. If Jack was gone, maybe I could help Anto or someone else. Anyone else, God help me.

I inched along the walls. A sniper on the corner of the building raised a gun but I held up my Red Cross flag.

"Hold fire!" a voice rang out and I was allowed to pass.

The old caretaker let me in through a tiny door in the large wooden gate. I saw motes of dust in the shaft of light as the door inched open. But it was hard to make out anything else in the gloom. I stepped into the stone courtyard and, lying on some dirty sacking, was a slumped moaning figure.

"Anto!" I exclaimed.

His face beneath the freckles was deathly pale. Beads of sweat stood out on his brow. He had lost a lot of blood. His eyelids fluttered and he opened them briefly.

"Am I died?" he asked. Then he groaned, "Me leg!"

The bottom of his left trouser leg was soaked in blood. I took out my mother's sewing scissors and cut his boot off. I felt a sudden calm. I washed his poor foot in surgical alcohol but my hands were trembling so much I used all of it up. I gave him a drink of water from my flask. His foot looked like something caught in a mangle. Trying not to flinch, I looked closer and saw that the flesh was torn open on the top of his foot. I spied a tiny silver bullet nestled among his tendons, like the centre of a blooming red flower.

I panicked, fearful I would gag. "Pull yourself together, Molly O'Donovan! Don't be a booby all your life!" I scolded myself out loud.

Remembering what Dr Ella had advised me about not disturbing the site of the wound, I checked to see if he was still bleeding. I saw beads of blood, so I laid him down and elevated his leg above his heart. I used a small stick and applied a tourniquet just below his knee. I did my best to remember what I had practised on my teddy bear from the manual.

There was a lot of swelling around his ankle, so I worried that he had internal bleeding. I felt his pulse; it was faint, his breathing shallow. I noticed his toes were purplish blue. His big toe was an unsightly pulp. But at least the bleeding had stopped.

I'd been so distracted when I heard about the dispatch riders I hadn't re-filled the iodine and I'd used up all the surgical alcohol. I remembered what Miss Huxley had told my mother about wound cleaning. So I applied sugar to the wound to fight infection. I gave Anto poor

Jack's belt to bite on. Dr Ella saying infection was the enemy came into my mind. So hastily I took out some water in a pail from a nearby butt and washed my hands. Then I rubbed them in a clean cloth that was in the kit.

"There, there, Anto."

I applied a dressing.

He came in and out of sleep, hovering, occasionally wincing with the pain. I thought it best to keep him awake. So I told him one of Mr Stephen's fairytales of how Fionn caught the Salmon of Knowledge, while I put a bandage around the wounded foot. For Fionn was in the original Fianna – the legendary band of warriors of Irish myth that had inspired the name of the Countess's Boy Scouts.

But Anto began to shiver and seemed to be fading fast. I desperately needed to get him to a hospital. I asked the caretaker to mind him as I sped across the dark narrow alley and rapped on the door of the Crown Alley Telephone Exchange. It was a faint hope but maybe they could call for help. And there was a slim chance my father might still be here or they might have news.

"Let me in!" I called. "I have a message from Mr Daniel O'Donovan, the Chief Technical Officer."

The door opened a fraction and I pushed in to be met by a surprised soldier. As we ascended the staircase the basement door opened, and I saw that it had been turned into a dormitory with mattresses on the floor.

"There's twenty brave women here, working all

around the clock. They don't flinch even when a bullet comes whistling in," said the soldier. He told me he was from Limerick and had been stationed at the Curragh. He was warm and open, but I realized with a sudden panic how foolish I was. If they saw Anto in his Fianna uniform they would arrest him! There was no guarantee he'd get medical attention.

A woman ran down the stairs and, to my great relief, it was Jane Killikelly. Was it really only two days before that I'd met her hurrying to work? She threw her arms around me and led me to the telephone room, all chat, asking me how I was.

"Is my father here?" I blurted out.

"I just spoke to him! I'm probably not supposed to tell you this but he's just left the Curragh. He's still going around surrounding counties to restore the lines. He can't say where in case there's any spies."

Relief flooded into my heart. At least my father wasn't in the thick of it.

"We are all holding the fort, thanks to your father," Jane continued. "The rebels have cut down all the poles and severed the wires, even smashing all the equipment. But he got us a guard before they could take this place," she said to me with pride.

My panic rose when she mentioned the guard and I hesitated, in a state about what to do about Anto, as she rattled on.

"We've borrowed mattresses from a nearby hotel and

are working around the clock. The rebels didn't cut the private lines that go through this exchange. So your father's diverted all the telegraph traffic through here. He's very clever –"

"Jane, I need your help but you mustn't let the guards know," I whispered to her.

I confessed to Jane that I had gained entry to the building under false pretenses. She looked at me so sympathetically that I found myself sobbing.

"I think Anto, my . . . brother's friend is badly hurt," I said. "He needs urgent help."

"I know the boy. There's a small hospital at Dublin Castle. They are the closest. I will put a call out for an ambulance." She went off to do that.

The seconds felt like hours. Although I badly wanted to talk to somebody, I decided not to tell her about Jack. I would tell my parents in person, since it was entirely my fault. I tried to concentrate on the exchange to take the edge off the agony of waiting.

I glimpsed about fifteen girls at their desks in the telephone room. Each one faced a switchboard of lights, jacks and small sockets studded with pins. There was a low steady buzz of conversation into mouthpieces.

"Caller, please hold the line."

"Caller, transmit your message now."

"Connecting you to Amiens Street, go ahead."

The windows were boarded up and the lights were dimmed so as not to attract sniper fire. Each girl, earpiece at the ready, seemed to work almost by instinct.

Jane dashed over to me from her small cubicle that was set off from the rest. "They are overloaded but they will see what they can do," she said. "But, Molly, you must go somewhere safe."

"Is Dublin Castle a military hospital?" I asked urgently, remembering all the chaos up there. Jane nodded.

"Anto is in the Fianna. He's wearing his uniform. They'll arrest him. Couldn't we take him to Dr Webb at Merrion Square? They're well set up there and it's not much further."

Jane looked grave. "We'll ask the ambulance to take him and you there."

I thanked her from my heart as we headed down the stairs.

"You know, our grandfather still has his old policeman's nose for trouble. He was right to whisk Christy and Gerard away or else it could be one of them lying there."

"You can tell my father I am safe with Dr Ella," I said hastily.

"I'll telephone your aunt in Belfast to tell your mother you are fine. Your Great-aunt Bessie is quite a character!" she laughed. "If there's interference on the line she says it's all those Catholics with their heathen prayers!"

As we neared the front door, we heard the ambulance drive down the narrow street. But just as we opened the door, there was a sudden volley of gunfire.

Although it was pitch black, I could see by the light of the moon that the ambulance car was armoured. The troops and rebels must have taken it for an army vehicle. Shots rang around it as it came to a halt.

"Hold fire! Ambulance!" several voices rang out.

But the ambulance crew was taking no chances and the driver parked broadside across the street. A woman stretcher-bearer jumped out of the back and I crawled on my hands and knees across the cobblestones to join her. Jane shouted out at them to head to Merrion Square and the driver said that was a good move.

We wriggled across the street, pulling the stretcher after us. A random shot pinged off the metal exterior and ricocheted round, raising brick dust, just as we closed the ambulance doors behind us.

"I bet it's worst than the Western Front," said the woman, laughing with relief as we settled Anto into the rear of the ambulance. Her hair was cut in a bob.

Anto was now breathing raggedly, pale as the dawn beneath his freckles.

"Come on, Anto," I tried to rally him. "We can't afford to lose our future national bard."

He opened his eyes briefly and I thought I saw the ghost of a smile.

As we drove by O'Connell Bridge, I peeked out the lookout slit and saw fireworks erupt and light up the sky. A girl strutted in a sable fur coat with a top hat on her head, while two snipers shot at each other from the roof of the corner buildings. And beside me Anto fought for his life.

7 a.m. Wednesday 26th April.
Merrion Field Hospital.

It was a nerve-racking drive through the south of the city to the Merrion Field hospital last night. Much of the south of the city, we learned, had been plunged into darkness by the rebels dismantling the Gasworks.

It was a mercy Dr Ella was still there when we arrived. Anto was taken straight away into a back room. She surveyed the wound to his foot. Luckily the hospital had some electric light, on account of being a supply depot. By now, many places in the city had none.

"By gosh, Molly, you have not only saved that boy's life but maybe also his limb." She signalled to the nurse to give him chloroform. "The site around the bullet wound looks clean. But, alas, he will lose his big toe." She pointed to the injured toe, which looked badly infected.

"Is it gangrene?" I asked.

"That usually takes about twenty-four hours, after the cells begin to die. Wet gangrene can then spread very quickly. I don't think it's that. But I don't like the look of that infection. It might be gas gangrene that spreads very rapidly. But we don't have time to wait for a second opinion." She felt his pulse. "He is cold and clammy and

173

his pulse is rapid and weak. If we do not remove the toe, it will infect his whole leg and go into his bloodstream. We can't take the risk. And the bone is so badly shattered it is unlikely to heal."

She allowed me to assist her during the procedure. I held Anto's hand and urged him to be brave, as much for my sake as for his.

She disinfected the tweezers and then removed the bullet in one swift movement. Then she sawed through the bone of his big toe quickly with a circular saw just above where the big toe joined the foot. It was done in the blink of an eye, the sound worse than the sight. Mercifully there was little bleeding and enough of a flap of skin to cover over.

"Now, young man, you will have to go in goal and avoid taking penalties. But you will regain most of your mobility and your leg will develop new muscles to compensate."

Even though Anto was barely conscious, I valued her good humour under the most trying circumstances.

She allowed me to hold the bottle of antiseptic solution while she cleaned the wound. She placed a dressing over the middle of the foot from where the bullet was removed. Then she threaded a needle to sew back over the flap of skin of the missing big toe. No sooner had she begun threading than a nurse ran in.

"Dr Ella, quick! A child has come in with a gunshot wound!"

Dr Ella handed me the needle. "Molly, after sewing, you can bandage his foot. We'll put a dry dressing and a stocking over the toe. And a splint on his leg to stop him moving around. We want complete immobility to help him heal. I'll get the nurse to put your name on the charge sheet at the front door. I'm trying to keep track of our volunteers coming in and out."

My hands shook but I breathed slowly to calm my nerves for Anto's sake. Dr Ella's confidence in me gave me the courage to finish the job. All the time, even under anesthetic, Anto held onto the belt. Even Miss Nugent would have been surprised at my deft sewing under the circumstances. I applied the dry dressing treated with iodine over his toe. A nurse glanced at my efforts and seemed satisfied. Then she bandaged the whole foot and made a simple splint from his heel to his knee using two slide rules and bandages.

I anxiously watched his breathing as he slept. Despite my best efforts to keep awake, I dozed beside him for a few hours, my eyelids feeling like they were stones.

As dawn broke, I heard my patient stirring.

"Where am I? Am I dead?" he murmured.

"Oh Anto!" I cried, my tears splashing onto his face.

"I had a dream you were an angel," he said.

I brought him some water and he winced when he saw his bandaged foot.

"You have just lost your big toe," I said.

"Sure what do I need that for? I could never score

175

goals anyway." His laugh was a whisper.

"You'd better stick to poetry," I said. "You know, your poem really was a bit good."

He grinned with pleasure, and I was relieved to see the old cocky Anto back again.

"Where's Jack? Did he drag me to the yard?" he said. "Why I am holding the Sam Browne?"

I bit my lip to hold back the tears and showed him my brother's initials: JFO'D.

But he shook his head.

"No, that's Gerald Keogh's. He won it at cards on your roof. Saturday night – just before you warned us your mother was coming."

Was it possible? I felt terrible for wishing it were Gerald and not Jack.

I took his hand and looked intently into his eyes.

"But, Anto, I saw the body just now in Trinity College."

"No, no. Jack wanted to hang onto the belt as long as possible and promised to give it to Gerald when the scrap started," he murmured. "We were teasing Gerald about it as we marched, saying he'd never get his hands on it. But Jack had to give it to him. It was Gerald wore the belt. I saw him put it on meself."

I jumped up, electrified. Could it be true? I remembered the image that I had tried to suppress in my mind. The handsome waxen face covered in blood. But so swollen, battered and bruised it was hard to make out the features. The matted hair – I had only glimpsed it from the door – it was so drenched in blood, in truth it was impossible to tell the original colour in the dim light. I looked into Anto's eyes.

"Did you see Jack?" I searched his face.

"He had orders to speak to Connolly in person. He's lost a few lives . . . slipped on Jacob's Tower . . . Check my jacket pocket . . ."

But he began to groan again. The nurse came in and settled him on his pillow.

"Let him rest," she said.

He closed his eyes in sleep. I found the tin of humbugs I'd given him in his pocket – dented with a bullet mark. This may have saved his life. And then in the left pocket – a small tin soldier painted green! I felt the tiny bird of hope take wing.

Jack is still alive! It's not certain. But there is a chance.

I felt light-headed. I blew my nose and wept. Poor George! My hope was his parents' nightmare. Another boy was dead. I could not blame Private McHugh. He is a soldier, shooting is his job. But what a wretched business is war! Between the two sides of life and death, only a breath.

I will pick up Jack's trail again but it's eight o'clock in the morning now and the most awful sounds are rending the air.

Later, Wednesday 25th April.
Field Hospital Merrion Square.

An ambulance brought some casualties from the side streets.

"They're shelling Liberty Hall," the driver told us. "The gunboat Helga has come up the Liffey and they're firing big guns from the opposite bank."

I raced up to the roof where there was a little balcony in front of a parapet. This was a new noise – a heavy dull pounding as if the very axis of the earth was tearing apart. That must have been the shells from the Helga.

But there was also a weird sort of wave of sound, more like a whistle. An arc of fire crossed the Liffey, there was a delay, then an explosion. I watched it a few times and realized the flash was coming from Butt Bridge. It must have been the big guns they brought from Trinity. There was a rhythm to it. Flames leaped up from Liberty Hall as the sun rose in the sky.

"I pray to God there is no one still in Liberty Hall," I said, clutching the parapet.

The woman stretcher-bearer from the night before joined me. She introduced herself as Linda Kearns.

"I've heard Liberty Hall's been evacuated and there's nobody in there," she said. "But nobody told the British. But sure they'd probably do it anyway to show who's boss."

Then the ground began to shake. We clung to each

other. Even from this distance we could hear the tinkling of a thousand glass panes after the shelling ceased.

We looked across as the smoke cleared and saw that Liberty Hall was now a fireballed shell, like the face of a skull. Flames raged within. Only the façade was untouched. The roof began to cave in.

"The sooner this is over the better," she said. "There's madness on both sides. They've arrested Sheehy Skeffington."

"What! But he's trying to stop the looters. He's the most innocent man in Dublin!" I cried.

"He was detained last night at Portobello Barracks, as he was being followed by the usual bowsie crowd of Dubliners jeering at him and making fun of him." Linda rubbed her eyes in tiredness. "Some officer by the name of Captain Bowen Colthurst took him hostage and was using him as a human shield."

She barely finished her sentence before she began to sway. She was so tired she was nearly falling asleep standing. I helped her down the stairs and took her to a room set aside for staff needing a rest.

"One of the other stretcher-bearers is a very young fellow too. An Englishman, Neville." She yawned. "I heard his father is head of the Post Office."

The son of Mr Hamilton Norway! I breathed a sigh of relief that he had not come from the Castle in the ambulance, as he might have told about Anto. But then I felt comforted that I wasn't the only young one out and about.

"Can you take over from me? You seem a girl with a head on her shoulders and there's no one else," she yawned.

"Dr Ella told me to stay here," I said. But she was already asleep

Somewhere out there, Jack was still alive, I prayed God for it to be so. Martin had been told at the College of Surgeons that Jack had been sent to the GPO. The head porter at Trinity College said that the three dispatch riders had been shot at when they came pelting down from Stephen's Green. Anto said Jack had orders to speak directly to Connolly. He was the next link in the chain.

I went to look for Dr Ella to beg her to let me take over from Linda.

In the 'ward' a couple of the nurses were hiding Anto's knapsack and changed him from his Fianna uniform into an old pair of trousers and shirt. He was in a deep, deep sleep and oblivious to their efforts.

"Just in case soldiers come to check. They're already suspicious of us," one of them said to me. "Look at him, sleeping like a baby."

"Dr Ella's been called over to Baggot Street," the other one said.

They moved Anto's mattress onto the floor.

"We're trying to stay away from the windows," the first nurse explained. "There are so many random bullets flying about, you're not even safe indoors. A few people have been shot in their own homes!"

At that moment the ambulance driver came in, holding a charge sheet.

"Molly O'Donovan? You're down for the next ambulance shift."

I looked up, surprised. "But Dr Ella told me to stay here."

The driver, a young man in his twenties called PJ Cassidy, with a pleasant face and wiry build, showed me the sheet, and there indeed was my name. I couldn't believe my luck.

"You're on the young side," he said.

I fished in my knapsack and pulled out my First Aid Certificate.

He looked at my name and smiled. "That's good enough for me."

"Are you going to the GPO?" I asked.

"Among other places," he smiled wryly.

Dr Ella must have changed her mind and, delighted, I got ready straight away and didn't need to be asked twice. I could ask Connolly at the GPO if he'd seen Jack. And I could ask around a lot more places if I was in an ambulance. Even in all the chaos and confusion, someone must have seen my brother.

I was glad my mother had bought me a cream coat, as this was the colour the medics wore. It was getting rather dirty but was passably clean. So I donned a fresh Red Cross tabard, put on my Saint John's Ambulance armband and, pulling my hat down low, went out to the vehicle, proud to be of service.

PJ asked me if I'd crank up the engine as he sat into the drivers seat. I asked if it was okay to sit beside him in the front cabin, which was open at the side. He said I might be better in the back. Our vehicle was a proper armoured ambulance and had a Red Cross flag on the nose and a big red cross emblazoned on each side. I asked him how we were to get through the barricades and cordons and he held up a sheaf of documents that were permits from the British Military to be let through. I jumped in the back and we were off.

Some time Wednesday night.
Saint Patrick Dun's Hospital, Grand Canal Street, South Dublin.

The day has been a storm of shifting images, like a kaleidoscope. I have seen things no person, let alone a child, should see. But I pray to God to make me strong so I can take it.

PJ drove the ambulance up Westland Row and across from Liberty Hall, to the terrible sound of cannon pounding. We saw the gunboat Helga – more of an armoured yacht. PJ enquired of the military guard at Butt Bridge opposite if there were any casualties.

"It's all been a waste of toime," the soldier said in a Cockney accent – I recognized it from having lived in London. "There was just a caretaker and he ran like billyo!"

So Linda had been right!

At O'Connell Bridge we had to come to the aid of one of our Saint John's Ambulance men, Henry Olds, who was attending the blind beggar who I often pass on the bridge, God help him. He must have just wandered out, unseeing.

Mr Olds was shot in the shoulder but astonishingly continued to treat his patient. He managed to stagger with him to O'Connell's statue. I dressed Mr Olds' wound in the ambulance as best I could, as he talked me through the folding technique for bandaging his shoulder. But after my talk with Dr Ella, at least I was reassured that doing a little was doing a lot. The poor blind beggar was shot in the abdomen but I was relieved that Mr Olds had already treated him as best he could.

At the Richmond Hospital, where we dropped our casualties, it was so dangerous that the mattresses were placed on the floor to avoid sniper fire from the housetops.

"The shelling's not as bad as the Western Front," PJ, who had served with the Ambulance Brigade in Flanders, said as we unloaded supplies for the hospital. "But the machine gun and rifle fire is worse. It's impossible to tell in these narrow streets where it's coming from."

"The rebels aren't out in the open. Once they occupy the buildings they dig in and defend them like fortresses. They have some outposts and forays to outside," I said.

"They are tunneling through the buildings."

PJ looked at me with interest. "You know more about them than the military," he joked.

There was an ominous lull as we set out to drive up Sackville Street and I risked sitting in the seat beside him. Gone was the mad circus of looters. But odd shoes, a rainbow of torn clothing and abandoned broken toys were scattered all around. I thought the looters were not bad people but just overcome with a frenzy of greed because they have nothing. We saw the corpses of horses buzzing with flies.

When I told PJ that there was a First Aid unit in the GPO, he said we should check if they needed any supplies or had casualties that needed hospital treatment.

"Our code is to treat whoever needs it no matter what side. I'm from Ringsend and my brother and school friends are with the rebels in Boland's Mill."

I admired his humanity and resolved to make it my code too.

We were admitted easily when there was a break in the firing. I was struck once again by the ominous air of waiting. I noticed a group stuffing tins, not with explosives but with metal letters.

"It's type from the Freeman's Journal Office across in Middle Abbey Street. We've run out of fuses and detonators," said the rebel.

"I thought we'd sent over to Jacob's for some?" said his companion.

"We'll be lucky to get a few crates of broken biscuits," laughed the rebel.

Another young boy spat out some tea he was drinking and was teasing Louise Gavan Duffy and Min Ryan.

"You're called what sounds like the 'Cumann na Man', but you are the Cumann na Monsters! That's the worst tea I ever tasted!"

Louise laughed behind her hand. "Oh no, we used the old water from the turnips."

"And served it in the bucket for Jeyes Fluid," said the boy, pointing to the makeshift teapot in disgust.

"I'll have to send you over to my brother Jim Ryan," said Min to the lad. "He's only a medical student yet he's running our field hospital over by the Prince's Street entrance. At your own risk!"

None of them had seen Jack or Connolly.

We called over to their field hospital where several wounded lay on pallets. PJ and I gave them some lint dressings and bandages. Jim the medic, a burly fellow with dark hair, was making up a syringe and gave me a friendly nod. PJ stopped for a chat with him but as there were plenty of Cumann na mBan women helping out, I decided to have a good search for Jack and see if I could speak to Connolly.

It seemed nothing had changed much in here since yesterday, yet outside everything was changing.

As I went up to the first floor, I passed the private quarters of the Post Office Secretary, Arthur Hamilton

Norway. The rebels were breaking open his safe. A man took out a bloodstained second lieutenant's British Army uniform and a .45 revolver. There was also a bunch of letters and in an envelope marked "Fred", a lock of fair hair.

"They belong to his son. He was killed in battle in France only a few months ago," I blurted out.

The men, to their credit, replaced the items respectfully, except for the revolver.

I saw the leaders all in a huddle, Joseph Plunkett in riding breeches and green volunteer shirt looking deathly pale with a brightly coloured new bandage on his throat that made him look like a cowboy. Pearse, distracted and otherworldly. Ancient, grizzled old Tom Clarke, in civilian clothes with his bandolier around his shoulder, resolute and grim. I wondered if they realized the British army was forming a cordon around them, tightening its grip like an anaconda. Battalions a stone's throw away in Trinity College were just waiting to strike.

I searched high and low for Jack or Connolly but nobody had seen either. I went down to the kitchen to get something to eat. There seemed to be no shortage of food and down there the girls were still carving joints and the Tommies were still washing up. But large pails of water were now everywhere about, in case the water supply was cut off.

"Pearse is punishing me because I said didn't support the rebellion," Louise Gavan Duffy joked, giving me a ham sandwich. "I'm stuck in the kitchen with four hundred mouths to feed!"

"But they probably think there's thousands of us here, so maybe they will smoke us out with a gas attack," said Min.

"They've bombed Liberty Hall," said Louise, "but they'll never bomb Sackville Street and the GPO."

She told me to ask Mary McLoughlin about Jack's whereabouts as she was also a courier. She was the girl I'd last seen hauling flour with Hannah, Skeffy's wife. Her brother Seán was also running messages up to the Mendicity Institute.

So many things that were unthinkable had come to pass. Maybe our own home would go up in smoke! A sudden impulse gripped me to check out our house and get a change of clothes for Jack. He was wearing a Fianna uniform. If he were captured, maybe they would kill him. If they could arrest Sheehy Skeffington, anything was possible.

There was a lull in the fighting. I looked out. The Citizen Army flag of the Plough and the Stars was flying from the Imperial. That had to be Mr Connolly's idea. William Martin Murphy, who had been his enemy in the Lockout, owned the hotel. But the flag was already riddled with bullets from the Trinity sharpshooters.

I dashed across the road, telling the sentry I had to speak to the officer at Reis's under orders from Connolly. As I pelted full steam, I saw that they were fortifying the pagoda tower of the DBC with cases marked "raisins" and "currants".

I clambered over the barricade by the ruins of Noblett's sweet shop and let myself into our house from the back by North Earl Street. Our house seemed just as I had left it but, when I checked the hallway, I spied large holes cut in both walls at an angle from each other. So you could now crawl through to Richard Allen Tailors and O'Farrell's Tobacco Importers on the other side. I wondered if they'd done the holes zig-zag in case someone coming from the opposite direction could shoot them if they faced each other.

Upstairs, I ran around like a demon, seizing up Father's and Mother's papers at random to put in our large strongbox kept in my parents' room. I grabbed mother's jewelry box and my music box. Then I carefully wrapped Mother's little porcelain baby dolls in the beautiful silk shawl, with its intricate Celtic knot design, that she had bought from Mr Mallin, and stowed them all inside. I even scooped up Jack's violin, as many tin soldiers as I could cram in and my father's toolkit for tinkering with electrics. Then I raced to Jack's room and grabbed his second-best suit, shirt and tie. Rolling them up tight, I stowed them in the pillowcase that was "Ireland" just days ago in Jack's explanation of all the armies, with my cambric lace dress. For I had run out in such a rush, I hadn't thought to bring my knapsack, which was still in the GPO. If I'd been thinking, I suppose I could have stored away the four tin soldiers from Jack in the strongbox. But in truth I didn't want to part with them – my link with my dear brother

As I made my way back, running with the Red Cross flag and holding the pillowcase, I saw Connolly in company with another rebel standing at the corner of Abbey Street, near Eason's Stationery. I was about to turn towards them when there was an unearthly explosion that threw me forward.

A shell had struck the Catholic Blind Boys' Home and a gaping hole appeared in the house.

I heard Connolly joking, "It's the heavy artillery now!"

An unearthly roar exploded. Then a whistle, a pause and another shell pounded the building. Shrapnel cascaded like sparks from a burning log.

I looked over and saw molten lead stream along the ground. Another shell erupted and the chimneystack was hit and fell in on the house. Panic rose like bile in my throat, but I remembered that the blind boys had been evacuated to the Customs House. More shrapnel spewed out from the house.

Connolly was now just a few feet from me and was almost beaming with pride.

"You know you've shaken the British Empire when they start to bomb you in the streets. Even if we lose now, we have won."

An old man was gathering up the molten metal as it

hardened. "Souvenirs," he said winking at me. "I'll make a packet."

Frankly at that moment I didn't know who was madder, him or the rebels.

I followed Connolly. But as I got inside the GPO, the very building shook to its foundations.

"There must be a bomb in the lower room!" exclaimed a rebel soldier.

There was a second and third explosion. The noise was truly awful.

"No, it's definitely artillery. A scream, then a bang," Mick Collins, the Big Fella, said. "Now back at your posts."

It was striking how quickly the rebels became accustomed to the bombardment, while I felt a sickening sensation, as if I was on a small vessel tossed on a high sea. I struggled to control my nausea as some of the rebels discussed the different noises guns make. I too had become good at distinguishing the different sounds of gunfire. With so much shooting there was plenty of opportunity for practice and it helped me calm my nerves. The stormy roar of the artillery was another noise to add to my collection – the shotgun with a bark all of its own – the German Mauser with a loud explosion and a distinct echo – and the sharp crack with a ring to it of the British Lee Enfield.

Amidst all the noise I heard The O'Rahilly tell Min Ryan and her sister from Cumann na mBan, in his soft Kerry accent, to deliver a message to three wives of

British Officers on the Drumcondra Road that their husbands had been taken prisoner and were being treated properly. The O'Rahilly is such a gentleman – he is like a courtly knight from days of yore. It's hard to believe he would ever shoot anybody.

"It's madness," I heard him say. "But a glorious madness."

In the Comptroller's Office Connolly was closeted with the Big Fella. I listened intently at the door, summoning up my courage to challenge them about Jack.

"Our outposts are coming in for increasing attack from the big guns at Trinity," said Collins, "and we have nothing to answer them with."

"Call in all outposts, south of the GPO," said Connolly. "Tell the men at Reis's doing the radio to go to the Hibernian Bank to Captain Weafer."

At that point a young Volunteer ran in, breathless.

"Diarmuid Lynch, sir. We've captured three English generals." He paused.

Connolly and Collins looked at him, incredulous.

"At the waxworks!" he finished with a grin.

The rebels all exploded with laughter.

But I thought, oh no! They must have tunnelled through to my friend Mr James's Waxworks Emporium in Henry Steeet and he would be most upset.

"They've put Lord Edward Fitzgerald and Wolfe Tone in the windows downstairs, sir," said young Diarmuid.

Mr Connolly thought this exceedingly funny and I

could see he was really a very jolly man. Then they ran down to see the sport. I followed them down the stairs, just as a hail of bullets pelted the waxworks. How Mr James would have cried to see his figures treated so! But even I had a giggle.

Mr Collins and Mr Connolly immediately returned to business.

"There's a field hospital in Hoyt's Druggists. Shall we bring the wounded back to the GPO?" said Collins.

"Yes, get the Red Cross and Saint John's Ambulance crowd to escort them so they're not shot at," commanded Connolly.

"What about in the event of a gas attack? We need to obtain chemicals to make up an antidote. Shall I send Jack the Cat out on that errand?"

Jack! I held my breath.

"That young fella with the nine lives!" laughed Connolly. "He's already on his way to the Long Fella over in Boland's Bakery on a special. Dev needs all the help he can get." He whispered something in Collins's ear.

I thought I heard the name "Roddy" and the word "messenger". They must have been talking about some other courier.

But I had heard what I needed. Jack had been sent to Boland's Bakery near Ringsend. I wondered what "on a special" meant.

There was a tap on my shoulder. It was PJ, the ambulance driver.

"Let's help with the evacuation of wounded from the field hospital at Hoyt's."

I ran out with my Red Cross flag. Then picked up one end of a stretcher being dragged by a young lad across the street to Hoyt's Druggists and Oil Supplies. There was a temporary cessation of fire and some of the rebel volunteers ran out from the Imperial, covering themselves with mattresses. But they weren't just temporary shields: they picked up some wounded in Hoyt's and the mattresses served as makeshift stretchers, It saved us a trip or two.

Halfway over from the Hibernian Bank, shots rang out again. I heard someone shout "Mercy, Lord Jesus!" I looked back and saw a rebel officer slumped in the window who I later learned was Captain Weafer, shot dead. I had heard his last words and it gave me a sorrowful pang in my heart to think of those who would be left grieving for him.

One poor fellow in hobnail boots fell over in the middle of O'Connell Street as he dashed from the DBC. I saw with a start it was Liam Tannam, the roguish joker who had complained about hauling ledgers. I said a silent prayer for him as I thought he was a gonner, but miraculously he got back up again, and zigzagged his way to the GPO. He talked to George Plunkett, the brother of Joseph.

"We took out that McBirney's sniper, thanks to that young fellow who suggested the pagoda of DBC as a lookout," he said.

I moved closer. I was sure he was talking about Jack.

"He borrowed a pair of binoculars from Hopkins and Hopkins and brought them back to me. I was able to see the sniper was operating from deeper in the second floor and using the tailor's dummy as a decoy," Liam Tannam continued. "I think we nailed him."

Before I had a chance to talk to him, he noticed he'd left behind his knapsack.

"Oh no, I've left my shaving gear behind," he groaned.

To my astonishment, he ran back out again and crossed the road to get it! Jack wasn't the only rebel with nine lives.

I ferried a young Volunteer across with his hand in a sling. He looked at me closely and when he got inside the GPO I redressed his wound and gave him a drink of water. My bandaging had improved. He gave me heartfelt thanks.

"You're Jack the Cat's sister, aren't you?"

My heart skipped a beat. "Have you seen him?"

"He's a legend!" the young soldier said. "I was on the first floor of Kelly's ammunition shop on Bachelors Walk overlooking O'Connell Bridge in the early hours this morning. And do you know what he did? He went under the bridge to avoid a patrol car going over. He went down from Eden Quay. Then I saw the hook come up on the stone wall on the other side of the river on Burgh Quay. He hauled himself up and disappeared up by D'Olier Street. I couldn't believe my eyes. It was like he could walk on water."

But I know how he did it. He must have swung across the three stone arches with his grappling hook, landing at the foot of each semi-circular span. I've seen him do it once before. I remembered now that he had gone out in a small boat with Gerald Keogh a few months ago and they had girdled the spans of the arches with ropes. The ropes would probably still be in place. I wondered why he did it at the time.

"Was he going to Boland's Mill?" I asked.

"He comes and goes like the Scarlet Pimpernel!" he laughed. Then he whispered more seriously, "He's always with the leaders. If he comes again, I'll let him know you're looking for him."

I was now desperate to get to Boland's Bakery and the scene of action over on the south side of the city. Meeting de Valera was my next move.

There were British Howitzers posted on the roof of the Rotunda now, so PJ drove the ambulance around to the Maternity Hospital by Henry Street and Moore Street. The snipers on the roofs held fire as we passed. The Rotunda was desperately short of food, so we dropped off our supplies and said we'd tell the next British Officers or rebels we saw to let food supplies get into the hospital. Judging by the groups of khaki, it looked like there were British army barricades all the way down Little Britain Street to Church Street.

But no sooner had we passed on the message at Trinity College front gate, than we were told to get to

Patrick Dun's hospital as soon as possible. There were reports of a big skirmish.

As I left Trinity, something made me turn back. I noticed a little tin soldier standing just at the foot of the entrance arch of Front Gate. I almost passed out. Only one person would have the audacity to place it there. Another one of his lives risked. I bent down as inconspicuously as I could and put it in my pocket.

As we sped through the streets, I scanned for any sign of Jack the Cat. But I didn't see any rebels at all.

There were some other strange sights. A portly man who PJ told me later was a well-known pompous High Court Judge, scuttled around the corner of Dawson Street clutching a fish in either hand. Another respectable gentleman pushed a pram full of groceries. There were children waiting in line at a bread van, Kennedy's Bread, that my father joked "stuck to your tummy like lead" – and not just street urchins and shoeless slum dwellers but respectable children in wool suits. The chaos and disruption had caused widespread hunger. There was nothing in the shops. There were no shops!

We proceeded to Merrion Hospital and were hailed at the National Gallery by Dr Ella and Dr Lumsden with their medical bags. Their faces were so grave it made my stomach lurch.

"As quick as you can," Dr Ella told PJ. "A regiment of two hundred Sherwood Foresters has run into a unit of rebels at Mount Street Bridge and there are heavy casualties."

They jumped in the back where I was sitting.

"Molly!" Dr Ella cried, embracing me. "Thank God you're safe. The nurse accidentally put your name down on the wrong charge street. There's no time to drop you back at the hospital. Be a good girl and stay with the vehicle."

Dr Lumsden was a tall man in his forties, and I was immediately struck by his composure and kindness. "We hope to broker a ceasefire to rescue the injured," he said.

Less than two streets away from Mount Street Bridge, the ratatat of gunfire assaulted our ears. From the lookout slits at the sides of the armoured ambulance, the doctors tried to piece together what was going on as we drew nearer. I was surprised to see that there was quite a crowd gathered near the bridge.

"I'd say most of the rebel gunshot seemed to be coming from Clanwilliam House," said Dr Lumsden, peering out through a small window that looked out over the driver's cab. He pointed to an imposing house on Mount Street, overlooking the bridge.

"But there's also firing from a house on the other side of the bridge on the corner with Haddington Road," said Dr Ella.

Haddington Road is a beautiful tree-lined suburb full of big houses that we have often cycled up on our way to Ballsbridge.

PJ stopped the ambulance at a diagonal from Clanwilliam House. The doctors got out and crouched behind the vehicle.

From my vantage point in the ambulance I took in a scene of carnage through the small window.

No words can do justice to the awfulness of the sights I witnessed. It was hard to believe that this bloodshed was unfolding in a leafy suburb of Dublin by the banks of the Grand Canal. It looked like the wholesale slaughter of one of Jack's games of soldiers. A whole battalion felled like at the Western Front. The dead and injured were piled up on the road. Those who had managed to get past the house in Northumberland Street took cover anywhere they could find it, on house steps, behind trees. They even lay end to end in the gulleys of the roadway like a giant human khaki-coloured caterpillar.

There were also rebels in the nearby schoolhouse and the parochial hall. Any soldiers who managed to make it that far were fired on like ducks in a pond, at close range. Smoke filled the air as the British soldiers had tried to blow up the rebels by throwing hand grenades into the buildings.

Those who made it to the bridge by sheer force of numbers were met with more hails of bullets, and were falling like ninepins in a bowling alley. The rebels fired volley after volley into the khaki ranks. The men fell. They could not return fire, I later learned, for such was their haste departing from England, and their unpreparedness for battle, that their rifles were unloaded.

The sounds and smells were awful. Groans, screams, the metallic scent of blood. Dozens of khaki-clad bodies lay on the bridge, piled on top of each other.

A Saint John's Ambulanceman called Mike joined us, his face flushed.

"Thank goodness you're here," he said. "They were sitting ducks. The regiment was in full military kit and marching into the city. Barely trained they are, from the slums of Nottingham and Derby. Some have never fired a gun."

"There are so many injured and dying," said Dr Lumsden, aghast. "Our hospitals will be overwhelmed."

"The British soliders were pushed forward by their officers with fixed bayonets and slaughtered like cattle. Some idiot of a general is on the phone giving them orders to keep going!"

The firing continued. "We will have to have a ceasefire to rescue the injured," Dr Lumsden said.

"The rebels are holed up in 25 Northumberland Street. And Clanwilliam House."

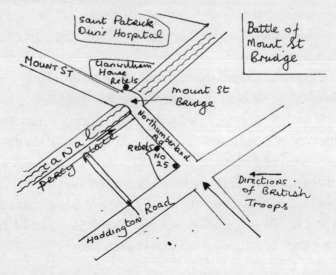

199

I looked through the window of the ambulance. I thought I also saw firing from Boland's Mill across the way and Robert's Builders Yard.

Dr Ella said she would go to the barricade at the lower bridge crossing to Percy Place to see if she could find a senior British Army Officer.

But then PJ, who had been speaking to some of the other crews, ran up to give some sad news to Dr Ella and Dr Lumsden.

"Holden Stodart has been shot dead at Carisbrooke House when going to the aid of a British Soldier," he said, his hat in his hand.

Holden Stodart was Commander of the Saint John's Ambulance.

Tears sprang to Dr Ella's eyes. "A brave man. He leaves a young wife and young child. He worked for Guinness Brewery."

Dr Lumsden was visibly shaken. "We must try to get him a pension."

PJ raked his hand through his fair hair and composed himself. "He died as he lived, doing his duty."

"Molly, stay here," Dr Ella said, wiping her tears. "You can help with First Aid when they ferry the injured back to the ambulance."

But Dr Lumsden could wait no more. When he heard a lull in the firing, he rushed onto the bridge trailing a white flag. He was the bravest man I ever saw, and I had seen many brave people. He coolly and calmly knelt in the middle of the road, attending to the wounded soldiers, feeling pulses to check the live from the dead, while bullets were fired from the houses on both sides. My heart was in my mouth, waiting to see if he could bring the injured to safety.

"Medics on the bridge. Hold fire!" a voice rang out.

Rebels and soldiers both took up the call. Soon there was a hush.

A group of nurses arrived from Patrick Dun's Hospital, Mother's friend Miss Huxley among them. I waved to her and she gave me a nod, then spoke to the nurses with her. There was a break in the firing. A proper ceasefire. Dr Lumsden stood up, supporting an injured soldier, walked toward us and waved to us on the side of the bridge.

As if with one body, all of the nurses and Saint John's Ambulance, led by Miss Huxley rushed onto the bridge. Nurses ran with white sheets and quilts to ferry up the injured as we did not have enough stretchers. I pulled out the stretcher from our ambulance and two strong men took it from me. I waited for the injured to be brought to the ambulance. I did not have to wait long.

"This man has a shoulder injury – dress it and we'll ferry him to Patrick Dun's Hospital," Dr Lumsden said to me, immediately returning to the bridge.

The soldier, no more than seventeen, his ashen face streaked with blood, winced with the pain. It was heartbreaking seeing him trying to smile.

"We said 'bon jour' to everyone when we arrived. We thought we were in France," he said, his voice a croaky whisper and his accent soft like a countryboy's. "My captain, Dietrichsen, is gone. Saw his wife and kids in the crowd at Ballsbridge – she's Irish and he broke ranks to embrace them. He sent them away from the Zeppelins bombing London. Now one hour later he's dead!"

I put his arm in a sling and patched him up as best I could.

"My mum's Irish. From Nenagh in Tipperary. Me granddad's still on the farm," he said quietly. "I thought I was going to get it in the killing fields of Flanders, not the aul' sod." His voice faded to a whisper.

And then the awful ritual was enacted again and again. As soon as the medics cleared the bridge, the awful shrill whistle sounded and the British soldiers charged the Volunteers' position. The shots rang out and the wounded and dying lined the bridge. The place was literally swimming in blood.

It seemed to me hundreds of soldiers lay dead or wounded. The living, who tripped over the dead, lay beside them for cover from the hail of bullets whistling through the air. During a break in the firing, a woman who was the image of Louisa Nolan, the Gaiety girl, ran out from an adjoining house with a jug of water to attend to a fallen British soldier. The combatants mutually withheld their fire. However, many of the wounded lay unattended for hours.

There was a strange noise from Clanwilliam House that we could hear from where we were parked. Random notes, ping-pinging with some of the shots. It sounded as if a crazy musician was accompanying the slaughter.

"What is that weird noise?" I asked a British soldier with a flesh wound on his arm.

He listened for a moment. "It's a piano – the bullets are snapping the wires," he smiled grimly. "Death music."

And after enough had been mowed down, there was a temporary ceasefire and the doctors and nurses and ambulance workers once more waded in among the fallen.

I am writing it all down in the hope of exorcising the awful images in my head. For the most part I was behind the firing line, set up at a makeshift First Aid station behind the ambulance. I did what I could to help organize the transport to Patrick Dun's Hospital as other vehicles arrived. PJ was working flat out as a stretcher-bearer. Dr Lumsden, Dr Ella and Miss Huxley were in the thick of it.

But there was one young woman I knew who was as brave as the medics. For it was indeed Louisa Nolan on the bridge – a singer and dancer more used to gracing the stage. Her father was former Chief Constable Nolan of Ringsend and he is a friend of Mr Killikelly, Addy and Jane's father.

She went calmly though a hail of bullets and carried

water and other comforts to the wounded men from the other side of the bridge. It was almost as if she was protected by an invisible shield.

"I don't know where you get your courage," I said to her when she brought a soldier with a shoulder injury to the ambulance.

"My two sisters are war nurses in England, I have one brother in the army and the other in the navy. My other brother was killed on the Western Front last year," she said matter of factly. "They are the brave ones. I see my brothers' faces in every single one of these men and I cannot leave them to die like dogs."

Towards evening, just as it seemed we had cleared most of the casualties, Louisa ran to me with great urgency. "There are a group of wounded soldiers in a house just over the bridge. The owner, the grocer little Mr Hayter, is dead. He was shot when he went to help the wounded inside his house. Hurry!"

PJ was nearby so I called him and he agreed to drive, seeing it was possible to get across. I jumped in the ambulance with Louisa. As the engine was cranked up and we rattled off, she started to sing a song I'd heard her perform on stage only a month before.

"'Daisy, Daisy, give me your answer do,

I'm half crazy, all for the love of you.'"

"'It won't be a stylish marriage,'" I joined in, in a faltering voice, as the noise of gunfire pinged off the ambulance.

"'We can't afford a carriage . . .'" We both laughed at this.

"'But you look sweet, upon the seat,

Of a bicycle made for two!'"

"We might as well enjoy the song, Molly," Louisa said sadly. "For there will be no young men left for us to marry."

"You are as good a singer as Marcella the Midget Queen," I blurted out. I was rather in awe of Louisa, having seen her on the stage. For she is very glamorous and pretty, even in a battle.

"You love the theatre, I can see," she said and her eyes were smiling.

"You should be a star," I babbled.

"It's my dream to appear on the West End," she said. "I'm the featherbrain of the family and it would please my dear old dad." She laughed softly.

I reached across and placed a reassuring hand on her arm. "You have the courage of a lion."

But the ambulance came to a sudden halt and I was thrown on top of her. She laughed once again but her face was rueful when we got up and opened the door to the new horror that lay ahead.

PJ drew the car up as close to the house as he could and we crouched behind the vehicle. We inched our way inside the house. I saw PJ wince as a small piece of kerbstone, thrown up by a ricochet, hit him in the cheek.

Seven soldiers, panting and covered in blood, were

inside the house. They were shaking and subdued. One was very badly injured, his uniform drenched with blood from a stomach injury. We moved him first. There was an officer with them who had been shot in the shoulder.

"It's worse than the French killing fields," he said. "For at least there we know where the enemy is. Here they are behind every chimneypot and tree."

As we went back in to pick up a soldier with his knee shot off, a hail of gunfire whizzed right past us. It was only when we got back in we saw the bullet-shaped holes in our clothing. I had one in my new coat, clean through the skirt. And Louisa's had passed through her hat!

As we got the last wounded man in, and pulled the stretcher in after us, its handle was shot off. Several bullets struck the armoured car as it left.

"What's your name?" the soldier asked Louisa. "I am Captain Gerrard. I want to commend you to my superiors."

As he shook out his pocket book to take a note, a bullet fell out. This struck us all as very funny, and despite the awful circumstances we all laughed.

"At this rate, I will never get to my rehearsal in the Gaiety Theatre," Louisa said and began to sing.

"'It's a long way to Tipperary,

It's a long way to go,

It's a long way to Tipperary

To the sweetest girl I know!

Goodbye, Piccadilly,
Farewell, Leicester Square . . .'"

It was her best performance ever. The seven men, broken, bleeding, faces grimy and nerves wrecked, looked at her with adoration. Even if she does get to sing at the West End, she will never have a more appreciative audience.

In Patrick Dun's Hospital, we were given bread and butter in the canteen and I confided in Louisa my fears for Jack. She looked at me earnestly. "You must do what you can to save him," she said. "For brothers cannot be replaced." A tear slid down her cheek but she brushed it away with the back of her hand.

I was restless so I offered to wash down the ward and went outside for buckets. A young woman approached me. She was very agitated and wouldn't go inside.

"Are there any Volunteers here?" she asked me in urgent tones.

I told her I hadn't seen any, though there were maybe hundreds of Sherwood Foresters injured. And just as many of them dead in the morgue and at least four civilians.

She was very jumpy but held my hand. "But there's less than twenty rebels taking them on!" She gave me a sharp look, trying to appraise which side I was on.

"My brother's in the Fianna," I said quickly.

She counted on her fingers, "Jimmy Grace and Malone in Northumberland Street, Reynolds and six volunteers in Clanwilliam House, three in the schoolhouse and another three at Carisbrooke House. There's another couple at Roberts Builders Yard and roving about . . ."

I was incredulous. "Less than twenty men have fought this battle?"

"The Fianna boys had been sent away."

"Was one called Jack?"

"No. They were Paddy Rowe and Michael Byrne. Sure, they sent them out through the skylight at half past two in the morning with messages for Michael Malone's mother and ours. Paddy Rowe called to us and was gloomy as anything. That's how I knew where to bring the food. There was another one or two with Commander Reynolds. I don't know who and they were sent off too."

I grabbed her arm. "If you know, you must tell me. One might be my brother."

She relaxed. "We just called to Northumberland Road about noon. Meself with May Cullin. Gave them hot steak from Mam." She lowered her voice again and looked furtive. "My brother is Jimmy Grace and I am out of my mind with worry! I'm Bridget Grace. We had a dispatch about the five hundred troops approaching from Kingstown. They could see them coming." She told me how they wouldn't let them in so they put the food and the dispatch through the letterbox.

"Do you know where the Fianna boys went?"

"Paddy Rowe, the young lad who gave us the

message of Jimmy's whereabouts was very upset. They were given orders that on no account were they to return to Mount Street. Jimmy was amazed when May and meself turned up, I can tell you, but I had to see him," She stifled a sob. "My brother and his comrades thought they would meet certain death facing the might of the British army."

I placed my hand on her arm and she composed herself.

"The young fella Reynolds sent away still came back with some fruit cake for the fighters holed up in their positions. I heard that brave young fella went back to Boland's Bakery," she said. "That's their command centre."

"I was going to go there any way," I said.

But Bridget Grace shook her head. "You've no chance. No women allowed there."

"Why? Everywhere else I've seen women alongside the men."

"Imagine seventeen brave volunteers holding off a regiment of hundreds!" said Bridget Grace, her eyes shining.

"Slaughtering them more like," said a voice.

We both jumped. Louisa had crept up on us on her dancer's feet.

"They are patriots fighting for Ireland's freedom," said Bridget. "They have redeemed Ireland's honour."

"As have the fallen in Flanders," said Louisa, almost in a whisper. But her eyes were hard, challenging.

"Shoneens, traitors, fools!" said Bridget fiercely.

I saw Louisa's eyes blazing and I thought she would strike her across the face.

"They are all our brothers," I cried. "Flesh and blood. A bullet doesn't know what side you are on before killing you."

There was an uneasy silence.

Both women looked down, each lost in her own thoughts.

"I came to tell you that the battle is over," said Louisa. "There are over two hundred British soldiers dead or wounded but only a handful of the rebels. They think some of them even escaped."

"Oh merciful God! I pray my brother is among them," said Bridget. Louisa looked at her with a certain amount of compassion.

"The officer in charge said they were brave fighters. Astonishing, actually, considering how outnumbered they were," said Louisa.

There was a sudden eruption and we looked over towards Mount Street Bridge. Clanwilliam House had burst into flames and lit up the whole sky. We were all subdued but the two women had reached some understanding.

"You won't be let into Boland's Bakery and de Valera won't see you," said Bridget. "We have to think of a way to get you in."

I took out my scissors and handed it to Louisa.

📖 📖 📖

I am writing this before I go to see de Valera in Boland's Bakery. I have cut off my hair and put on Jack's clothes, with a cap that Louisa had found somewhere, to help with my disguise. If Mr de Valera won't see a girl . . . then he will see a boy.

Thursday 27th April – early afternoon.
The GPO.

I waited until 5 o'clock in the morning to get into Boland's Bakery because martial law has been declared and anyone on the streets between seven at night and five in the morning could be shot.

All I knew about de Valera, the Long Fella, was that he was reserved and distant. And that he no longer wore a hat because he'd given his to a young soldier.

The territory they held was a nightmare, spread out over several acres, not compact like the GPO. Mary told me that Boland's Bakery and the Stores were the base of operations. The rebels had made themselves popular by distributing bread to civilians until the military started shooting at the shawlies. If de Valera had any personal headquarters, it was the dispensary adjoining Grand Canal Street and facing Sir Patrick's Dun's Hospital.

The railway track was next to railway yards, and across the lines there was a disused distillery building. There were several other sheds and outbuildings. Most of the railway track had been torn up. The large grey mill facing down to Ringsend held just a small outpost. The rebels had also seized the gasworks and broken up some of the machinery, which was why large parts of the city had been plunged into darkness. Westland Row Station was also occupied.

I got in over the wall from Patrick Dun's hospital. British snipers were posted on the roof, but Louisa took them up tea and sandwiches to distract them.

I peeked into the dispensary where May said de Valera was based. But there was no sign of a tall man. Two volunteers were arguing.

"He's deranged. He keeps changing his mind and disappearing. He's jumpy as hell, is Dev."

"No, the Long Fella's smart. He fooled the Helga into firing at the tower of the distillery house and not us. He just can't sleep. And we are all jumpy."

I moved quickly, down by railway sidings and sheds, as dawn broke. I was worried that both sides might shoot at me. At one stage I trembled so much with fear that I crawled down beside a disused railway carriage and had to stay there to recover my nerves. I don't know how long it took. But I forced myself to keep going, yard by yard, shed by wall by building. The only relief was that I was wearing trousers. I knew now why boys moved so freely, and why the Countess was so keen on them.

Near Westland Row, I came across the Royal Carriage and, overcome by curiosity, peeped in. A long-legged man in red socks was lying there, on the red royal seat under the paintings of nymphs and cherubs. His clothes were dusty with flour, his face haggard. I guessed he was de Valera, "The Long Fella" from the height of him.

I went in. He leaped up like a madman, wild-eyed and quivering.

"Is that angels I see? Am I in heaven?"

"No, they are paintings of nymphs and cherubs –" I realized how high and girlish my voice sounded. So I coughed and tried to sound more masculine. "This is the Royal Carriage."

He looked at me wild-eyed but quickly came to his senses.

"Boy, are you back already? And you've released the horses from the bakery stables and the dogs and cats from the pound as well? They have a better chance of survival out in the open and we can't provide the manpower to feed them."

I wondered if he thought I was Jack.

"This is a man's war. I don't want boys caught up in this. I have four children myself. But since you've come back I see you are determined to risk going back over to the GPO."

So, he had mistaken me for my brother.

He unfurled his jacket and took out a battered old tin

of Jacob's Cream Crackers.

"Pass this on to Tom Clarke. For the Yellow Bittern. We haven't needed it."

I grabbed the tin of Cream Crackers, and pushed it deep into my knapsack, thinking it a very strange souvenir. We have some exactly like it at home, yellow, with a picture of a smiling maid on the front. Jack uses them to store his soldiers in. I was utterly mystified by de Valera's reference to the Yellow Bittern, which I think is a bird, but I was relieved that I hadn't been given a gun or a bomb.

De Valera patted his pockets, took out his spectacles and stepped forward to take a closer look at me, but I sprang out the carriage doorway. I might pass muster when he was shortsighted and half asleep but I would not stand close scrutiny.

I should have known it – Jack was going back to the GPO, the centre of operations, where all the webs were spun. I gambled that when Jack got back to de Valera he'd be sent to the GPO and I would be there waiting for him.

As I passed out of Westland Row Station, I saw a rebel using a handful of coppers to get sweets and cigarettes out of the kiosks on the station platform. I was struck with how honest these rebels were – paying their tram fares, issuing receipts. If they hadn't been carrying guns, I would have thought them the nicest group of people I had ever met.

When I got outside, I crouched in a doorway, took out the tin of crackers and opened it. The lid was quite stiff and I glanced in hastily because I saw the khaki uniforms of British soldiers in the distance. But the tin just had crackers in it. I pressed on.

I saw the British troops passing down towards Trinity College on both sides of the street, so I decided to cut back up past Stephen's Green via Merrion Square, hoping to loop over by a western route. There were several soldiers' barricades but I picked my way carefully across the square and, at this early hour, I was unnoticed by the sleepy soldiers.

As I came towards the Merrion Street junction with Stephen's Green, I heard the clatter of hooves. At first I thought it was a new gun, but then saw a troop of horses pass in a cloud of dust. I thought they must have released the Boland's horses. I took out my spyglass and tried to focus and saw the unmistakable shape of Jack on horseback, leading them towards the park. I ran at full pelt.

"Jack! You are to give this to Tom Clarke!" I screamed after him, brandishing the tin of Cream Crackers like an eejit.

Most of the horses stood panting outside the park gate but Jack emerged again from the park in a cloud of dust. He rode up to me. I stood stock still, more out of nerves than bravery, and he grabbed the tin from my hands, like we were a circus act. Jack, rising on his horse from the cloud of dust, smiled at me like an angel and gave me a thumbs-up, then shoved the tin inside his buttoned-up jacket.

Bullets from the Shelbourne Hotel whizzed through the air, raising brick dust where they hit the granite kerbstones and the walls.

Jack's horse broke away and went up Grafton Street, bullets hitting the ground behind him as he went. Bullets and hoofs like twin drums beating out a tattoo. Jack rode on – his horse vaulting over a makeshift barricade of bicycles as if in a steeplechase. Past children bizarrely holding huge bunches of bananas looted from a fruit shop, women with aprons full of oranges and apples, boys holding boxes with tins and bottled fruit. A whirl of silver, pink and white paper shaving used for packing fruit rose like multicoloured snowflakes under the hooves. A clatter of broken crockery and glass rang out as a sniper missed Jack and fired into a china showroom.

Stunned soldiers looked at him in amazement – scratching their heads, not believing their eyes at the mad audacity of rider and horse. One even cheered. A tat-tat-tat of surprised sniper fire snapped at the horse's heels, marking Jack's route. I ran to the bend in Grafton Street, panting. I saw him whoop and holler as he swerved down Suffolk Street. Clearly, he wasn't going to risk going past the death trap of Trinity College once again. I ran to the next barricade and followed him in my spyglass.

But no – it was a feint. He continued on round by the bank at College Green and down Westmoreland Street. The snipers at Trinity were silent – caught unawares.

Onlookers were now cheering him on from windows and street corners. Fairyhouse Steeplechase come to war-torn Dublin.

At O'Connell Bridge an armoured vehicle blocked the way. Guns trained on him. He was snookered. But then out of alleys and doorways, people flocked onto the bridge in a wave of excitement.

"Hold fire!" roared an officer.

In the blink of an eye, Jack disappeared into thin air!

Everyone else was looking at the riderless horse. But I saw the splash in the water.

I knew instantly what he had done. Jumped into the Liffey, no doubt clambering to the arches under the bridge. .

My mad, wild brother was dicing with death. It was fifty-fifty if he had survived. But if he had – for how long?

Later Thursday afternoon 27th April.
The GPO.

"Clear the streets!"

I saw a bewildered soldier holding the horse. The crowd dispersed and we were ordered to go back up Westmoreland Street. But before I departed, I ran to the barricade and craned to look into the water. I could have sworn I saw the glint of a tin soldier caught in the grip of a wave before the current pulled it under. Another life gone – if he was lucky. It wasn't yet nine o'clock in the morning.

But I was wrong. There was a tin soldier, standing to attention between two of the columns of the balustrade of the bridge. All I had to do was bend down and reach beneath the barbed wire to snatch it. Another one for my collection.

The soldiers pushed us right back up Westmoreland Street but I slipped left onto College Green.

A man ran down from his house.

"Did you see that boy!" he exclaimed. "I hope he made it. I saw you following him from my skylight."

He ushered me inside his house, the Provincial Bank on College Green. He saw my look of surprise but put both his hands out in a disarming gesture and I decided to trust him. We went to his top room on the fourth floor and he pointed to the skylight.

"The soldiers are very jumpy and are afraid of snipers," he whispered. "But you are concealed here and you can see out the skylight." He pointed to a spot and pulled over a chair. He had rigged up a crude periscope with mirrors to scan the battlefield that Dublin had become.

I climbed up and scanned about. There was no sign of Jack. The horse, however, was still being held on the bridge.

I scrambled back down to join the man.

"My name is George Duggan," he told me. "I'm a reputable banker, but yesterday a drunken sot of a soldier thought I was a rebel." He tried to control himself but his hands shook. "They threatened to shoot me."

I looked at the man. He was dapper and well dressed and so clearly a respectable citizen, it made me realize just how nervous the soldiers were.

"After the massacre at Mount Street Bridge yesterday, the rest of the Sherwood Regiment will be looking for revenge," he said. "They will take it out on innocent civilians. I was nearly one of them."

We went down to the second floor, and in the drawing room, his hands still trembling, Mr Duggan held out photographs of his sons.

I looked at the photographs of two fine-looking men. "My fifth son was a captain in the Royal Irish Fusiliers. My youngest boy, God rest his soul, was a lieutenant. He was killed last August in Suvla Bay in Gallipoli." His voice faltered. "Same day as his brother . . ."

The poor man poured himself a shot of whiskey to steady his nerves.

I looked at the shining young faces of his sons, their genial natures evident.

"One was the best runner Trinity ever saw and the other the best shot, by God. I don't support the rebels, but I can see why young lads like you don't know who to fight for."

I was at a loss as to his meaning but then I saw a

puzzled young boy under a cap reflected in the mirror over the mantelpiece. I was still wearing Jack's clothes! I'd noticed that the British soldiers were more sympathetic to girls and women trying to get through barricades. I needed to become Molly again.

I explained to the kind gentleman that the boy on the horse was my brother and needed my help. He accepted my simple explanation.

"Under any other circumstances, I would prevent you from leaving, but when a respectable banker isn't safe in his own home, I cannot guarantee your protection," he said. "Now let me offer you any assistance I can."

"If you could lend me a lady's hat," I said.

He merely smiled and fetched me a range of bonnets and hats, plumed, buttoned and beribboned. I settled on a simple green felt cloche. Nor did he blink an eyelid when I transformed back into a girl. My new cream coat, which was crushed in my knapsack, was streaked and caked with dried blood. I could not bear to put it on. So he gave me a new coat, a good woollen cape in a drab grey-and-brown plaid belonging to his wife. He insisted she no longer wore it. I thanked kind Mr Duggan from the bottom of my heart and promised to visit him when all this chaos was over.

The cordon was tightening around Sackville Street and nobody was being admitted. I decided to try a route keeping west to get to Sackville Street, reckoning I could cross at the Four Courts Bridge. Little did I know I was walking further into the lion's den.

I wheedled and cajoled my way through every barricade in Dublin. Begging and entreating to see my sick uncle, or mother. Crying my eyes out where simple requests failed. Pretending I lived at a range of addresses. At around eleven thirty, I heard the sound of heavy gunfire once more in the direction of Sackville Street. It sounded like rifles, the stutter of machine guns and heavy artillery.

As I weaved passed the Saint James Gate of the Guinness Brewery, an extraordinary vehicle nearly ran me over. A cylindrical iron lorry used to transport stout had holes drilled in the side to create an armoured vehicle. It headed up the quays towards Sackville Street.

I spoke to a Guinness worker who was stationed at the gate and he was surprisingly unsympathetic to the soldiers. "The Dublin Fusiliers killed two of ours and are trying to pretend they were rebels. Bad cess to them!" he said in disgust.

I learned that the City Hall had surrendered on Tuesday and I wondered how Jack's friend, young Matthew Connolly, was and prayed he hadn't met the same fate as his brother.

I soon found out. At a barricade at Parliament Street there was a very chatty fusilier, who was boasting and regaling his fellow sentry with tales of his derring-do. I stood among a group of shawlies trying to pass through.

"Caught a young 'un we did, up at the Castle end of City Hall. They left him behind. Fast asleep he was, with 'is bugle around his shoulder. Bunch of kids they are."

I blessed myself in relief. Matthew had survived. For now.

His companion shook his head in amazement. "They were young blighters held out at the Mendicity Institute an' all. Threw out all the old down-and-outs they did. They ran out of ammo and threw our grenades back at us. Heuston was one of their leaders – little runt. I coulda killed 'im with my bare hands when I saw how small their force was."

"The rebels are still holding out in the South Dublin Union and their outposts all around the Four Courts," said the other. "They've got women fightin' too. General Maxwell's not going to show them any mercy." He punched his fist into his hand in demonstration.

Their words made the blood ice in my veins and I felt a sudden nausea. I walked back down an alley and retched. But I forced myself to go on. I had to find Jack before it was too late, tell him to lie low and go into hiding, that he was more valuable for Ireland alive than dead. Even if he wouldn't listen to me, I had to see him. The thought of never seeing him again was unbearable. I saw an abandoned milk jug on a windowsill and grabbed it. The milk was on the turn and the smell nearly made me throw up again but would be a useful prop.

I approached the sentry and held up my milk jug.

Unfortunately it was the mean fellow, with hooded eyes in a narrow face and sharp fox's teeth.

"My mother sent me out for a twist o' tae and some milk for the babby. We live over on Henry Place. Please let me back."

The sentry raised his rifle at me. I stared down the dark nothingness of the barrel and raised my eyes to see pure hatred. My legs turned to jelly, I broke out in sweat.

I started to wail. This time I wasn't acting. I was really frightened.

"She's just a kid," said his companion.

"They're all just kids. Like that blighter on the horse. He's been making a monkey of us all week. Captain's offered ten guineas to whoever pots him."

I saw the mean one tighten his grip.

The friendly fusilier pushed away the gun and gave his companion a warning look. "Don't come out again, if you know what's good for you," he said to me, not unkindly.

I raced over the bridge and had to sit down for a long time to recover, by the back of the Four Courts. The sound of sniping came regularly from nearby, mixing with the thump of my heart in my ears. My head was swimming, I felt hot and cold at the same time and thought I would pass out. But then the cruel soldier's words came back to me. Ten guineas for whoever shot the blighter on the horse. I needed to try with every bone in my body to warn Jack.

I saw many children also scurrying around, searching for food. There was a little fellow of no more than seven, his trousers in rags and a little mother, a girl my own age, carrying a toddler in a shawl, probably her brother or sister.

"We're trying to get to Father Matthew Hall in Church Street," the girl said. "They have bread there." The child in her arms was listless and pale. The girl had a dirty face and no shoes on her feet. I gave her the jug of sour milk. She rewarded me with a warm smile. We were allies in the strange lunatic asylum Dublin had become. I realized I was able to move about because I was no different from a hundred other young people drawn by curiosity or necessity to roam the streets.

It gave me courage. I sneaked along from door to door, sitting down sometimes in tenement hallways. I passed some dead bodies, some covered with sacks, Lord have mercy on their souls. Then a Red Cross Ambulance collecting some of the dead. I wondered how many innocent citizens had been caught in the crossfire. Hundreds, I guessed. I had heard the nurses at the hospitals talking about some of the poor victims. A man on a stairway bringing a glass of water to his sick wife. A nun closing a window at dusk in a convent. A mother and daughter, sitting frightened by the fire, the same bullet killing them both. A baby in a pram. Death was stalking the streets.

At Richmond Hospital there was a barricade manned

by Volunteers. Private Chapman who I'd given dressings to on Monday recognized me as the "First Aid Girl" and let me through. There was a crunch of glass underfoot as he led me to a hole in a house in Henry Street and I crawled through the holes in the buildings. I came out at the side entrance of the GPO.

I got through just in time. Two Cumann na mBan women, Min and Phyllis Ryan, the lively sisters of the medical student Jim Ryan, were hanging about outside the side door on Henry Street. Two beautiful girls that should have been going to a dance.

"We're sneaking back in. If the men are going to die, we will too," said Min. "I have a safe address for The O'Rahilly if he manages to get out."

I remembered The O'Rahilly whispering something to her when he sent her out to visit three wives of British soldiers being held prisoner. It must have also been a mission to set up the safe house. She waved the piece of paper and I saw the address in Drumcondra.

"She just wants to go back in to see her sweetheart, Seán Mac Diarmada," teased Phyllis.

Mac Diarmada was always closeted with Tom Clarke. He walked with a limp because of polio but he was the handsomest of the rebel leaders. I suddenly thought of Anto's line about his gammy leg, and it made me smile.

I was surprised to see a line of women and children from the slums of Henry Street file by holding a white flag. To my great delight, one was Nancy, our char, with

225

her baby and three youngest ones. I ran to her.

"Nancy, Anto is safe!"

She embraced me, then looked into my eyes with a look of pain on her face. "I haven't seen May since she marched those kids back on Tuesday. Said she'd lose her job if she didn't go back to the Imperial."

I reassured her that I would look out for her eldest daughter.

"I'd be lost without May," she said. "She has never given me a peck of trouble. If anything ever happened to her . . ." Nancy shook her head.

I told her I couldn't find Jack.

She smiled briefly. "I've been cursin' all them rebel fellas, as I haven't had any money this week. But someone has been leavin' bread and milk. They didn't come today, but yesterday I found this." She handed me a little tin soldier, painted green. "Sure, aren't I always pickin' them off the floor in his room." She kissed me gently on the cheek. "Don't forget he has nine lives."

She handed me the soldier and I gripped it tight and put it with the others. No doubt another life risked.

The door of the GPO opened and we were admitted. I bumped into my friend with the hobnail boots, Liam Tannam. He was in a state, clutching his eyes.

"I'm blinded! A bullet from the Gresham Hotel struck the granite and the dust got into my eyes!"

I took him to the First Aid station inside by the Prince's Street entrance and met a young Indian Army

Officer called Lieutenant Mahoney with the medical student Jim Ryan. Lieutenant Mahoney told me he'd been taken prisoner, but felt it was his duty to tend the sick. I admired him for his dedication in his makeshift hospital, his equipment an odd assortment of sterilizing needles, forceps and surgical knives. There was even a vet's thermometer for a cow! He took a quick look at Liam and reassured him he would be fine and asked me to bathe his eyes.

I got most of the grit out and made Liam lie down with a handkerchief over his eyes.

"Have you found your brother? Jack?" he asked.

I shook my head. "I'm looking for him here."

I heard a snore. Liam had fallen instantly asleep.

The Indian Army doctor came up to me.

"I heard you talking to Liam about your brother Jack," he said. "A young lad of that name came in soaking wet. He was closeted with Tom Clarke for a while but I sent him to Jervis Street Hospital. Shivering, he was. I am worried he has a fever."

Liam murmured in his sleep, then woke and told me that Jervis Street Hospital was accessed through a hole in the wall from Henry Street and over the roof of the Coliseum Theatre, then down the alleyway. I dashed off like a mad thing, desperate to get to Jervis Street before Jack eluded me again.

The nurses at the hospital had hidden the access hole from Henry Street with screens. I careened about the

227

wards searching for Jack. But saw no one but women and nuns.

I was about to speak to the matron when I noticed one of the women looked rather whiskery. I leaned in closer and the strange creature opened her eyes and winked at me.

"You're a man!" I gasped.

"Shush," he said. "You'll get the nurses into trouble. They're disguising us as women. Now fix my plait like a good girl. One of the nurses cut hers off to give me."

On closer inspection, a lot of the patients looked distinctly boyish and ugly. A couple were wearing old-fashioned caps and one had a five o'clock shadow. A cleaner, forgetting his disguise scratched himself in a most unladylike manner. A big nun came in who looked like a rugby player. But when I winked at her, she scowled at my impertinence. I think she was just a rather horse-faced woman!

I laughed on my way back to the GPO. Then I went back to the grim task of scouring the building. Everyone's nerves were on edge, expecting a full frontal attack. A sudden rumour of an armoured car coming down Henry Street had everyone insanely hanging out the windows. For nothing. Then an explosion. More frayed nerves. Stuttering machine-gun fire. Then more nervous waiting. I resumed my anxious search for Jack around the GPO, feeling like I was in a nightmare, where everything was familiar but strangely altered.

At around 3 o'clock, Pearse gave a rousing speech from the balcony above the main floor about how a large band of fighters were coming from Dundalk to Dublin, police had been captured and there were grand battles all over. There was a deafening outburst of cheering. Did they really believe him? Within seconds his false claims were shattered by a burst of shellfire.

I went up to the Instrument Room to search for Jack but instead saw Liam Tannam leap eighteen feet from the hole in the ceiling the rebels had made to gain access to the roof

"There's Howitzer guns mounted at Findlater's Church," he roared. "Molly, there's wounded coming down!"

The injured were lowered with two ropes. I stayed with them, and got busy removing peppershot shrapnel from a man's face. It was Lieutenant Mick Boland who'd asked me to send him tea before. Surely he hadn't been on the roof since Monday!

"It's just a bit of shrapnel," he said. "I was in the Boer War in Africa helping the Africaans fight the British so I'm an old warhorse. It's only a scrape." He flashed me a grin but winced in pain.

Lieutenant Mahoney the surgeon came to tell me that James Connolly the Commander was rounding up a crack unit to go to the Independent Newspaper offices on Abbey Street. There was a fair chance that Jack might be among them as they'd need a messenger. Seán McLoughlin, one of the other messenger boys, was being promoted. He was only about twenty. They must have been getting short of men.

I raced through the building, jumping two steps on the stairs at a time to get down as quick as I could. But I was too late! Connolly was standing at the corner of Abbey Street, watching the troops go in.

I sank to my knees. The fatigue now was going into my bones. I only came around when I heard a great shouting.

"Connolly's wounded!"

A group of rebels ran out the door and dragged Connolly back into the GPO. I immediately ran to get Lieutenant Mahoney.

A sniper bullet had caught Connolly on the ankle. The surgeon examined his injuries. He had lost a lot of blood. I handed Mahoney the bandage and stick to make a tourniquet, which he applied to his leg. The bones were protruding so it wasn't possible to fix a splint.

"He needs an anesthetic," said Mahoney urgently.

I ran upstairs to the First Aid post and came back with a small amount of chloroform and anaesthetic ether. Ryan, the medical student, gave it to Connolly, while Lieutenant Mahoney released the tourniquet. But I don't think there was very much of the chloroform so he was in a lot of pain.

I helped him clean the wound, holding the disinfectant, while the surgeon fished out the small fragments of broken bone and tied off the small blood vessels with thread. I watched fascinated as Mahoney fashioned a back splint with a foot-piece out of bandage and stick. I felt a kind of awe watching his deft fingers and precision. In that moment, I vowed to be a surgeon. If I survived this madness, nothing could stop me.

Connolly at first refused anything stronger for the pain, but the surgeon insisted and gave him an injection of morphine.

"It's a compound fracture of his left shinbone," the surgeon said to Jim Ryan. "He needs serious medical attention."

Jim Ryan spoke quietly to Connolly and it was clear that he wasn't going to be moved anywhere.

Lieutenant Mahoney was to stay with him and I volunteered to help nurse him. I needed to know if Jack had gone out to Abbey Street and the only person who knew for certain was the wounded Connolly.

I was beginning to lose heart and, when I carried a glass of water for Connolly, a fit of trembling came over me. The water sloshed about and I just managed to put it down. I gripped the edge of the iron bedstead.

Shortly after, shelling began again, moving ever closer. My nerves were stretched to breaking point and I was glad I had the duty of looking after Connolly to keep me focused. A shell hit the barricade on Abbey Street. The cycles and crates caught fire like tinder and carried the blaze to the Hibernian Bank where poor Captain Weafer had died. The building went up in flames.

Multicoloured fireballs of terrible beauty burst into the sky like fireworks. Then Hoyts' Druggists caught fire, engulfing the whole of the block of Earl Street. There was a lot of turpentine there and the colours leaped up, blue and gold and flaming red. An oil works near Abbey Street was next, and a solid sheet of blinding flame leapt a hundred feet in the air. There was a heavy bombardment as drums of oil exploded. It was only a matter of time before my own house was engulfed. And yet I watched, mesmerized by the rainbow flames.

"The Imperial's next! We need to get a message to them!" I worried that May, Anto's sister, might be there and without thinking charged onto the street with a couple of others.

Bullets still fell on the street like hailstones but we made it across to the hotel and gave them the message. Most of the guests and staff had been evacuated already, including May no doubt, but some of the rebels came back with us. Somebody gave me a large mattress as a shield against the bullets and a group of us made our way back across the street to the GPO underneath it. We must have looked very odd indeed. As I turned to run, I saw the huge plate-glass windows of Clerys store run molten into the channel of the street kerb, a river of liquid glass.

As we ran in through the Prince's Street entrance, a rebel from the Imperial who had crossed the street with me said, "There was a phone and I rang the fire brigade like an eejit. They told me they were going to let the fires burn out!" I wondered if my father had managed to repair the telephone lines.

The noise of bursting glass, the fall of burning masonry was terrible, the heat appalling. Despite dousing the barricades outside the GPO with water, they kept bursting into flames.

Steam rose off the windows, the ledgers smouldered. The smoke was terrible, choking and acrid. Sackville Street was an inferno.

I went back to Connolly who slept fitfully. I mopped his brow and tried to get him to take some water, as Lieutenant Mahoney was worried he would become dehydrated in the heat. The light in our room was as bright as day now in the lurid glow of the flames.

The flames engulfed the tower of the DBC, the copper and glass twisting and bending and falling like a melted icicle. I thought of their delivery boy, stout little Tommy Keenan, on Stephen's Green. If he was still alive, he would have no job to go to.

Patrick Pearse, his face flushed by the heat, came to see the surgeon about Connolly. I knew it was useless to question Pearse about Jack.

He looked at the flames intently and spoke to one of his soldiers. "It was the right thing to do, wasn't it?"

His companion replied slowly that it was.

"When we are all wiped out, people will blame us for everything. But without our protest, nothing would have been done after the war. After a few years, people will see the meaning of what we tried to do."

He had voiced the same thoughts all week, but now with his face lit up with fire in the heat of battle, his words were like a terrible prophecy fulfilled. It had gone from wiping out the stains of history to this. It was indeed going to be a wipe-out.

I fear we are all doomed to burn to death, like Joan of Arc on the stake. Except some of us never chose this.

Huge mountains of billowing jet-black smoke rose in the air. The world was ending. We were trapped in a ring of fire.

Mr Connolly was dreaming at one point and started to call out, "Mona! Mona!"

I held his hand and he awoke briefly, searching my face with pain in his eyes.

"I thought you were my wee Mona coming out of the flames. How old are you, child?" he asked in his soft Scottish burr. For Mr Connolly had been born and bred in Edinburgh and had never lost the accent.

I told him.

"I had a girl like you. Died when she was thirteen. Her apron caught fire when she was helping a friend boil water for the washing. Just before we went to America."

I mopped his brow. "I'm so sorry for your trouble."

"My first born. My wife wanted a boy but I was always as happy with girls. My boy was here. I sent him away on Wednesday.'

"Did you send my brother Jack over to the Independent offices in Abbey Street?" I asked him but he didn't seem to hear me.

"My wife said Roddy was too young too fight but I said he was fifteen and could decide for himself. But it got too hot . . . and to please her . . ."

He was talking about his own son Roddy, the name of the messenger I had heard him mention to Mick Collins.

I tried to ask him about Jack again but he was wincing with pain and anxious to say what was on his mind.

"We might still make it. But if you do and I don't, will you visit my Mona's grave for me?"

I held his hand. "I will try."

"She's buried in plot JL174 in Glasnevin." He paused and winced the shadow of pain in his eyes. "A pauper's grave. No headstone. That's how poor we were. She would have been twenty-four and I pray we do not face her fate."

He was exhausted from the effort of speaking and fell back asleep.

📖　📖　📖

I recall my dream less than a week ago, of Jack consumed by fire. As the flames leap and jump, the whole of Dublin lit up by the glare, I too pray I will not die in this inferno. I am too tired to write any more.

Friday 28th April – late afternoon.
The GPO.

I was glad to awake to another dawn this morning and the first thing I saw out of the windows was Nelson's Pillar emerging faintly from smoke. The weather promised to be fine and sunny as usual this week. There is still the acrid smell of burning in the air, which gags in the back of my mouth.

While I slept on a pallet on the floor beside Connolly's iron bed, I dreamed that Jack came to me and roused me by the shoulder.

"Molly, I have one more mission to fulfill. Special orders. Do not try to follow me. If I fail, console our parents."

As he leaned over me, his head framed in the arch of the window, a ring of blue, orange and crimson flames surrounded him.

"Tell father and mother I did not fire one shot but have died for the cause I believe in."

I heard Connolly groan in his sleep and opened my eyes to see Jack's beautiful face break into a smile. He kissed me lightly on the brow.

That kiss awoke me. I leaned up on my elbows, my head groggy with sleep, my eyes swimming. I looked at the doorway to see an elusive shape disappear.

"Jack!" I jumped up and called his name, the dream was so vivid.

I returned to my bedside vigil by Connolly.

The illusion was so real, I almost believed it was him. But I am so tired, my nerves so wretched, I was sure my mind was playing tricks on me.

I went as close as I dared to the window. I could not see our house from the GPO. It will be a miracle if it still stands. Smoke billowed like from a volcano down the wide thoroughfare.

Connolly wasn't much better but he was more lucid. Ryan has prevailed on him to take morphine, a powerful drug for the pain. All morning people came and went to his bedside.

I tensed when I saw Seán McLoughlin, the young dispatch messenger who was at the Independent offices.

I hovered close to the bedside and heard Connolly say to him, "You have seen more of Dublin than any of us. We better keep you with us. You are calm under fire. Give the order to withdraw all outposts. We will make one last stand."

As Seán left to give the instructions, I followed him and asked him if Jack had gone to the Independent.

"I sent him here this morning at the crack of dawn, about six. He came back straightaway with a message for our outpost to fall back to the GPO. That's why we're here."

My hope rose once more. "Is he resting somewhere?" I asked eagerly. But he shrugged and departed with greater urgency.

I went back to Connolly and questioned him gently. He had not seen Jack since he sent him to the Independent. So someone else must have issued the order for him to go back to Sean McLoughlin at the Independent offices with the instruction for them to retreat to the GPO.

I once more searched the building inch by inch. The smoke cleared as the day wore on. The fire is burnt out and my beloved Sackville Street is gone! Only rubble and ruins remain and facades of burnt-out buildings.

Pearse issued more fanciful bulletins about saving Ireland's honour and even Connolly, propped on his iron bed, dictated a pronouncement about how the men of North County Dublin had occupied all the police barracks.

There is a lot of chaos. While some people have food, others are cursing the quartermaster in charge of food for being so sparing in his rations. But he has a difficult job. How do we know how long we have to last out?

I searched among the prisoners in the basement and all the secret places I know of in the GPO – out in the yard, among the old mail sacks. Still no trace of my brother.

Like a pebble tossed in a pool, the rippling image of my brother that came to me in my dream fanned through my mind. As I searched, I began to believe that my dream of Jack was real. As real as the breath on my forehead. I went back to sit by Connolly's bed. When I bent down to retrieve a spoon, I saw the little soldier standing sentry, top left by the leg of the bed. Jack had left his calling card! That makes eight tin soldiers in all.

I was going to question all the leaders, determined now to find out where he was. I saw Pearse as he sat quietly writing. Even as everything disintegrated around him, there was a stillness surrounding the man that I was afraid to interrupt. But I was desperate.

"Mr Pearse, sir. Have you seen my brother? I know he was here this morning."

There was a faraway look in his eyes that told me he didn't have a clue what I was talking about.

"Willie is about somewhere." He thought I was speaking of his own brother. But then he looked at me candidly. "My brother is devoted to me. I can only hope that my mother will be consoled that both her sons died for Ireland. I am writing a poem for her."

I did not dare to ponder what my own mother would think. She would find a poem a poor substitute for her children.

Neither Connolly nor Pearse knew where Jack was. That left Plunkett, the one with the throat operation, Seán Mac Diarmada, Michael Collins and The O'Rahilly. There was also Tom Clarke. Jack had been sent to Fairview with a message for his wife on the very first day.

If Jack had been sent out again while the British were tightening the ring of steel around the GPO, it would be a suicide mission. He was running out of lives.

But there was lots of confusion and disarray. At some stage I saw Tom Clarke instruct a young Cumann na mBan woman called Leslie to go fetch a priest. She didn't want to go but he looked into her eyes, almost hypnotizing her. She went out to cross Sackville Street, suppressing her tears.

Then Mac Diarmada rushed up to him and they were locked in discussion. I could not get near them.

I gave up running around the building and decided to stick by Connolly, figuring everyone would come to see him at some stage.

At around 3 o'clock serious shelling started. Someone said the GPO wouldn't burn as the roof was made of concrete. I ran into the Instrument Room and looked up at the arched ceiling. There was a little hole burnt in the plaster about the size of a teacup. The O'Rahilly and Liam Tannam went out through the skylight to take a look at what at caused the breach. I climbed up behind them on the ladder. Blackish smoke was starting to billow.

"I think it's steam," The O'Rahilly said. "There's no flames."

"No, it's black, sir."

"Get the fire extinguishers!"

The blaze grew. So much for the concrete roof. Time was running out.

In the Telegraph Room, they were dousing the floor with water in the hope it wouldn't catch fire.

I collided with Michael Collins but the big Corkman, his clothes singed, was in a terrible temper. He softened when I asked him about Jack but he knew nothing either.

"The gunboat Helga has come up the Liffey and is bombing the living daylights out of us. If he's off somewhere, he's well out of it, for we're going to have to evacuate. It's madness being holed up in these buildings. We'd stand more chance in small units in the streets." He looked miserable and angry at the terrible end that was facing us all.

I thought about speaking to Joseph Plunkett but, when I approached him, he was giving a large ring to Connolly's secretary, Winifred Carney.

"For my fiancée Grace, if I don't make it," he said.

I knew in my heart he was half in the next world already and knew little of the details of the fighting, though he spent a lot of time making notes in a little book. So I left him to his sorrow.

Liam Tannam, who'd been up on the roof, ran down. "We need to get all the bombs and homemade grenades from the top floor," he shouted. "Get the Citizen Army and the prisoners to bring them down to the basement!"

The place became a seething pit of confusion. The prisoners, terrified and hunched, carried the home-made bombs, tin cans with pieces of match sticking out of them, back down to the basement only for someone to re-direct them out into the courtyard. They looked terrified they'd explode in their hands. Burning masonry was now falling from the ceiling. An officer suggested to The O'Rahilly to let the prisoners go, but he did not want to expose them to the danger outside.

I took the opportunity to ask him about my brother. But he didn't know. But I was touched that he'd noticed I'd cut off my hair.

I saw the priest, Father Flanagan, going around listening to confessions, and soldiers were making their wills. Liam Tannam swaggered about smoking a cigar, trying to cheer everyone up. But he was one of the few able to keep up morale.

I decided to try to speak to Tom Clarke again. He was sitting holding his revolver in the main hall. Mac Diarmada was arguing with him.

"I am not leaving here," said Tom Clarke. "I will go down with the building." So he was determined to be Joan of Arc.

"But, Tom, there is always a chance we might make it," argued Mac Diarmada passionately.

Despite the fraught nature of their talk, I had to seize my chance.

Mac Diarmada realized that I was standing beside him.

"Is it about Connolly?"

"My brother Jack . . . the messenger . . ."

Tom Clarke lifted his face, his eyes penetrating, and he gave me a look of infinite sorrow. I could not finish my questioning but stood there silent, on the verge of tears.

His old face, weathered by fifteen years in British jails, looked so stricken.

"We have not seen your brother," Mac Diarmada said gently.

I ran out and sat in a corner, shaking. All week the urgency to find my brother had driven me to seek him through hails of bullets, in strange corners and maximum danger. But my courage was beginning to fail me. I could not walk through fire.

Luckily for me, Jim Ryan came to find me to help with looking after Connolly whose pain was worsening. It was hard to breathe with all the smoke swirling about.

As I mopped Connolly's brow, Lieutenant Mahoney looked intently at me.

"You said your surname was O'Donovan, didn't you? You are very like your late grandfather, Molly," he said.

I looked up, astonished.

"He gave us a lecture at the Royal College of Surgeons when I was a student. He had a high reputation in Goa."

"He died before we knew him," I said sadly.

"He was famous for running a clinic for the natives and never turned a sick person away. He would have been proud to see how you have worked to help the wounded."

It was as if, through Lieutenant Mahoney, my grandfather had reached from the world beyond to give me a tender hug. His words turned the tide of despair and gloom for me. I felt a spark ignite again in my heart.

I would not give up on Jack yet.

I was helping Lieutenant Mahoney change Connolly's dressing when we were told to go to the main hall. The supplies were running low and I thought about how it was only a few days ago that I'd dried out the moss in the basement. We used a broom handle broken in two to fix the split for his leg. Connolly thanked me for my work.

Pearse now told all the women, the wounded and the prisoners to leave.

"Go to the Coliseum Theatre – it is fire proof," he instructed them. "And from there to Jervis Street Hospital."

Lieutenant Mahoney and Father Flanagan led the wounded and the prisoners out.

I was about to go back to Connolly, when Liam Tannam put his hand on my arm. "Molly, that means you too. You have more chance of finding your brother alive than dead."

Reluctantly, I joined the evacuees. Where would I start to find him, now that the rebellion was collapsing? Even if Jack had made it out, searching for him was going to be like looking for a needle in a burning haystack.

With terrible urgency, the group of women, medics, prisoners and wounded went through the tunnelling and across the roofs into the Coliseum Theatre.

It felt so strange and eerie to be in that large, empty theatre of three thousand seats. It had only been open one year exactly and the nap of the plush red velvet was still fresh. We had nothing but matches to illuminate us. But the flickering shadows showed we were in the main auditorium.

It was hard to manage the prisoners. One fellow who was carried in a blanket had severe wounds: shrapnel under his eye, a bullet wound in his chest and one in his abdomen. I prayed he didn't die during the evacuation.

I could tell the priest and the doctors were nervous and tense. We felt like rats in a trap.

Then Father Flanagan groped around and tried to lower the safety curtain in case the fire spread inside. As the curtain fell we all jumped and to our horror it was smouldering. Our ragged group struggled out of the auditorium with the wounded and Father Flanagan saw a light under a doorway. We pushed against it and it flew open. We were staring down the barrel of a gun.

"Halt."

It was a rebel unit that had been sent to check out the theatre as place of refuge. They were scared and twitchy. One of them was raving in the corner.

"Put away those guns and help with the wounded," the priest said to them angrily. "We've got to get out of here to the hospital."

After an argument, the soldiers did as he asked and prepared to carry the wounded who were in blankets.

I looked around at the chrome and mirrors of the bar, the groaning injured men, the priest, the shaking and frightened rebels, and I had a sudden memory of my last visit here, sneaking in to see the gymnastics.

"I know the best way out," I said in a small voice.

But the priest heard me and I led them to the side exit where Jack and I sometimes crept in. This led to a shortcut into Abbey Street.

While Father Flanagan was making a Red Cross flag from a nurse's apron and a broom handle, a rebel took out a cream cracker wrapped in a hankie. He broke it and handed me half. I thanked him and ate it. I suddenly smiled to myself.

"The British will think we eat nothing but cream crackers, if they find the crumbs," I said. "Even the leaders share them with each other."

The rebel soldier grinned amiably but I had a sudden revelation. I remembered the tin of cream crackers from de Valera. Connolly had said that Jack was on "a special", no doubt meaning special operation. De Valera had said "Yellow Bittern" to me. Was it a code word? Maybe Jack wasn't just carrying messages but something else in that battered old tin of cream crackers? Documents maybe? And he had been sent to Fairview with a message for Tom Clarke's wife. And what about all the tin soldiers? I knew I had to speak again to Tom Clarke. He held the key to Jack's destination.

Nobody noticed me slip away in the dark Coliseum Theatre.

There was falling, burning masonry across the GPO yard as I dashed back inside.

I am writing down the day's events to calm my nerves, crouched at the bottom of the stairs in the main hall. Even though it's likely both diary and I will perish in the flames. I might die without ever having solved the mystery around Jack.

Midnight Friday 28th April.
Moore Street.

I'm still alive, thank God! Who knows for how much longer but it's a miracle any of us got out of that inferno.

Inside the GPO, there was pandemonium as the evening drew on. Everyone was gathered near the Henry Street exit, screaming and shouting at the top of their voices. Liam was still there, smoking his cigar, spluttering now in the smoke-filled building.

"The O'Rahilly has gone down to Moore Street to find a retreat. It's a suicide mission," said young McLoughlin.

I heard the O'Rahilly shout, "For the Glory of God and the honour of Ireland!" Then a fusillade of gunshot.

I felt sick. It would be a miracle if he survived.

I ran back into the main hall and frantically searched round for Tom Clarke. There was grave danger now that the ceiling would collapse. Suddenly, Liam Tannam began to sing: "Soldiers are we, whose lives are pledged to Ireland . . ."

The song by Peadar Kearney who I'd met in Jacobs' Mill. I looked at the blackened, haggard faces of the rebels, most of them young and beautiful, and I felt a deep deep sorrow. They were all so amazing and pure of heart. What had brought them all to this madness? Surely we were not going to perish in this deathtrap?

I went back to the Henry Street entrance.

"The O'Rahilly has fallen!" a rebel soldier at the door roared.

I heard Patrick Pearse shout, "We must evacuate to Moore Street!"

Volleys of shots rained down Henry Street, so I did not know how this was possible, as the best way down was through Henry Place, an L-shaped alley about seventy yards to the right and opposite. But machine-gun and rifle fire raked down Henry Street. Crossing it would be a suicide mission. Bullets boomed and ricocheted in the narrow canyon of the street.

Another group of soldiers including Liam Tannam went out to reconnoitre. Seán McLoughlin was gone too. I did not expect to see them alive again with machine gunfire sweeping the street.

I do not rightly know how I got to Moore Street. Events became a blur of fleeting impressions. Someone, I think the medic Jim Ryan, grabbed my arm and I was in the party with the leaders, the wounded and James Connolly.

There was a crush, a panic. People were carrying odd provisions – a leg of ham, a case of eggs – and crossing the lane in twos and threes.

I saw the bullets like hailstones hopping on the streets. With head down, as if running against heavy rain, I ran as I had never run before and got into the L-shaped Henry Place.

I heard Seán Mac Diarmada say, "My God, we are not going to be caught like rats and killed without a chance to fight!"

Behind us, the GPO was a burning pyre and the only light in the lane was the terrible glare in the skies. The wounded were groaning but we could not attend to them.

"I've lost all my medical supplies! They were in a basket," I heard Jim Ryan shout out in anguish.

Here there was more panic. The sky was darkening at dusk, the shadows rising. But we had to pass through a cloud of white dust, shot off a whitewashed building in a hail of bullets. Some of the rebels created an obstruction with a motor van to block the shots raining down on us and we crossed into Moore Street.

"Occupy the buildings!" instructed Tom Clarke.

We were behind Cogan's Grocers at Number 12 at the corner of Henry Place and Moore Street. Someone shot the lock off a cottage door at the back of the shop. I heard later that the sixteen-year-old daughter Bridget McKane was shot dead by the bullet but I walked through the building in a blur and didn't see anything. I followed with the group, as the men broke their way through the bare walls using a crowbar. The work was so exhausting some of the men fell down asleep. From the greengrocer's, the men tunneled though all the way to O'Hanlon's fish shop.

I stayed with Connolly who was brought into Cogan's Grocers. We were taken into the kitchen and Connolly was laid on the stretcher on the floor. Sitting with us were Miss Julia Grennan, Elizabeth Farrell, Seán Mac Diarmada, Tom Clarke, Patrick Pearse, Willie Pearse and Joseph Plunkett.

Seán McLoughlin came in. "We are surrounded," he said.

They had a conversation among themselves. He told us all to sleep.

There was talk of a "death or glory" squad to break out through the streets and head to the Four Courts for a final battle, leaving the wounded behind.

There were seventeen wounded in the retreat from the GPO and I spent the night helping Nurse O'Farrell and medic Jim Ryan, attending to their needs.

Jim Ryan was very upset about losing the morphine to help Connolly's pain in the retreat down Moore Lane. When Nurse O'Farrell asked him how he was, Connolly said, "Bad." When I helped Jim Ryan change a dressing I saw that his leg was turning grayish-green. There was a putrid smell. Gangrene was setting in, Jim said. Connolly spent most of the night groaning in pain.

Around us, the roar of burning buildings, machines guns and hand grenades crashed like violent waves on a tiny boat. But even as everything came to its bloody end, I still was not going to give up my fight to find Jack. It was my duty and I clung to it as the only thing to keep me going. There was a lull during the night and all was eerie and still for a time. The silence was almost worse than the guns. I pinched myself to stay awake. Pearse and his brother had gone upstairs and made their bed on a wide table. McLoughlin slept on the floor.

When Connolly dosed fitfully, I crept up the stair, terrified to make a sound in case someone shot me out of fright.

Tom Clarke was sleeping on a mattress in a room further upstairs but, as I summoned my courage at the door to speak to him, I heard a whispered conversation between him and Seán Mac Diarmada.

"All is lost," Tom Clarke said. "But if the boy makes it, at least the women and children can be cared for."

I did not need to question him. The women and children would be cared for . . . I remembered that long-ago conversation between Kathleen Clarke and Patrick Pearse when I ran into the shop. I had been puzzled about de Valera sending Tom Clarke an old tin of Jacob's Cream Crackers, thinking perhaps it was a peculiar souvenir for Mrs Clarke. And Jack had been sent to her in Richmond Avenue on Easter Monday. The pieces of the puzzle fell together in a shape.

With a flash of insight, I knew what was being smuggled. I grappled in my knapsack and felt for one of the toy soldiers belonging to Jack. Using my scissors I prised off the bottom. Inside was a rolled-up crisp banknote. I opened it out. A hundred pounds! I had solved the mystery of Jack's mission. I opened the others, eight in all, and they all had rolled-up banknotes. I noticed one of the tin soldiers, which was rather larger than the others also had a tiny piece of paper with list of numbers that I guessed were some sort of code. He was smuggling money, gathering all the funds of the rebels for the safe keeping of Kathleen Clarke.

I also knew with blinding certainty where I had to go to find Jack. I knew the why and the where. The real problem now was how.

Dusk, Saturday night 29th April.
From Nelson's Pillar overlooking the ruins of Sackville Street.

The sun rose once again. Mercilessly. I was reminded of that quotation of Shakespeare that Miss Nugent tried to drum into our heads: "Time and the hour runs through the roughest day."

I helped Nurse Elizabeth O'Farrell prepare breakfast for the men who had spent the night tunnelling through the houses.

"We've only got as far as the fishmonger's," one whispered to me.

After breakfast, Connolly and the other wounded were moved to Number 16 Moore Street – Plunkett's, a butcher's and poulterer's. Connolly was in frightful agony. The gangrene was creeping up his leg. The houses were very small and the stairs very narrow, and sometimes we had to lift the stretcher over the top. Connolly was roaring with the pain. Plunkett's was owned by a man from County Meath. He was a rough, kindly butcher and no relation to the aristocratic Count's family. Anto had worked for him before he got the job at Findlater's. Thankfully the family wasn't there. I was glad too that Nancy and her children had been led to safety.

Connolly and the other wounded, three volunteers and a British soldier who was badly injured stayed in the back room tended by Julia Grennan and Nurse O'Farrell. I tried to help too. I was told the British soldier had been heroically rescued by George Plunkett, Joseph's brother. He had braved a hail of bullets in Moore Street, knowing full well the soldier was an enemy.

The leaders came in for a council of war. Pearse came to Connolly's bedside and consulted in private.

Just after noon, the medic Ryan and I changed the

dressing on Connolly's leg. Nurse O'Farrell borrowed some sheets from the household to tear up for bandages.

"It's all over," Connolly whispered. "Pearse doesn't want any more civilian dead and is preparing to surrender."

Jim Ryan and I looked out the window. Lying dead on the opposite footpath of Moore Street with white flags in their hands were three elderly men. They had been shot down by machine-gun fire when trying to reach safety, fleeing from a burning building on the opposite side of the street.

I looked closer and with a start saw my father's old jacket on one of the men, a crimson bloodstain on the lapel. It was Mr Hanrahan who had joked about Mother being a 'cracker' when we had visited him on Easter Sunday. I cried for his poor soul and hoped his end was quick.

"It was the sight of those men that has convinced Pease to surrender," Jim Ryan said to me. "And he hopes by giving up that, though the leaders will be shot, the rank and file, the ordinary soldiers, will be saved."

I gasped. They expected to be executed. Would there be no end to this bloodshed?

"For God's sake, has someone got a white cloth?" called out Mac Diarmada.

James O'Reilly, one of the men who was shaving, produced a none-too-clean handkerchief out of his breast pocket.

I gave them one of my Red Cross insignias to put on a

nurse's apron to make a flag. The first time the flag was stuck out the door it was met with a hail of bullets. But the next time the guns were silent.

Nurse Elizabeth O'Farrell bravely went out into the street at 12.45 with a note from Mr Pearse.

The silence after all the gunfire was unsettling. The leaders were each in their private space, preparing themselves to face their enemy after a week of battle. Tom Clarke was distraught. Tears ran down his face as he sat waiting. I did not want to disturb him so I spoke to his loyal friend, Seán Mac Diarmada.

"The wives and children of the people in the rising," I said to him softly, "how will they manage?"

He looked at me kindly. "Kathleen, Tom's wife, is in charge of a fund for the wives and dependents. She is a strong and able woman and measures have been taken. I can tell you no more than that."

I left him to his preparations. I had guessed correctly. Jack was gathering together all the funds to help the families of the fighters, to be administered by Kathleen Clarke. I felt a surge of pride in my brother. He was risking his life for a worthy mission for, after all, the children in particular were innocent and would surely suffer. He had done so without firing a shot.

I too had preparations to make to carry out my plan. I found a spot in the attic and put my new cambric frock on under my clothes. I put all the money from the soldiers together and, disconnecting my spyglass, hid the roll and codes in the barrel. It could still be creakily extended but the lens was now cloudy. If anyone tried to use it, they would just think it an old dud.

As I tucked the soldiers back in my knapsack, something fell out. A rolled-up piece of paper, battered and creased. I opened it and was astonished to see it was the 'proclamation' I'd picked up at the pillar only a few days ago. I don't even remember how it got from the big front pocket of my mother's Red Cross apron to my knapsack. Somehow, through the gunfire and the conflagration, the chaos and the killing, I had kept it with me and it had stayed intact. A little piece of history. I would have to read it with more care at a future date. So I hid it in my shoe for safekeeping.

After about an hour, Nurse O'Farrell returned, her face pale.

"I have met with General Lowe but I have only half an hour to return with Commandant Pearse," she said. "They want an unconditional surrender. Hurry! They thought I was a spy at first and held me prisoner at, of all places, Tom Clarke's shop! Of all the places in Dublin, they have made that their headquarters."

I gasped. I had to find a way of going with them. For I was convinced that was where Jack would be. I had conceived a very dangerous plan.

The leaders conferred and Pearse shook everyone's hands and prepared to go. I took my courage in my hands and approached Nurse O'Farrell.

"Take me with you," I begged her. "I am with Saint John's Ambulance. I am not part of this."

She looked stricken. "The officer at the barricade asked me how many other girls there were down there and I said two. I forgot about you, poor Molly, you are so quiet and discreet, writing away in your book. But they are very jumpy and if you come with us now, they will think it a trick."

"Please," I begged. "Look! I have my own flag."

She smiled. "I will go with Pearse and tell the British officer they must let you go, as you are but a child."

I waited with the others. Despite the circumstances, I smiled to myself at her calling me quiet and discreet, for no one had ever called me that!

All was quiet and ominous and the men got ready by cleaning up, trying to shave, summoning their dignity. Each was locked in his own world, calling up the courage to face whatever lay ahead.

But I was tense and keyed up. My battle wasn't finished. And I wasn't going to give in before I'd done everything to achieve my goal.

I went to the doorway. I saw Nurse O'Farrell reach the barricade and speak to the officer in charge. His small nod was enough for me.

I was relieved and rushed out, not thinking to say goodbye to anyone. I was so used to behaving like a shadow, hugging doorways, that I passed up the street unnoticed.

So intent was the focus on Pearse, nobody paid me much attention. Even Nurse O'Farrell was all but forgotten. I slipped through the barricade as the soldiers watched history unfold.

The British general, all sharp features and spruce uniform, was there with a dashing younger officer who looked like his son. The young man was very devil-may-care, as if he was at the races, and lit a match and smoked a cigarette as Pearse in his slouch hat and dark overcoat approached with Nurse O'Farrell.

The general was cross. "You are a minute late."

Nurse O' Farrell calmly showed him her watch. She was on time and an officer set his watch by hers. The General apologized. But he had established his authority.

Pearse handed his sword to General Lowe and they were passed to another captain called de Courcy Wheeler, who I later learned was a relative of Countess Markievicz. Pearse also handed over his automatic pistol and holster and his canteen, which contained two large onions. They were believed to be high in nutritional value by the rebels. But the sight of them made me sad. They were so ordinary and domestic, so out of place among the carnage.

"I will allow the other commandants to surrender," said Lowe. "I understand you have Countess Markievicz down there."

"She is not with me, sir," insisted Pearse with great dignity.

It was agreed that Pearse would supply a list of the addresses of the other rebel positions and Nurse O'Farrell would be given safe convoy to travel around to carry the surrender notice. I saw a photographer capture the moment from an angle that seemed to obscure Nurse O'Farrell. Pearse turned to the nurse and asked would she travel around to the other posts with the notice of unconditional surrender. How harsh those words sounded, even to me who had prayed for the madness to stop.

"Will you agree to this?"

"If you wish it," she replied.

"I do wish it," he said with great sorrow and shook her hand.

Instantly he was whisked away to a motor car with the general's son. Then General Lowe and Captain Wheeler got in another car with an armed guard on the footboard motor.

As they pulled off a British Officer remarked, "I wonder how many German marks that fellow has in his pocket. It's all a German plot."

It made me think how little they understood Ireland.

Nurse O'Farrell was put into the care of a Lieutenant Royall and the group proceeded up Great Britain Street.

Once again, remarkably, nobody paid me much attention as I tagged along. As we got to the familiar shop, now stuffed with British officers, Nurse O'Farrell turned to the Lieutenant and whispered, "She is my special charge."

The officers barely glanced at me, so busy were they staring at Nurse O'Farrell, the bold and pretty Irish rebel. They didn't even ask to search my knapsack.

We were taken to a back room and the lieutenant sent a private to get us some tea. We sat silently. I had to make my move.

"Lieutenant, I need to be taken to my aunt in Drumcondra," I said. "I am Saint John's Ambulance, an innocent girl caught up in the troubles."

He looked at me suspiciously.

I played my trump card. "I stayed to help the wounded. My father is Chief Technical Officer Daniel O'Donovan at the GPO. He is an assistant to Mr Norway, the Head of the Post Office. I hope to tell them you treated me well."

"We will arrange for your transport," said the officer. He looked closely at me. "I can see you are but a child. A shrewd one."

"I am twelve, sir."

He looked astonished that I was so young. I knew this would put him off the scent.

I drank my boiling tea, and once again it scalded my mouth and made me gag.

"I feel sick," I said.

"Molly hasn't been eating proper food," said Nurse O'Farrell.

I began to retch.

"I need the privy," I moaned.

Luckily for me, there was a flurry as General Lowe arrived back outside. Nurse O'Farrell was taken out to deliver the surrender orders and I was a forgotten footnote.

The private assigned to look after me kept his distance as I retched into my hankie and walked out the back door. He was so disgusted by me that he hung at the back door, smoking a cigarette.

There was just enough light to see the false panel at the back of the privy that concealed the hidey-hole. My nausea had abated but I kept up the pretense. Making loud groaning noises as if I was throwing up, I sprang the catch.

After all this time, Jack was curled up fast asleep like a cat. His face was innocent and childlike in the shaft of light, but there were deep shadows under his eyes. I put my hand over his mouth and shook him awake. His eyes opened in terror, but creased into a smile when he saw me.

I tapped out in our private tapping code my plan and the part he had to play. He smiled at me, as if it was just another one of our many games. I passed him our father's spyglass, which I had hidden under my clothes, now stuffed with the money and code numbers. He understood without me having to spell it out.

I took off my outer clothes and handed them to Jack, and showed him the piece of paper with the safe address in Drumcondra that was meant for The O'Rahilly. Then I ate it. I already had my new cambric frock on underneath.

"Hurry up in there," shouted the private in an English accent.

I pretended to throw up with great theatricality as Jack changed into my clothes like a true Houdini. I took his place and crawled into the tiny space lined with blankets. He pulled my green felt hat down on his head, kissed me lightly on the forehead, then took my proffered hankie. Jack took my hand and tapped out in my palm our Code – G-B-U – God *Bless You*. The message was carved into my heart. Then he sprang the cover back over the hidey-hole.

I heard him go back out towards the shop, bent double and groaning. I had to bite my hand not to cry in the darkness.

"General Lowe's car will take you to your aunty," the private said. "But stay away from me – I don't want to catch anything."

The private didn't seem to notice that the retching girl had grown a good six inches and acquired the trace of a moustache while visiting the privy.

I needed to figure out how to get out of there. But I could bide my time. For now, I was bone weary. I tucked up in the hidey-hole, oblivious to the stench and fell into a deep dreamless sleep.

A month later – 26th May.
Buswell's Hotel, Dublin

It is a month since the events of which I wrote took place and all has changed so much.

Mother returned to Dublin within a week and how great was our joy!

Father too has been spared and braved many a bullet to keep the lines of communication open. But we no longer have a house and are currently residing in apartments in Buswell's Hotel off Kildare Street. Our strongbox that I had stuffed with random things survived, however. For this we are all glad.

For attacking the forces of the crown and openly declaring an alliance with an enemy, so many of the people I have come to know and in some cases greatly admire for their courage, if not their actions, have been shot.

Pearse, MacDonagh from Jacob's Garrison, old Tom Clarke – all shot as traitors. General Blackadder was moved to say to a friend, "I have just performed one of the hardest tasks I ever had to do. Condemned to death one of the finest characters I ever came across. A man named Pearse. Must be something very wrong in the state of things, must there not, that makes a man like that a rebel?"

Poor James Connolly was strapped to a chair, already mortally wounded and in agony from his gangrenous leg, to face the firing squad.

Joseph Plunkett, already very ill, was allowed to marry his fiancée Grace Gifford just before the execution.

Mac Diarmada, Pearse's brother Willie, MacBride the soldier, Michael Mallin – all shot.

But their executions have had a curious effect. If yesterday they were dangerous poets and dreamers, now they are martyrs. As the wits of Dublin have always joked about the statue of Justice at Dublin Castle who has her back to the city:

"Here stands Justice,
Regard her station,
Her face to the Castle
And her backside to the nation."

Some have been spared. The Countess because she is a woman. And Eamon de Valera because he is an American. But they all must go to jail. And so must those who showed me kindness including Liam Tannam and the Big Fella Michel Collins. Thousands are going to jail, many who weren't even in the Rising but who are members of the Volunteers or the Citizen Army. Even some who are just supporters of independence like members of the Sinn Féin Party. Even Addy and Jane Killikelly's nephews who weren't even in Dublin have been rounded up and sent to Frongoch in Wales because they were members of the Fianna. Addy and Jane are beside themselves for they are delicate boys not used to rough living.

Anto is still recuperating in hospital, too ill to be

moved. We are worried that someone will denounce him but Mother and Nancy are cooking up some plan to get him offside. Mother and I also plan to pay a visit to Mr George Duggan who showed me such kindness.

I will be waiting a long time for my ice cream with Martin Walton because Matassa's Ice Cream Parlour is burnt down and Martin is in Frongoch prison camp. But he is alive to play another tune for Ireland. I hope some day he gets to set up his music school.

Matthew Connolly the bugler has also gone to prison. Poor Gerald Keogh's family mourns their son.

There is an outcry over the death of our brave friend, Mr Sheehy-Skeffington. Hanna his wife wants an enquiry into the circumstances of his death at the hands of a deranged British Officer.

Mrs Kathleen Clarke has set up a Fund for the Women and Dependents. I learned later that "The Yellow Bittern" is a famous poem translated from the Irish by Thomas MacDonagh about a little bird that died of thirst. It could also be the code name for a plan, could it not, that the little birds left behind by the rebels will not suffer?

I am one of the few people who know the role that Jack played in this. I still don't know what the code numbers related to. My guess is bank account numbers, perhaps some in the United States. I mean to ask Mr Duggan what bank account numbers look like when we pay him a visit. Jack must have smuggled a lot of money around, between biscuit tins and soldiers and who knows what else. I still marvel at the audacity of Jack's plan. And I wonder, once he knew I was on his trail, did he enlist me as his unwitting accomplice? Knowing I would keep them in safekeeping for him. Either way, I do not mind. He didn't expose me to any risk I wasn't already taking. Tin soldiers were after all an ingenious hiding place that no one would think to look in. If I hadn't collected all the soldiers, he would have hidden them for someone else to find and get the money to the right people. Though I was safer and quicker! The truth is, he knew I would have done it for him any way. For in truth, I may not have been prepared to die for a cause or a country but I was willing to risk my neck for my beloved brother.

I am glad for all the people who will benefit. Mr Mallin at Stephen's Green had four children, Tom Clarke three children and James Connolly was also a father. I was told that his son Roddy had got out of the GPO but was arrested. He had been well instructed by his father to keep a low profile, gave his name as Carney and was released. I am glad for I'm sure his mother could not bear to lose her only son as well as her husband. Some day soon, I will visit Mona's grave. And I am glad that all those other young children, who do not choose the colour of the flag their parents swear allegiance to, will have some help thanks to Jack.

The people who I most admire through all this, the doctors and nurses and ordinary people, the Saint John's

Ambulance and First Aiders have been nominated for awards, including Dr Lumsden and Dr Ella Webb. The widow of Lieutenant Holden Stodart will get a pension.

Miss Louisa Martin will I think get a military medal and I hope she gets to sing in the West End.

My father wants to stay to rebuild the Post Office – so I think we will stay in Ireland. Though there is talk of us going to America.

I will study hard now because I am more determined than ever to be a surgeon or the very least a doctor. For I have seen life and death but I want to make a difference.

I am but a child but I have witnessed things a child should never see. I have seen people killed. I have seen brave men and women take up guns to fight for freedom. But I am not so sure if you can win real freedom down the barrel of a gun. And once you unleash violent rebellion, it is a mad dog that will not do your bidding.

We are still burying the dead. The fatalities in the Rising on the rebel side – fifteen executed and sixty-four dead. Seven of these were young members of the Fianna. On the British side one hundred and thirty-two soldiers and police. There were well over a thousand injured. The greatest amount slain was two hundred and thirty innocent civilians. At least thirty-eight of them children. The words of Skeffy echo in my heart and I intend not to die for Ireland but to live for my country, whatever it is called. And I will try to live well for those I saw lose their lives.

For this one thing I learned in this terrible week. You may swear allegiance to a flag of green or gold or march under a standard of red, white and blue. But the blood spilt on both sides is all the same colour red.

And as for Jack? I got a postcard just this morning, a picture of a big top. The address is the winter quarters of Mr Barnum and Bailey's circus in Florida. He did well to get to Cobh and was smuggled aboard Uncle Edward's ship to America. Jack has joined the circus. No message, just the drawing of a little tin soldier – standing on his hands. Jack the Cat still has one life left. The most precious – his own.

The End

THE PROCLAMATION OF

POBLACHT NA H EIREANN.

THE PROVISIONAL GOVERNMENT
OF THE

IRISH REPUBLIC
TO THE PEOPLE OF IRELAND.

IRISHMEN AND IRISHWOMEN : In the name of God and of the dead generations fro m which she receives her old tradition of nationhood, Ireland, through us, summons her children to her flag and strikes for her freedom.

Having organised and trained her manhood through her secret revolutionary organisation, the Irish Republican Brotherhood, and through her open military organisations, the Irish Volunteers and the Irish Citizen Army, having patiently perfected her discipline, having resolutely waited for the right moment to reveal itself, she now seizes that moment, and, supported by her exiled children in America and by gallant allies in Europe, but relying in the first on her own strength, she strikes in full confidence of victory.

We declare the right of the people of Ireland to the ownership of Ireland, and to the unfettered control of Irish destinies, to be sovereign and indefeasible. The long usurpation of that right by a foreign people and government has not extinguished the right, nor can it ever be extinguished except by the destruction of the Irish people. In every generation the Irish people have asserted their right to national freedom and sovereignty ; six times during the past three hundred years they have asserted it in arms. Standing on that fundamental right and again asserting it in arms in the face of the world, we hereby proclaim the Irish Republic as a Sovereign Independent State, and we pledge our lives and the lives of our comrades-in-arms to the cause of its freedom of its welfare, and of its exaltation among the nations.

The Irish Republic is entitled to, and hereby claims, the allegiance of every Irishman and Irishwoman. The Republic guarantees religious and civil liberty, equal rights and equal opportunities to all its citizens, and declares its resolve to pursue the happiness and prosperity of the whole nation and of all its parts, cherishing all the children of the nation equally, and oblivious of the differences carefully fostered by an alien government, which have divided a minority from the majority in the past.

Until our arms have brought the opportune moment for the establishment of a permanent National Government, representative of the whole people of Ireland and elected by the suffrages of all her men and women, the Provisional Government, hereby constituted, will administer the civil and military affairs of the Republic in trust for the people.

We place the cause of the Irish Republic under the protection of the Most High God, Whose blessing we invoke upon our arms, and we pray that no one who serves that cause will dishonour it by cowardice, inhumanity, or rapine. In this supreme hour the Irish nation must, by its valour and discipline and by the readiness of its children to sacrifice themselves for the common good, prove itself worthy of the august destiny to which it is called.

Signed on Behalf of the Provisional Government,

THOMAS J. CLARKE.

SEAN Mac DIARMADA.   THOMAS MacDONAGH.
P. H. PEARSE.   EAMONN CEANNT.
JAMES CONNOLLY.   JOSEPH PLUNKETT

Author's Note

Fact and Fiction in Molly's Diary

There is probably no more documented week than Easter Week 1916 in the history of the world, never mind Irish history! Not only was it the foundation of the Irish State but also Dublin was teeming with writers, diarists and letter writers. Indeed, several of the leaders were themselves noted poets and writers. So while this is a work of fiction, there was a wealth of material to draw on.

Molly, Jack, and their parents are an imaginary family grafted onto my own family history, but aspects of their situation were typical. Most families had someone on both sides of the struggle for independence, either working for the government or fighting in the First World War. Several participants in the Rising were themselves ex-soldiers or government employees. So conflict between family members was woven into the events.

Nancy their char and her family are invented, though their circumstances are representative of the majority of slum dwellers in 1916. Dublin had the worst slums in Europe with a third of families living in one room.

Many of the other major and minor characters are real. I have tried to follow documented accounts of the actions and speech of the principal players. But this is, after all, a work of fiction. I have depicted them through the eyes of a larky twelve-year-old and taken a few liberties. But where I have invented encounters and conversations, I have tried to make them plausible. There are sometimes inconsistencies in the records, but the mistakes are all my own!

Children in the Rising

Children played an astonishing role in the Rising. Hundreds roamed about Dublin, with nearly forty losing their lives. But also quite a few took part directly on the rebels' side.

Given the chaos of Easter Week, the central plot involving Molly and Jack is not entirely farfetched. Many eyewitnesses reported several young Fianna boys directly involved in the Rising, mainly as messengers, some as young as twelve, (Tommy Keenan in Stephen's Green, an unknown fourteen-year-old boy in the GPO, several in Jacob's Factory including a twelve-year-old who escorted prisoners). There are many accounts of daring young dispatch riders, and even of a teenage girl escaping from a locked bedroom to work as a courier (Mary McLoughlin, aged fifteen).

There were also hordes of children out foraging for food – many sent out by their desperate mothers. By Wednesday there were severe food shortages in Dublin, with a danger of famine conditions in the north of the city.

There are photographs of youngsters swarming over barricades for firewood and standing at barricades. It was often the children who got caught in the crossfire. Many children were also enthusiastic looters and it was noted at the time how many of the looted premises were sweet shops.

Women, many of them still in their teens and early twenties, were also active and involved. There are stories of smuggling ammunition in a violin case and food supplies ferried for the rebels from one side of the city to the other. As late as Thursday, with fires raging in Sackville Street, Pearse sent a young woman out to give a message, and Tom Clarke dispatched Leslie Price from the GPO to fetch a priest from the pro-Cathedral. There is even an account of one Cumann na mBan member taking her seven-year-old niece as a decoy when transporting ammunition (Marie Perolz).

Large amounts of funds were transported around the city, according to several testimonies. For example, one Cumann na mBan member tells of money intended for the Dependents Fund being hidden during a raid in a feather bolster. Kathleen Clarke did indeed set up the Women and Children's Fund from such monies. She herself hid a substantial amount of money in the bra of an old lady who was a friend of hers, when British soldiers came to arrest her!

Likewise, Jack's physical prowess and derring-do on

Dublin's rooftops is not so unlikely as it might appear. The 1916 Rising was in James Connolly's plan "a battle fought on the rooftops". Snipers on both sides were posted all over the city. Many of the Irish volunteers and Citizen Army soldiers and messengers performed extraordinary feats. Jimmy Grace, for example, who escaped from the battle of Mount Street leaped out of the window and swam across the canal. The "Boy Commandant" Séan McLoughlin ran messages all week through enemy fire between the Four Courts and the GPO. There were even two cyclists the Walker brothers, who had represented Ireland in the Olympics working as dispatch riders. Seven young Fianna boys were killed during the week and many of the participants, such as Con Colbert and Sean Heuston, had started as Fianna Boy scouts.

Even some of the minor details appear in the records, from de Valera's red socks and sleeping in the Royal Carriage in Westland Row to the use of a cow's thermometer and the British Tommies doing the washing-up in the GPO. While I invented some of the critical plot details of Tom Clarke's shop, there is no doubt his tobacco shop was a "hotbed of revolution".

I have tried to accurately reflect events and stick to the documented chronology of the Rising. Occasionally I have compressed details, but only if they remained true to the general tenor of events.

For more information log onto *www.poolbeg.com*

https://www.facebook.com/pages/Mollys-Diary-The-1916-Rising/277254289106782

Glossary of Main Groups in Ireland in 1916

The Ulster Volunteers – a ninety-thousand-strong group of armed Ulstermen led by Edward Carson who supported staying in the United Kingdom. The majority of them enlisted in the British Army.

The National Volunteers – a large armed group that supported Home Rule for Ireland but who fought for Britain in World War I. They took part in the war against Germany in the hope that it would lead to Home Rule for Ireland.

The Irish Volunteers – a group of fifteen thousand volunteers led by Eoin MacNeill who refused to fight for the British Army in World War I. The majority did not turn out for the Rising, following an order issued by Eoin McNeill.

The Army of the Irish Republic – a breakaway force of the Irish Volunteers led by Pádraig Pearse, who were the main group in the 1916 Rising. One thousand three hundred of their members took part, joining forces with the tiny Irish Citizen Army.

The Irish Citizen Army – a small armed force of trade-union volunteers set up to defend workers against the police during demonstrations. Led by James Connolly, they became committed to the idea of achieving an Irish Republic through armed insurrection. Two hundred and twenty of them, including twenty-eight women took part in the Rising.

Cumann na mBan (League of Women) – a women's military organization that supported the Irish Volunteers. Around seventy of them took part in the Rising, mostly as Red Cross workers, couriers and cooks.

na Fianna Eireann – a group of military Boy Scouts led by Countess Markievicz. Several members took part in the Rising, mostly as couriers and dispatch riders. Six of their members were killed and two former members who had gone on to be leaders in the Irish Volunteers were executed.

The Irish Republican Brotherhood (the I.R.B.) – a revolutionary secret organization known as the Fenian Movement founded in the 1850's. They were committed to the use of force to establish an independent Irish republic and carried out bombings and assassinations with funding from their American wing, **Clan na Gael**. Thomas Clarke, who had spent fifteen years in British jails for bombing offences, was one of their leaders. He played a leading role in organizing the 1916 Rising. All seven signatories of the **Proclamation of the Irish Republic** were members of the secret military council.

Sinn Féin ("We Ourselves") – a political party founded by Arthur Griffith. They were not involved in the Rising although large sections of the media, government and the public mistakenly called the Easter Rising the "Sinn Féin Rebellion" and the rebels "Shinners". The party did subsequently become the rallying point for supporters of an independent Ireland.

Main Historical Figures Featured in *Molly's Diary*

The Seven Signatories of the Proclamation

Pádraig Pearse – a poet, teacher and barrister. Founder of Saint Enda's Nationalist school. Leader of the Easter Rising who was executed for his role.

James Connolly – Irish socialist, renowned Marxist, and trade-union leader who became committed to the Republican cause. He was born in Edinburgh and spoke with a Scottish accent. He was executed for leading the Irish Citizen Army in the 1916 Rising.

Thomas Clarke – member of the Irish Republican Brotherhood and one of the chief organisers of the Rising. He ran a tobacco shop in Dublin, after serving fifteen years in British jails for bombing offences.

Sean Mac Diarmada – national organizer of the Irish Republican Brotherhood, he had been afflicted with polio and walked with a limp. He was executed for his part in the Rising.

Joseph Mary Plunkett – the son of a papal count, and a poet, journalist and nationalist. Despite a lifetime's ill health with tuberculosis, he joined the IRB and was one of the leaders of the Rising. He married his sweetheart Grace Gifford in prison, hours before his execution.

Eamonn Ceannt – a master of the uileann pipes and founding member of the Irish Volunteers. He led fierce fighting at the South Dublin Union hospital and workhouse during Easter week and was executed in Kilmainham Jail.

Thomas MacDonagh – a university lecturer, poet and Irish language enthusiast, he was a founder of the Irish Volunteers. He led the garrison at Jacob's Biscuit factory and was executed with the other leaders.

Other Prominent Figures Involved in the 1916 Rising

Countess Constance Markievicz – born into the Anglo-Irish ascendency, Constance Gore-Booth married a Polish count. She became a socialist and nationalist and founded na Fianna Éireann boy scouts. Her sentence of execution was commuted because she was a woman. She supported the Republican side in the Irish Civil War in 1922.

Michael Collins – took part in the fighting in the GPO and was subsequently imprisoned. He later emerged as the leader of the Irish guerilla forces in the War of Independence 1919-1921. He played a prominent role in the negotiation of the Anglo-Irish Treaty in 1921 and was later killed in an ambush in 1922 by anti-treaty Republican soldiers.

Eamonn De Valera – commander of the rebellion in Boland's Bakery and Mill. His sentence of execution was commuted because he was an American citizen. He became a prominent leader during the War of Independence and the leader of the Republican anti-treaty side in the Civil War. He founded Fianna Fáil in 1926 and served numerous terms as Irish Taoiseach and President.

Kathleen Clarke –the wife of revolutionary Thomas Clarke and founding member of Cumann na mBan, She set up the Irish National Aid Fund to provide financial assistance to the families of all the nationalists killed or imprisoned because of the Rising. She became Lord Mayor of Dublin in 1939.

Professor Eoin Mac Neill – head of the Irish Volunteers. He did not support an armed Rising and cancelled the planned march that was supposed to lead to the insurrection. This led to widespread confusion.

Michael Joseph O'Rahilly – known as "The O'Rahilly" in the manner of ancient Irish clan leaders, he was initially involved in the cancellation of the Rising. Once he knew it was going ahead, he joined the rebels in the GPO and was shot dead in the retreat at Moore Street.

Francis Sheehy Skeffington – 'Skeffy" was a well-known pacifist, writer and supporter of women's rights, married to Republican Hannah Sheehy. He was opposed to the Rising and tried to organize a citizen's militia to control the looting that took place during Easter Week. His murder by an unstable British Officer caused an international outcry.

Dr Ella Webb – was a pioneering Irish doctor and Lady Superintentent of The Saint John's Ambulance Brigade.

She won an MBE for her bravery in attending the wounded and setting up a field hospital in the 1916 Rising. She was the first woman MD on the staff of the Adelaide Hospital, a founder of St Ultan's Children's Hospital and of Sunshine House for Sick Children.

Sources

Primary Sources

Primary sources provide first-hand accounts or direct evidence concerning the topic under investigation. Witnesses create them who experienced the events being documented or who consulted those who took part. Often these sources are created at the time when the events or conditions are occurring, such as newspaper accounts or letters. But primary sources can also include autobiographies, memoirs, and oral histories recorded later, such as radio or television programmes.

Diaries – give valuable first-hand accounts of the times with vivid descriptions and eyewitness accounts of people who were there.

Those consulted include:
James Stephens – a writer and journalist who witnessed the whole rising
http://www.gutenberg.org/files/12871/12871-h/12871-h.htm

Lily Stokes – a young woman caught up in the Rising
http://archiver.rootsweb.ancestry.com/th/read/IRELA
ND/2001-07/0995840602

Cesca's Diary 1913 - 1916: Where Art and Nationalism Meet
by Hilary Pyle, Woodfield Press
Mrs. Hamilton Norway – the wife of the head of the Post
Office. Hamilton Norway kept a diary during the Rising
https://archive.org/stream/sinnfeinrebellio00norwrich
#page/22/mode/2up

There are several books that include vivid and wonderful
testimony from contemporary eyewitnesses.

1916 – What the People Saw by Mick O'Farrell
(Mercier Press)
Rebels – Voices from the Easter Rising by Fearghal McGarry
(Penguin)

The Bureau of Military History

http://www.bureauofmilitaryhistory.ie/

This is an amazing online resource including nearly two
thousand witness statements, hundreds of photographs
and many documents collected from direct participants.

Some of the ones I found particularly vivid and useful were:

Liam Tannam who was in the GPO

Séan McLoughlin – the twenty-one-year-old "boy commandant"

His sister Mary McLoughlin – a dispatch courier

Mary Mulcahy (Min Ryan) dispatch courier

Jimmy Grace who fought at Mount Street Bridge in Number 26 Northumberland Road and survived to tell the tale.

Louise Perolz

Mairin Cregan

Maire Smartt

The Sinn Féin Rebellion Handbook
https://archive.org/details/sinnfeinrebellio00dubl
This was published by the Irish Times in 1917 a year after the rebellion and is a remarkable source of contemporary interviews, documents, inventory of buildings destroyed etc.

Biographies

Kathleen Clarke, Revolutionary Woman, first-hand account by wife of Thomas Clarke, signatory to the Proclamation (O'Brien Press)

Prison Letters of Countess Markievicz (Virago Press)

Secondary Sources

These are documents that recount or analyse information recorded elsewhere, and are based on primary sources. This usually means books but could also be exhibitions, television documentaries or docu-dramas.

The Irish Times Book of the 1916 Rising by Shane Hegarty and Fintan O'Toole (Gill and Macmillan)

The Easter Rebellion by Max Caulfield published in 1964 and still the best minute-by-minute narrative of the Rising by a journalist who interviewed many of the participants (London 1964; Dublin Gill & Macmillan paperback edition 1995)

Easter 1916: The Irish Rebellion by Charles Townshend (Penguin)

Dublin 1916: The Siege of the GPO by Claire Willis (Profile Books)

The Easter Rising: A Guide to Dublin in 1916 by Conor Kostick and Lorcan Collins (O'Brien Press)

Business as Usual – GPO Staff in 1916 by Stephen Ferguson (Mercier Press)

Online Resources

There are a wealth of sites and resources available online. Some of the primary and secondary sources are listed above.

Websites
http://www.nli.ie/1916/pdfs.html
Overview online exhibition from the National Library of Ireland
http://resources.teachnet.ie/dhorgan/2004/thursday.html
Great day-by-day diary of events

http://www.easter1916.ie
Very good online resource including day-by-day events and portraits of participants

http://irishmedals.org/gpage.html
Participants in 1916 Irish medals

http://irishvolunteers.org/2012/06/dublin-1916-then-now-pictures-from-the-1916-rising/
Comparison pictures of Dublin – then and now

http://www.bbc.co.uk/history/british/easterrising/aftermath/af06.shtml
Summary of events

http://comeheretome.com/about/
Website about history of Dublin with many fascinating and quirky pages documenting the Rising

http://www.irishtimes.com/archive
Newspapers of the time

http://multitext.ucc.ie
This is an innovative project from the Cork History Department at University College Cork and is a growing resource of written and visual information on the 1916 Rising and Irish history in general.

Biographies

Constance Markievicz – an Independent Life by Anne Haverty (Pandora Press)
   Terrible Beauty – a Life of Constance Markievicz by Diana Norman (Poolbeg)
   Michael Collins by Tim Pat Coogan

http://www.historytoday.com/anthony-fletcher/young-nationalist-easter-rising
   Account of Cesca Trench, an English born Irish Nationalist who visited the GPO during the rebellion

Audio Visual Resources

http://shop.rte.ie/Product/The-Story-of-Easter-Week-1916-CD/1273/2221.0

A CD of interviews with participants and witnesses

http://thecricketbatthatdiedforireland.com

has a list of quirky objects and photographs at the National History Museum, including a toffee hammer thrown from a confectionery shop during the looting of Sackville Street, and memorial cards of Charles Darcy, aged 15, who was killed in action at Dublin Castle

http://digital.ucd.ie/get/ivrla:30626/pdf

An old article on the members of the Fianna who were killed in action

https://www.rte.ie/radio1/liveline/generic/2013/0215/367956-special-features/

Broadcaster Joe Duffy has researched the 38 children killed during Easter Week – the forgotten children of 1916

http://www.irishlifeandlore.com/result-collection.php?collectionName=The%201916%20Rising%20Oral%20History%20Collection

This is a wonderful collection of 111 interviews

associated with the 1916 Rising, many with the descendants of those who took part in the Rising.

http://www.flickr.com/photos/nlireland/
Some great photos from the period, including shots of the shoe shops, and ruins of Dublin

Acknowledgements

Heartfelt thanks to Paula Campbell who asked me to write this book in the first place and to editor Gaye Shortland for her diligent work in getting it into shape. Much thanks also to David Prendergast for typesetting and layout.

I am indebted to my brother Neil Murphy for his close reading of the first draft and helpful suggestions. Thanks to Dr Elizabeth Orchard, Consultant Cardiologist at the Oxford University Hospitals NHS Trust who gave me advice on medical matters and Alice Channon and William Murphy for reading early chapters. Thanks also to my mother for family memories and reminiscences. Also to Aoife, Patrick, Cian and Senan O'Leary, Daniel, Isabella and Alex Cassidy, Conor Murphy and Henry Murphy.

I am grateful to Aideen Ireland, Head of Readers Services at the National Archives of Ireland, who not only helped me with tracking down sources but gave me the best student summer job ever at the Public Record Office many moons ago.

Thanks to my husband Marc and daughter Rosa for their tolerance while I have been living in 1916!

For permissions:

Thanks to Rev Dr Norman E Gamble Honorable Archivist of the Irish Railway Record Society for permission to use the 1910 tram timetable.

For permission to use the 'World's Fair Varieties and Waxworks" advert first used on the 9th June 1913, I am grateful to Irish Newspaper Archives & Irish Independent© 2014. With special thanks to Phillip Martin for his help.

The Illustration of a First Aid tourniquet was sourced from www.publicvectorsdomain.org and published under Creative Commons licence.

Also coming Soon 2014

Seeds *of* Liberty

Three countries - three revolutions - three children caught up in the struggle for freedom.

Boston 1770s: All Jack wants is to stay out of trouble – but when the fighting breaks out, he knows he'll need to pick a side.

Paris 1790s: Catherine is thrilled by the Revolution. But terror will soon take over the city.

Wexford 1798: Robert's brothers tell him he's too young to take part in the Rising, but he's determined to prove them wrong.

Liberty can come but there's always a price to be paid.

CLAIRE HENNESSY

If you enjoyed this book from Poolbeg why not visit our website:

www.poolbeg.com

and get another book delivered straight to your home or to a friend's home.

All books despatched within 24 hours.

POOLBEG

Why not join our mailing list at www.poolbeg.com and get some fantastic offers, competitions, author interviews and much more?

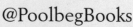
@PoolbegBooks